THE CENTER OF THE WORLD

. . .

THE

Center

OF THE WORLD

Thomas Van Essen

OTHER PRESS

NEW YORK

Production Editor: Yvonne E. Cárdenas
Text Designer: Jennifer Daddio/Bookmark Design and Media Inc.
This book was set in 11.65 pt Deepdene
by Alpha Design & Composition of Pittsfield, NH.

1 3 5 9 10 8 6 4 2

For information write to Other Press LLC, 2 Park Avenue, 24th Floor,
New York, NY 10016. Or visit our Web site: www.otherpress.com

Library of Congress Cataloging-in-Publication Data

Essen, Thomas Van, 1952–
The center of the world / by Thomas Van Essen.
pages cm
ISBN 978-1-59051-549-5 (pbk.) — ISBN 978-1-59051-550-1 (ebook)
1. Turner, J. M. W. (Joseph Mallord William), 1775–1851—Fiction.
2. Art—Psychological aspects—Fiction. I. Title.
PS3605.S6757C46 2013
813'.6—dc23
2013003848

Publisher's Note:
This is a work of fiction. Names, characters, places, and incidents either
are the product of the author's imagination or are used fictitiously, and
any resemblance to actual persons, living or dead, events, or
locales is entirely coincidental.

For Bob, WITH LOVE

... no man ever painted or ever will paint well anything but what he has early and long seen, early and long felt, and early and long loved.

JOHN RUSKIN, *Modern Painters*

. . .

... here his intention seems to have been one of private gratification rather than preparation for a more developed work.

ANN CHUMBLEY AND IAN WARRELL, *Turner and the Human*
Figure: Studies of Contemporary Life, DISCUSSING TURNER'S
"SHEET OF EROTIC FIGURE SUBJECTS C. 1805"

. . .

It is no discredit for Trojans and well-greaved Achaeans to suffer long anguish for a woman like that.

HOMER, *Iliad*, TRANSLATED BY ANNE CARSON

. *(1856)* .

⟨⟩ SHE WAS NO DOUBT the most wicked of women. They were the most wicked of pictures. I knew Ruskin was right and that they ought to be consigned to the fire.

"Wornum," he said, "I have been entrusted with the memory of England's greatest painter. These images are the products of a diseased mind. We must destroy them. If we do not, the world will not remember Turner as the transcendent genius of his age."

He instructed the boy to gather some old lumber and kindle a fire in the brickyard behind the gallery. Ruskin said that he himself could not bear to see these sketches burnt, although he knew it was his duty. He was quite distraught and asked me, as a special favor to him, if he could excuse himself and if I would place the offending material in the flames.

Ruskin withdrew and one by one I let the sheets fall into the fire. Most were drawings on paper, some were oil sketches on canvas. A mournful black smoke rose into the sky.

I was not sad to see most of this material go. I had been to Paris when I was young, and, being no better than most young men, I had seen material of this sort for sale on the banks of the Seine. Most of what I burnt was no better than that.

But there was a set of notebooks that gave me pause. They seemed a study for a painting of some evil queen of antiquity. Ruskin said she was Jezebel. I did not say so, but I believe she was Helen. She was more beautiful than I can say. More wicked too, no doubt.

One by one I placed the sheets from the notebook on the fire and watched her disappear in the flames. It was as if I had cast her into hell myself.

After the last piece was burnt and the fire extinguished I went inside. Ruskin offered me a glass of sherry which I gratefully accepted. There was a look of suffering on his face. I had done him, he said, a great service. I said it was nothing, but my looks must have given the lie to my protestation.

I am sure we did what was needful. But I think of her often during the day and by night she haunts my brain.

. 1 .

❧ IN ORDER THAT I should feel the pangs of hell most fiercely, Providence, in its wisdom, has decreed that I should taste heaven before I die. This is, to be sure, a peculiarly English heaven, but it is hard to conceive of a French or Italian one half so comfortable or so pleasing.

The presiding genius of the place is, of course, Lord Egremont, of whom you have heard much. He is a most remarkable personage. I have spent only a few minutes in his company, yet I have felt the nature of the man in my bones. It is difficult to explain or account for. He exudes a sense of mastery so complete that he need not exert it. He is all kindness and welcome, but one knows by a kind of instinct that he is quick to anger and that his wrath, when unleashed, is most terrible. He takes, I think, a silent delight in knowing that all those around him live in fear, although, in spite of that, he appears a delightful old gentleman of the gruff old-fashioned school.

He is almost eighty, yet as active as a healthy man of fifty. Every morning after breakfast he buttons on his leather gaiters and goes out to inspect some part of his vast agricultural enterprise. It is curious to stand in one of the drawing rooms here and look out upon the park and see this English Maecenas making his way across the great lawn, his favorite brown spaniels following close behind. Behind the hounds comes a boy leading his horse, and other functionaries and factotums all waiting on his merest nod or grunt.

One's only obligation while a guest here, as near as I can make out, is to be agreeable and not to get in Lord Egremont's way. Those guests who delight in the hunt join His Lordship when he rides; those more peaceably inclined are given the freedom of the house and the grounds. There is much to do. One can play billiards in the Marble Room, find a comfortable chair in the library, or go to the North Gallery, which contains what many say is the finest collection of pictures in all England. One can also retire, as I have done, to one's own room. I have never before spent the night in a room so grand. There are high ceilings with curious carvings, crimson walls hung with paintings that would find pride of place in the drawing rooms of most noble houses, and various pieces of antique furniture. My bed, for example, could comfortably sleep six (although you know, dear David, that only a certain one, in addition to myself, would make my Paradise complete!). I almost fear that I am in danger of smothering when I lie down, such is the profusion of soft blankets and feather beds. There is a remarkable portrait of Lady Mary Villiers—by Van Dyck, no less—glowering over me, and despite her fierce expression I have taken it into my head that she will keep me safe from all harm.

Some time toward the late afternoon His Lordship returns, wet through and through and either cursing like a fishmonger or dispensing smiles all round, depending on what he has learned. He then disappears into his chambers and, as a general rule, is not seen again until about seven, when we all dine.

Dinner is the only time that all the guests and hangers-on are gathered together. His Lordship and Mrs. Spencer (more of her shortly) preside over an agreeable motley of about twenty people. The only sour notes in the composition are Mr. Wyndham, Egremont's heir and bastard, and his wife. He is fat and bilious; she is thin and shrill. Both are much given to disapproving expressions of piety and contempt. Wyndham seems to resent every forkful that his father's guests consume as some diminishment of his patrimony. One half suspects that he eats as much as he does because he knows that every morsel he devours will not be given to another.

But those two aside, it is a splendid company. There is Mr. Romney and his beautiful lady; Mr. Sockett, an agreeable divine; and Mr. Gedding, the member for Pulborough. Gedding and His Lordship have different views on certain agricultural matters which I do not profess to understand and get quite heated about them. Then there are the artists: Jones (whose sea scene you much admired when we saw it in London), Simmons, and the great Turner. Turner is an unprepossessing figure. Much below the average height (which seems somehow queer when you consider how grand and mighty his paintings are), he is a barrel-chested man with a large hooked nose, which is often red. He wears a suit of shabby and much mended black, and were it not for his dirty hands and the paint under his fingernails one would take him for a clergyman in reduced circumstances. His eyes, however, are wonderfully acute and he seems to see into the very heart of things. He says little and has a queer gruff way of speaking into his soup, but what he does say is worth attending to.

So now let me come to Mrs. Spencer. She sits by His Lordship's side and presides over the table. When conversation flags, she revives it; when it strays into unprofitable areas, she redirects it. She is His Lordship's mistress.

Egremont has always set conventional pieties at defiance. For many years Wyndham's mother lived at Petworth and bore His Lordship's children without benefit of marriage. He married her eventually, but when she died, his grief was so extreme that he went up to London to recover and returned with Mrs. Spencer. She is a great and ageless beauty. I would guess that she is forty years younger than her lord and master, but she looks and may be as young as thirty, younger than his son and heir. She has good teeth, fair hair, and wonderful skin. Her smile would bring cheer to a dead man, and even Wyndham is sometimes unable to resist her charms, although he makes no secret of the fact that he hates her with all the strength a small soul is capable of.

The food is good solid English fare, served out with a liberal hand. Fresh game and fish from Petworth's forests and streams and ponds; vegetables from the model kitchen gardens. There is good wine, but not extravagant, poured liberally, but not to excess. Between the wine and Mrs. Spencer the conversation is most delightful. She makes a point of drawing everyone out and manages to make the dullest person at table seem interesting. The only blemish on my happiness is the fear that I will be found wanting and cast out of this Paradise prematurely. Do not take that to mean that I do not miss you; far from it. Nothing could increase my joy more than to have you by my side to share it.

Last night after we dined I joined a small group gathered in the library. The conversation was of the usual sort to be heard in country houses: talk of land reform, of the state of the deer herd at Petworth and other agricultural topics, of the latest news from France—but it was all carried on in the most agreeable way.

At length everyone tendered their good nights, but I knew I should be unable to sleep for the sheer delight of my situation. I had found a beautiful edition of Pope's translation of Homer and settled down before the fire with the volume on my lap; it seemed the right thing to be reading in a room which also contained a bust of Aphrodite said to be by Praxiteles.

I was thus engaged for about half an hour when I heard voices approaching. It was His Lordship, Turner, and Mr. Jones. As I rose to greet them, Egremont waved me back into my seat.

"Well, Grant, what are you doing here?"

I said something to the effect that I was not yet tired and wanted to read. I offered to retire if he and his companions wished to continue their conversation in private.

"Nonsense," he said in his gruff manner. "I don't plan to say anything to these fellows that I would not say in front of any other gentleman." He settled himself into an armchair, as did Turner and Mr. Jones. His Lordship called for a bottle of brandy and a plate of biscuits. The three of them smelled like paint and mineral spirits. There is a room above the chapel to which Turner has been given a key and where he has set up his studio. No one is allowed in without his permission except, of course, Lord Egremont. I surmised that they had just been there looking at Turner's latest painting.

"I hope," His Lordship said, addressing me, "that you have found everything to your liking so far. I look forward to seeing what you will make of the collection here. That was a very pretty essay you wrote in the *Westminster*. Have you had much chance to look about yet?"

I said that I had seen very little, but already much to admire.

"Well, you must take your time and get to know the place. Turner here has studied our collection as well as anyone. You must have him show you round. But I look forward to your article. It will be a pleasure to see a good essay on the collection. Get it known more in the world, you know. No point hiding one's light under a bushel. But not too long, mind you."

I said that I would do my best to provide satisfaction, but it would be difficult to decide which pieces to single out for praise.

"That," he said, "is your job, not mine. So what are you reading that keeps you up after dark?"

"Pope's *Iliad*, my lord," I replied. "This is a remarkably fine edition. A pleasure to hold in one's hand, and the poetry, sir, is always nourishing."

"Well said, young man, well said."

Turner meanwhile had taken his first (and not particularly modest) swallow of brandy. I began to understand why his nose was so often red. His Lordship turned to the painter.

"Ah, Turner," he said. "You daubers and paint-smearers can never approach Homer and Virgil. The authors of antiquity show us all we need to know of men and morals. You poor present-day fellows can do nothing but embellish and illustrate what their genius proved."

Turner seemed at first somewhat taken aback by Egremont's sally, although I suspected that this was not a new topic between them. He looked at his patron sideways for a moment and then took another swallow of brandy.

"My compliments," he said. "This is most excellent brandy." He resumed his study of the fire. "But words," he said, "and images. Altogether different. Not even images. Light. Color. Paint. Shadow. A different order of things, sir."

Mr. Jones now spoke. He is a bluff and commonsensical sort of man. "But you have to admit, Turner, that the ancients knew more of the truth of things than most men of our time will ever imagine."

Turner fairly snorted. "Truth, sir? What is it? There is more truth between a woman's legs than there ever was between Homer's ears."

All of us were startled by this extraordinary remark. I began to think that the brandy had done its work too quickly. Turner held his hand out before him, extending it several times, like a man trying to reach for something in the dark. "All of us.

Painters. Poets. The world is before us. What is it? It is a damn hard business, gentlemen."

"But a woman's legs," said Jones. "What does that have to do with it?"

Turner looked at Jones with something like anger. He pointed one of his short stubby fingers and shook it at his friend as he spoke.

"The truth, sir, is what *matters*. My lord, you understand. Good night, gentlemen, good night!" And with that Turner, the man they call the greatest painter of the age, rose abruptly from his chair and left the room.

. 2 .

⋘ I AM NOT a remarkable person, but I have had a glimpse into the heart of things.

I was born in the same year as the hydrogen bomb; I grew up in the New York suburbs; I have lived an ordinary life. My parents got divorced in 1967, when I was in high school. It was a messy business: alcohol, unexplained charges on the company card, calls to the police. I was sent away to a third-tier prep school to join the other lost boys who were there for similar reasons. When I returned, my mother was living on a golf course in Boca Raton with most of my father's money and one of his partners. My father got me and the summer house on Saranac Lake in the Adirondacks.

I was an unhappy kid, my childhood wrapped up in my parents' miserable marriage, but the summers I spent at the lake were cool drinks in the desert. It was only when we were up there that they stopped fighting. They would play golf in the morning; my father would take me sailing in the afternoon. We would sit on the dock in the evening as they had their cocktails, chatting amiably until my mother was too drunk to stand. My father would laugh, offer her his arm, and drag her up to the house.

Except for the lake frontage, the house is a modest place. Upstairs are three small bedrooms and an old-fashioned bathroom; downstairs, a fifties-style kitchen and a living room with a view of the lake and a moose head on the wall. I spent hours when I was little staring at this sad and giant creature. It seemed, like me, to be trapped on the wrong side of my parents' picture window.

My father always claimed that the moose was killed by Cornelius Rhinebeck, the original owner of Birch Lodge, the estate next door. Rhinebeck, a banker and industrialist from New York City, built the compound in the early years of the twentieth century. In the 1930s the estate was broken up and the individual houses have changed hands any number of times since then. Our house and the barn were originally built for the groundskeeper. A small stream and a band of trees separate us from the main buildings, although an ornate stone bridge that connects us with the estate still stands.

My father was always a tight and controlling man, but from the time of the divorce until his death on January 27, 2002, he drank more and more and became tighter and tighter with his money. His whiskey got cheaper, and it became harder for him to throw things away. It was as if he had promised himself that, having lost his wife, he would never lose anything again.

By the time he died the house was a mess and the barn even worse. They were both filled with crap that reminded me of the worst of him and seemed like a stain on the lake and the only happy memories I had. I didn't have a lot of money at the time, but I hired two guys to take all his junk out of the house. Most of the stuff went straight to the dump, but the stuff that I couldn't decide what to do with I had them toss in the barn, on top of the junk that was already there.

It was a year and half later, on July 6, 2003, that I started to work on the barn. I had been up at the lake with my wife, and she was heading back to Princeton. I guess you could say that we had had a nice week together, in a middle-aged way. We had not quarreled. We made love once after a nice dinner without too much wine. But she had meetings to go to in New York and I had some vacation to burn. I had a dumpster delivered to the barn and started to fill it up. There was something deeply satisfying about taking my father's stuff and smashing it.

I had been working for about an hour when I saw Jeffrey Mossbacher walking up the driveway. He was wearing a pair of Bermuda shorts that looked as if they had just been pressed. Rita and Jeffrey had recently purchased the main house of Birch Lodge and restored the place to what it must have looked like when Rhinebeck was alive. Photographs, with Rita posed fetchingly in front of a fireplace, had been featured in *Architectural Digest*. They were nice enough people, but they made me feel embarrassed about who I was. They were not the sort of people who let their lives be encumbered by junk; they were able to use their money to make any troubling bits of the past disappear, while for me the past was always present. Jeffrey kept quiet about what he did, but Rita, who used to be a model, let it slip that he worked on Wall Street, something to do with hedge funds. They flew up for weekends in their plane.

"I heard all the banging and thought I would come over," he said as he held out his hand.

I apologized for disturbing them.

"I don't think I've seen you since your father passed away. I'm sorry about your loss. I never got to know your father very well."

I thanked him for his condolences.

"So you're starting to fix the place up?"

"That's probably a bit strong. Just cleaning up a bit."

"You have to start somewhere. These old places can take a lot of work."

"There's only so much we can do," I said. "The taxes up here are murder."

"It's the waterfront that's killing you. Fourteen K. That's a lot, given what you have, no offense. You guys pay almost as much as we do. From a market value perspective the two places don't compare, but from an assessment perspective, they're pretty darn close."

I asked him how he knew all this.

"My people were looking into our assessment—considering an appeal and all that—and so they were checking out 'comparable' properties." I found his use of air quotes annoying, but let it pass. "You're not thinking of selling, are you?"

"We're trying to figure out how to hang on to it," I said. "It's a lot of expense—and some debt. It's sort of complicated for us right now."

"Well, if you ever want to sell, I hope you'll give me the opportunity to meet any offer you get. One point three, one point four. It wouldn't be out of the question, the way the market's going. It would be fitting, in a way, to bring the old property together again. Good to close the loop, you know." He gave me his card. "It's got my email and cell number. If you ever even think about it, get in touch. You won't regret it."

I thanked him again.

"I'll let you get back to work," Jeffrey said. "But I'm serious. I've redone the old wine cellar. You should come over and check it out. We can have a glass of wine and talk."

. 3 .

EVERYTHING ABOUT STOKES was aggressively English, from the cut of his suit to the way he slicked back his blond hair and held out his soft right hand. He was pale, thin-lipped, and beautiful. And later, when the true and astounding—the absolutely remarkable—extent of the smash became known to the world, it was difficult to imagine such a perfectly groomed face so badly shattered that the blood and pieces of bone had to be cleaned off the Constable before it could be brought to auction.

Adversity had emboldened Stokes. He lived more richly now than he had ever lived before. His debts had reached such spectacular proportions that even Rhinebeck could hardly imagine them. They had become, in some profound way that only Stokes himself could appreciate, beautiful.

"I am informed," Stokes began, "that you have been peeking into the cabinets of broken-down families in France and

Italy, looking to exchange some of your plentiful cash for the odd Old Master."

"I did not come here, Mr. Stokes," Rhinebeck interrupted, "to be kept waiting five minutes in your antechamber nor to be insulted. I came, at your request, to discuss a matter of business between us. If you have something to say about that matter, please say it."

Stokes allowed the gleam of hatred which had been shimmering about his eyes to come into crisper focus.

"Very well, sir. My firm is in debt to yours for a considerable sum. You have also indicated through Mr. Manwaring that you are aware of a potential disagreement between His Majesty's government and myself. You are prepared, in the name of truth, of course, to provide to the government certain information with regard to that disagreement. Does that state the case?"

Rhinebeck nodded.

"Just before the turn of the century, never mind how, I came into possession of a remarkable painting by J.M.W. Turner," Stokes went on. "I can tell you very little about the painting, nor can I, in fact, prove that it is by Turner, for reasons that you shall appreciate shortly. The painting is hidden behind the bookcase in front of you. I am going to leave you alone in the room for fifteen minutes by my watch. Then we will discuss our matter of business."

Stokes moved with remarkable swiftness. With one light and gliding motion he rose from his chair and touched a hidden latch. The heavy and fully laden bookcase slid into the wall and disappeared. With a deft and showmanlike continuation of his original movement, Stokes opened a black curtain that the bookcase had revealed and left the room, closing the door noiselessly behind him.

When he returned, exactly fifteen minutes later, Rhinebeck had regained sufficient possession of himself to be prepared for his arrival, but had it not been for the stark evidence of his watch he would have been unable to say how much time had passed. All at once *The Center of the World* became the hub of a wheel to which everything, or at least everything that mattered, was attached. When he saw Helen's tunic fall in folds of gold and light about her incomparable shoulders, he saw Régine and that room in Paris when he was so much younger. He saw the very pulse of the world; he understood how empires rose and fell and that power and pleasure beyond his ability to imagine were before him to be grasped. Helen's eyes told him that he was both her slave and a man of destiny who could go forward without fear.

Stokes closed the black curtain so suddenly that Rhinebeck felt a physical sense of loss. His face was flushed, his heart was racing, and sweat beaded his brow.

"I see that you are able to appreciate what you have just been privileged to see. Now to our business." He proposed a transaction which, even then, Rhinebeck knew to be monstrous and outrageous. "And further: I insist that both of us never speak of this arrangement to any living soul and that— I am sure that this hardly needs saying—you will utter not a word to His Majesty's government on the matter about which you have threatened to speak. I also insist that we conclude this agreement within the next ten minutes. My terms are what they are; you will either agree within that time or I withdraw the proposal. The thought of parting with this painting is deeply painful to me. If I am to endure this amputation, I insist that the ax fall quickly."

For the first and last time in his life Rhinebeck felt staggered. There did not seem to be enough air in the room. In the upper left corner of the painting he had seen an eagle soaring in the blue sky. The two armies were stretched out below the magnificent bird, the armor of the heroes sparkling on the plain. He saw the battlements of the great walled city in which Helen awaited her lover.

He understood now that Stokes's financial difficulties were much greater than he had suspected. Only a desperate man would propose what he had.

He looked at his watch. Eight minutes had passed. He wiped his brow with his handkerchief. Stokes sat across from him as still as a statue.

"I accept your proposal."

"Damn you. I knew you would. You are a man of sense and feeling." Stokes rose. "I have a lorry waiting round the back. Within the hour my people will deliver it to your hotel. My business people will call upon yours. We are done with each other."

Rhinebeck saw in Stokes's eyes that he was a defeated man. A servant entered and ushered him out.

He crossed the square and looked at the house, trying to determine which curtained window hid the painting, which Stokes was surely looking at for the last time. London seemed vague and unreal. The sky was gray and unfocused. There were children playing in the park. An attractive young woman was looking at him. It all seemed like mere decoration, like the work of a third-rate Impressionist.

. 4 .

⟨⟩ **THERE IS NO PLAQUE** on the door of the elegant brownstone on the Upper East Side of Manhattan where Madison Partners does business. An attractive young woman greets those who arrive. She answers the telephone, keeps calendars, and makes travel arrangements. She hopes one day to sit at one of the nineteenth-century mahogany desks behind her, at which two or three other young people are working on silver laptops or speaking to clients on the telephone. These young people are always well dressed, usually in black, white, and shades of gray. Low shelves filled with catalogues and art books ring the room. The wall above is paneled, decorated with a changing collection of five or six top- or second-tier European oils from the eighteenth, nineteenth, and early twentieth centuries—a Sisley, say, or a Sir Thomas Lawrence. These works may be acquired, but the young people have been trained too well to say they are for sale.

Behind the front room is a small conference room, also decorated with three or four paintings, and behind that, with a view over the back garden, an office. A small kitchen completes the first floor. The two floors above are a private residence, the second floor being dominated by a large library.

The only dweller in this residence, and the principal of the firm, is Mr. Arthur Bryce. The office on the first floor is also his, for Madison Partners has no partners. When Bryce leans toward a client as if he is revealing a confidence, he often likes to say that he is a modest man who prefers to remain invisible, the one who disappears into the illusion of the many.

Although the paintings in the front room and the conference room are for sale, Madison Partners is not, in any conventional sense, an art gallery. It is, rather, a fine arts consultancy, specializing in European art. Bryce makes it his business to know who has what and who desires what. He brings parties together, often without either knowing who the other is. Payments are made and checks are written into accounts in Geneva, New York, or Nassau; shipments arrive from a secure facility near Kennedy Airport. Works not generally known to be available change hands without any of the inconveniences associated with auction houses or tax collectors. Those who might be tempted to raise concerns about the provenance of a work are not informed of anything that could cause them distress.

One afternoon in November of 2001 Bryce sat alone in his library, a cup of coffee by his side. A handsome man in his early sixties, with close-cropped gray hair, blue eyes, and a disarmingly clear complexion, he wore round tortoiseshell glasses, a custom-made shirt, and a silk tie with a Windsor knot. Bryce prided himself on his ability to stand above the fray and to take the long view, but he realized that even he had been knocked into something of a funk by the recent events. The smell of smoke and death still hung in the air; getting around downtown was, he found, inconvenient as hell, and conversation had turned horrid. He had, of course, been able to take advantage of the panic that had set in that September; he had assisted in several transactions in which savvy clients in Japan and the Middle East were able to profit from the nervous desire for cash that a number of Americans felt. The walls of Madison Partners were more densely hung with paintings than was usual, but Bryce knew it was only a matter of time before cash would seek a more beautiful refuge.

Bryce picked up a leather binder and reread a document he had read a hundred times before:

> *Petworth House*
> *November 16, 1837*
>
> *Dear Mr. Turner,*
>
> *Of your past greatness as an artist there can be little doubt, as there can also be little doubt of your pernicious influence on my Father in his declining years, or of your impudence. As for that infamous painting to which you had the audacity to refer, I beg you to think of it as no longer existing. Any payments you received from my father you may keep. If you provide Documents signed by him acknowledging further obligations to you they shall be examined*

carefully, for it seems to me, and so it would seem to all men of correct understanding, that no matter how lofty the title of artist you claim it is improper you be paid for debauching an old man in his dotage.

Thank you for attending my Father's funeral. I regret that the ceremony went on so long as to inconvenience you. I see no reason for you to trouble yourself with further visits to Petworth. Sketchbooks, paints, brushes etc. belonging to you have been packed up and will be sent to your address.

Yrs,

Geo. Wyndham

The writer of the note was the bastard son and heir of the Third Earl of Egremont. Egremont, who was born in 1751 and died, at the age of eighty-six, in 1837, was the most important patron of the arts of his era. He supported any number of British artists, including J.M.W. Turner, the greatest of all English painters, and, in Bryce's opinion, one of the three or four greatest painters who ever lived. Bryce smiled to himself as he remembered how he had acquired the letter, less at the ingenuity of the scheme than at the fact that it would not do if the circumstances became generally known.

If Bryce had been a conventional art historian or scholar, this document might have changed the general direction of Turner studies. But Bryce traded in information; information, like certain works of art, was precious and beautiful to him on account of its rarity. He was conscious of the fact that he knew something that no one else did, namely, that at the behest of

Egremont, Turner had created a painting that Egremont's boorish son had described as "infamous." And there was something curious about the phrase "I beg you to think of it as no longer existing." Not quite the same as "it has been destroyed" or words to that effect. If, Bryce thought, it had not been destroyed, it might still exist; if it still existed, it could be found.

Yes, it still existed. Bryce decided he would believe in this "infamous" painting and that he would find it. He knew that he needed some greater purpose to help him get through the dreary days of war and vengeance that were sure to come. Such a quest would serve that end.

. 5 .

THE THREE OF US who remained sat in silence for a moment. When His Lordship rose, we all rose with him. He seemed more than usually thoughtful as he led us to the staircase. A servant had appeared to lead us and light the way, while others had materialized behind us and were already cleaning up the brandy glasses.

"Turner, you know, is a brilliant man. He hits his mark more often than he misses it. It is time for bed, gentlemen. It is time for bed. Good night." With those words Egremont shot forward and disappeared up the stairs.

Jones and I followed at a more moderate pace and said our good nights at the landing. I left the candle burning by the bedside as I settled myself down in the enormous bed. Lady Mary looked down out of the darkness. I wondered who else had slept in this bed under her baleful gaze. Some Tudor knight, I thought, might have died where I was lying and the panels on the wall may have echoed the sound of a baby's first cry when Elizabeth was queen and Shakespeare's new work was the talk of London. Thinking of all those houseguests in tights and ruffs who must have known each other on this bed, I fancied that if it could speak we would have a history of noble life, death, and fornication to which I would be some insignificant footnote.

These cogitations led me back in due course (after a pleasant detour around your thighs and bottom) to Turner's remark about the truth that lies between a woman's legs. I have, as you know, only a theoretical knowledge of that location, but, thinking of you and what hangs between *your* legs, I half understand what Turner meant. When we are in each other's arms, David, I am, at least, aware of all that matters.

I woke just before dawn and went to the window, which overlooks the park. Earth, trees, grass, and water had been molded by Capability Brown as if all God's materials were putty in his hands. The result was Nature made more perfect than Nature itself. In the half light I could see the pond, silver gray against the darker gray of the grass. I could make out some ducks or geese. There were deer bending down at the water's edge. The hills beyond were black against the lightening sky, while the distant patchwork of cultivated fields was still invisible. As I stood there in my dressing gown, I could see the world begin to take on the colors of day, gray giving way to various shades of somber green. The sky behind the hills glowed with the faintest traces of rose as the fiery disk of the sun began to appear.

The sound of an opening door attracted my attention and I looked down. A figure dressed in black stepped quickly across the terrace. Turner, for it was he, has a queer stiff-legged trot, but he made his way with remarkable speed across the field and up the hill on my right. He held his hat onto his head with one hand while the other clutched a large portfolio which contained, I assumed, his drawing materials. When he reached the top he sat down on the bench and began to work. As I watched, the sun crested the hill and its image appeared in the glassy water. My words cannot do justice to the scene, and I was curious what Turner's chalk and pen would make of it.

I got dressed as rapidly as I could. It promised to be a beautiful morning and I wished to take up my lord's offer to accompany him as he went out for deer. There had been conversation the night before of the need to cull the herd. His Lordship had said it was "not the usual way of things" and that it might interest me. Before tendering the invitation he had asked me a number of sharp questions. I had told him that I could not shoot and had no desire to do so, but that I could ride tolerably well. My father, though a poor clergyman, had been, through the kindness of his friends, a keen hunter and had taught me to ride. That was enough for Egremont, who said, "Come along then. It will be good for a young puppy like you to take a bit of air." He said we would ride to the shooting grounds by a roundabout way so that I might get some exercise and taste the flavor of the neighborhood. "You will do well," he said. "Just stay out of the way when the game appears." I wish to God I had listened.

When I arrived at the stables, Mr. Hobb, the master of the stables, introduced me to my mount. He apologized for the quality of the beast, but said she was "a good-tempered old creature who knew her business well enough." I am no great judge of horseflesh, but I could see at once that in all his years of riding my father had never sat on so fine a horse. But such is the way of things at Petworth.

The morning lived up to its promise, one of September's gifts. We were a party of about five, with Egremont taking the lead, a number of servants bringing up the rear, and a cart following. In spite of his years, His Lordship took what seemed a young man's delight in showing us how to ride. At one point we came to a low hedge that bounded a meadow. There was an easy path around, but Egremont, after glancing back at the rest of us, took the hedge with graceful confidence. I tried to remember what I knew about riding, but in truth the horse knew more than enough for both of us and I cleared the barrier with no bad outcome beyond a delicious pounding in my heart. It was a glorious morning to be alive.

We rode on for about half an hour, sometimes at a gallop, sometimes at a walk, as Egremont pointed out some of the beauties of his English Paradise. Petworth Park is notable for the variety of its scenery: woods and forest, streams and ponds, glens and meadows and fields. Much of the park looks as cultivated as a city kitchen garden, but then you turn a corner and see a forest as wild and free as the farthest reaches of Canada. I half wished that the shooting would be put off for another day so that I could enjoy the riding uninterrupted.

At length we arrived at the edge of what I was later told was the greatest stretch of forest on the estate. Towering trees that must have been planted at the time of the current lord's father's father's father came to the edge of a delightful and uncultivated meadow. Wildflowers of yellow and white dotted the soft green grass.

Egremont and the others who had come to participate in the sport dismounted as their guns were brought forward. The shooters lined themselves up along the edge of the meadow, but I stayed on my horse to get a good view of the scene. Behind me the servants waited. Egremont pulled a watch from his pocket and studied it for a moment. At length he gave a signal and a gun behind me was fired into the air. We were all very still. After about a quarter of an hour we could hear the faint sound of human voices shouting in the distance. The sound grew louder and louder as a party of Egremont's tenants approached. Soon I could hear the faint thundering, if you will allow the phrase, of the frightened deer as they fled toward us and their doom. Egremont and the others brought their guns to their shoulders. Excitement visible on their faces, they glanced toward the forest and then at each other. The sound of the hoofbeats grew louder and then louder still, until all at once fifteen or twenty of the park's famous deer exploded into the meadow. Egremont was the first to fire, and then there was a fusillade as the others followed suit. I watched in horror as first one, then a second, and then a third of the speeding creatures crumpled to the ground, their motion carrying them forward as they died. The shots continued, more deer fell, until a cloud of gun smoke hung like a curtain between me and the meadow.

I turned my eyes away from the slaughter and toward the edge of the wood, where I saw one of God's great creatures, an enormous stag, almost twice the size of his murdered cousins, standing just off the verge of the forest. For a moment, the stag's eyes met mine and, I hardly know how to say this, I felt a flash of more than human sympathy as the noble animal seemed to be trying to decide which way to flee in order to save its life.

I had been hanging toward the back as I was instructed to do, but I must have unconsciously urged my horse toward the edge of the wood. I looked away from the stag and saw that Egremont had seen it as well and was reloading his piece. When this was accomplished he took aim. I cried out in alarm, for although I was more than twenty paces from the stag, I was uncomfortably close to Egremont's line of fire. Quicker than thought itself, the stag turned and disappeared into the darkness of the forest. I heard the sound of its hooves as it clambered into the shadows at the same time that I heard the blast of Egremont's gun. He missed his mark and threw the gun to the ground in fury. He turned to me, his face disfigured with anger and contempt. Even though I was seated on a horse and looking down at him, Egremont appeared to rise above me in his rage. He showered down a stream of invective unlike anything I have ever heard before. At length his anger began to subside and his face to return to its normal color (for he had turned an alarming shade of crimson), but he said, in conclusion, that I ought to be ashamed of myself for I was "a disgraceful young sodomite."

I cannot recall all the insults he heaped on me, but that last phrase is indelibly etched in my memory. A sense of shame and humiliation enveloped me like a dark cloak as I sat there waiting for the party to remount and head back toward the house. None of my companions, who had laughed and joked with me as we made our way across the fields, would now meet my eyes. I rode along behind them, looking, I suppose, like a man whose very spine had been stolen from him.

I knew that it was impossible for me to stay at Petworth any longer. I resolved to leave as soon as I could.

. 6 .

❧ I THREW STUFF in the dumpster for another hour, but Mossbacher's visit had taken the edge off my ambition. One point four million dollars. That seemed like a lot of money.

It was lunchtime. Susan would be around Albany. I made a sandwich with a thick layer of ham, some salami, a lot of cheese, lettuce, tomatoes, onions, and good olive oil. Taking a bottle of beer out of the refrigerator, I paused for a moment, feeling guilty, and then grabbed a second. I thought of my father being pretty well shit-faced by four in the afternoon, but then I remembered that I was on vacation and that there was nobody around to tell me what to do. I read someplace that married men lived longer than unmarried ones because their wives were always telling them to eat less and see the doctor more. It hardly seemed worth it.

Plopping myself down on the Adirondack chair, I settled the plate on my lap and looked out over the water. This was where I used to sit with my parents when I was happy. I took a sip of beer. The morning had started out damp and overcast, but the cloud cover had been carried away to the north. There were just a few white clouds in the blue sky. It was so pretty that it looked like a cheap postcard.

This was the afternoon of July 6, 2003, the day before everything changed for me. The last time I had been alone at the lake had been just six weeks after the attack on the World Trade Center. On that October weekend the trees were bare and a bone-chilling rain was falling so hard that I couldn't see across the lake. Everyone was still in a daze and trying to wake up to the new world. My father, who had only four months to live, had called from Florida and told me that I needed to drive to the lake house immediately and find a manila envelope that was hidden in his bedroom. "Don't open it," he said. "I want you to send it to me insured and registered mail. The best kind of mail there is. Spare no expense. And if you think you have better things to do, I have better people to leave the house to." There was, apparently, a set of cousins somewhere who hadn't disappointed him as much as I had.

I asked him what was in the envelope.

"Wouldn't you like to know?" he said. "But let me give you a hint. I want you to insure it for ten thousand dollars. You got anything worth insuring for ten thousand dollars? That's my point." I knew he was half senile and about to die, and yet I was still as afraid of him as I had ever been. I was fifty years old and still waiting for him to say he loved me.

I drove up through the cold rain and found the envelope where he had said it would be, buried under old pajama bottoms and a few *Playboy* magazines from the seventies. It was sealed at both ends with duct tape. My father had printed the words CONFIDENTIAL: DO NOT OPEN UNDER PENALTY OF THE LAW in block letters on both sides. I drove to town the next day and dropped it off at the post office. When we were cleaning out the apartment in Miami after his death, I found it unopened. It contained telephone bills from around the time of my parents' divorce. Some of the numbers were circled or underlined.

It was a good sandwich and plenty of beer, but I don't recall enjoying either. I remember I was still hungry when I was done. I am not as hungry anymore.

The Mossbachers waved as they took the powerboat out of their boathouse, and I waved back. Jeffrey was driving while Rita helped their two children into life jackets. I didn't care for Rita much, but I had to admit that she looked good in a bikini, even at a distance. I wondered how much Jeffrey had paid for her boobs. I realized that what he said about "closing the loop" and it being "fitting" that the old property be brought together again was a lot of crap. My house was nothing but a teardown as far as he was concerned. Their boat took off with a roar, the inflatable raft following in its wake and the Mossbacher children screaming with pleasure.

I spent the rest of the afternoon working in the barn and watched with satisfaction as the dumpster filled with the detritus of my father's past. Every time I tossed an object into the dumpster I got a kick out of thinking how upset he would be. I found a box of drinking glasses decorated with the Sinclair gas company's green dinosaur logo and smashed them one by one, remembering my father coming home from work and handing one to my mother. "It's no wonder there are so many poor people. They get some other gas when they could go to Sinclair and get something useful without spending an extra penny." It was only later that I realized that the glasses had a kind of retro appeal and would have fetched a good price on eBay. The fucking guy was always right. He was always right.

As I worked I allowed myself to fantasize about what I would do if I could afford to keep the place. With a little work I could turn the barn into a study. I thought about where I would put a desk and some bookshelves to hold that box of books and those notebooks that were up in the attic in Princeton. I could turn those two chapters I had completed into a modest article or two. My dreams that day were also modest: if I could only publish one article I might be able to lay some of the old ghosts to rest. It was really pretty pathetic.

At six the dumpster was almost half full. I took a quick dip in the lake to rinse off the dust. Still dripping, I came back into the house and took the silver Tiffany martini shaker engraved with my father's name from the kitchen cabinet. It was a memorial of those happy days when my parents drank together, a gift to him from my mother two years before she filed for divorce. I filled it with ice and poured about half a pint of gin and a tablespoon of vermouth into it. By the time I got down to the dock the shaker was beaded with moisture. I gave it a gentle shake or two, filled my glass, ripped open a bag of chips, and tried to be happy.

My father sat in that same chair at five o'clock every summer afternoon, staring at the perspiring martini shaker as we waited for my mother. "If your mother doesn't get here in three minutes, I'm going to start without her." When she finally appeared, he poured the drinks before she had settled into her chair. They clinked their glasses together and drank. As I sipped my martini I felt how much that first real drink of the day had come to mean to me. It was the golden moment at the beginning of cocktail hour that had allowed my parents' marriage to last as long as it did.

I sat on the dock until the sun started to go down. The Mossbachers had put their boat away; all the sailors had gone home. The green mix of firs and deciduous trees on the far shore started to glow in the light of the setting sun. It was as if someone had turned a switch and all the colors were suddenly saturated. My mother called it the cocktail hour miracle. As I sat there, unwittingly on the cusp of a new life, I was struck by how odd it was that I could be so sad in a world that was so beautiful.

. 7 .

MANY THOUGHT THAT RHINEBECK had aimed to compete with Camp Wonundra, the Rockefeller place down at the other end of the lake, when he built Birch Lodge. It was fine with him if they thought so. Birch Lodge sat on a small rise on the shore of Upper Saranac Lake. From his veranda Rhinebeck had a good view of the southern end of the lake, and if he turned to the left he had a sweeping view of the eastern shore and the wide expanse of water up to the Narrows, about two miles away. A few small islands dotted the view, and he sometimes thought that if God hadn't put them there, he would have done it himself. He could see the high mountains in the distance. In the evening the cries of loons echoed across the water.

Rhinebeck had been working on the place for three years now, ever since he had acquired the Turner, and the last of the workmen had just left. Durant had done a fine job. The place was all "twigged up" in the Adirondack style, but it hadn't been overdone. The rustic charm of the room appealed to him. He didn't think the ladies would mind; their comfort, too, could be attended to.

It was the middle of August. Rhinebeck sat on the veranda and lit a cigar as he waited for the coffee to be brought. He knew he was a different man than he had been. He had made himself into what the world called Cornelius Rhinebeck by keeping his eyes on the facts. Early on he had realized that every enterprise, no matter how complex, could be understood as a series of steps in a finite process. People spoke of the romance of industry, but it was all in the ledger sheets and how people moved about on the factory floor. Money was made by understanding how many steps they took and reducing the number of them. The human heart, he had believed, was also an enterprise devoted to maximizing return. It was a simple matter. If she was not willing, what could be done to make her willing? What were her scruples? How could they be removed?

But now the water seemed quick and alive as it responded to the color of the sky in a way that it had not before; the light was beautiful in a way it had not been before. Time, and perhaps his Turner, had taken the edge off the egoism and striving of youth.

He finished his coffee and left the cigar to burn itself out. Lottie and her friend would arrive in a few hours, and he needed to complete his preparations. Rhinebeck had told his wife that he'd intended Birch Lodge "for men only." He wanted, he said, a place where he could come with his friends and associates and they could go hunting and fishing without worrying about offending the ladies with their language and their cigars. She had been suspicious, he thought, but she knew him well enough to understand that it was not a quarrel worth having. He had appeased her, however, by suggesting that she might want to come up just once after the place was completed, to see it for herself.

The pride of Birch Lodge, and the reason he had built it, was a room on the second floor of the main building which Rhinebeck called his Snuggery. It could only be approached from a dark, narrow stairway that led off the main living room. Durant's gift for decoration seemed to have deserted him when it came to this stairway; the paint had been cunningly applied so as to look like second-rate workmanship of many years ago. At the top of the stairs was a low door, to which only Rhinebeck had the key.

This door opened into what Durant had described as a cathedral of manly comfort. Light poured in from doors on the balcony and from the clerestory windows that were cleverly set just below the steeply sloping ceiling. It was a large room, but cozy. There were half a dozen places to sit with a book and a glass of wine; some took advantage of views of lake or forest, others faced one of the three fireplaces, in the largest of which a small man could comfortably stand. The stonework around each fireplace showed craftsmanship of the highest order, but it was in the woodwork that Durant's genius had found its fullest expression. The walls were covered with strips of birch bark, cut and arranged so that pictures of the forest appeared on the wall. Borders and moldings were rioting bands of twisted twigs and branches. Stuffed animals of every description hung on the walls and peeked out from every corner. There was a raccoon walking carefully along one of the beams, a porcupine climbing up a pillar, and a bobcat crouched and about to pounce on a baby rabbit that seemed to be nibbling some grass on a mantelpiece.

All the furniture had been made especially for the room. Living wood had been twisted into easy chairs and sofas. Sitting in these chairs, surrounded by these walls and decorations, Rhinebeck had the pleasant sensation of being embraced by Nature in her very womb.

Rhinebeck opened the large cabinet that Durant had made to his particular specifications. He felt the familiar shudder of pleasure. He concentrated on the ships which sailed on the perfect sea. He had a vivid sense of the baskets of spices and the amphorae of fragrant wine that filled the ships' holds. He had never noticed them before. How odd that there, far out on the sea, the sailors and merchants went about their business, while the great warriors fought the greatest battle the world had ever known. The towers of Troy were surely a landmark that guided them on their way. What could they see? The towers and the plain before them, perhaps the smoke from the invading army's campfires, perhaps the fleet of Greek ships pulled up upon the shore. Perhaps they had heard about the quarrel and they were staying as far away from the Trojan coast as they could. Just merchants going about their business, trying to stay out of harm's way.

He looked at his watch. Twenty minutes had passed. He wondered how many hours had disappeared in front of his painting. It was a wonder that he still found the time to make any money at all.

He took it out of the cabinet and laid it on the billiard table. He wrapped it carefully in a piece of canvas, tying the bundle up securely with a stout cord. It pained him, but it just wouldn't do for his wife to see it. He went to a closet and took out an identically sized painting. It was a Renoir, one of his plump pink nudes, although a bit more risqué than most of them. The look on her face was more lustful than languorous, and there was a hint of pubic hair visible through her parted legs. The sense of moisture down there, Rhinebeck suspected, was not on account of the bath. Of course she was nothing like his Helen, but she would do for the purpose he had in mind. Closing her up in the cabinet, he thought it was almost a sacrilege to allow her into the space that had been built to contain his Turner.

He called for Mr. Kircum, the head groundskeeper at Birch Lodge. Kircum and his wife lived in a small house next to the main property. They had had a child, but she had died. He was a silent man who had seen things in the Great War that he would not speak of.

"Is everything in order?" Rhinebeck asked. Kircum nodded. "Will you go pick up the ladies at the station or will you send someone else?"

"I go in about an hour."

"Good. Take that bundle on the billiard table and bring it down to your barn. Be very careful with it. I'll come with you."

Kircum picked up the painting. He carried it with ease in spite of its size and the weight of the gilt frame. They crossed the stone bridge that connected the keeper's house with the main property and walked up the gravel path to the barn. Opening the door, Rhinebeck went ahead. He pushed against the back wall. There was a slight click and the door to the compartment opened. Kircum put the bundle inside and Rhinebeck closed the door. He stepped back to look at the place where his treasure was concealed.

"This will do nicely. Throw some old tools and lumber up against that wall before you go."

. 8 .

THE PART OF HER WORKDAY that Gina liked best
was the evening, after all her colleagues had gone home. First
Tracey, who sat by the door and answered the phone, said good-
bye at a little after six, and by seven she usually had the downstairs room at Madison Partners to herself. Often she would
turn off the overhead lights and sit in the cone of light that
emanated from her desk lamp. With the incessant telephones
finally quiet, she felt she was in a sacred circle, alone with her
catalogues and auction announcements, doing difficult work
that was beautiful and good. She liked to listen to the sounds
of the brownstone as it settled down for the evening: Rosaria
cleaning up or preparing Mr. Bryce's dinner, the faint notes
of an opera recording from the library upstairs, or the solitary
whir of the fax machine as it spat out some paper that would be
dealt with tomorrow.

Sometimes Bryce would pass through on his way out for
the evening and might compliment her on her outfit or ask

what was keeping her so late. Once or twice he asked if Rosaria should bring some coffee or perhaps a sandwich. He seemed pleased that she took her work so seriously, and Gina delighted in his pleasure, although she knew that his approbation probably meant more to her than it should.

For Gina, Madison Partners was an oasis of class and perfection in an ugly world. Bryce dressed beautifully and was devoted to his work. She felt fortunate to be paid so well for participating in that work and sitting in such a lovely room. She had been raised in affluence in New York, but she felt she had grown up in the circus of her parents' screaming fits, divorces, and love affairs. College had been better and graduate school better still, but nothing had ever been as satisfying as Madison Partners.

On Fridays most of "the young people," as Bryce called Gina and her colleagues, went home early, so Gina had been alone for longer than usual when she left at eight. She hoped that Bryce would come through and see that she was still there, but he seemed to have no evening plans. Eventually she took her bag of gym stuff from under her desk, turned out the lights, and made her way to the subway. She had stayed so long that she found herself on a bike in the last row in the corner of her spin class. She missed being able to lock eyes with the instructor as she tried to keep up, but she was so tired that she was happy enough to let herself disappear into the exercise.

There were three messages on her phone when she got home. The first was from her father. She could hear airport noises in the background. "Hi, Baby. On my way back to L.A.

I wanted you to be the first to know, but the damn rags never leave you alone and there was a screwup with Megan's publicist. I keep telling her to fire the fucker, but she's got her own ideas. Anyway, we're getting married. Not sure of the date yet, not sure where. We're thinking Napa, but maybe something a bit more fun. Tahiti, Iceland—we're still working on it. Morocco. But listen, I'm going to need you there, so stay tuned for the details and be ready to party. Gotta go, they're calling my flight. Love ya."

Her father was like a character in a bad movie, who also made bad movies in real life. He had been an entertainment lawyer in New York when Gina was young but had started producing films in Los Angeles while she was in middle school. Since his divorce from her mother, he had had one more marriage and a string of affairs with younger women, mostly actors. Gina had met Megan only once, when her father introduced them at a restaurant as they were passing through New York. She seemed nice enough, was certainly pretty enough, and although she was younger than Gina, she was, fortunately, a year or two older than the second Mrs. Bolton.

The next message was from her mother. She sounded drunk. "So Romeo is at it again. I don't know why he calls me; he thinks I care. He said he already left you a message—Mr. Sensitive. I'm sorry you have to deal with it. He's getting more and more pathetic. He just got all his teeth done—shiny white like a shark. Said it makes the world of difference, said I should try it. He's unbelievable. Give me a call when you get a chance. Love you." Gina decided that if her mother was still awake she would be too far gone to talk to. She would call her in the morning.

The third was from Mr. Bryce. "This is Arthur Bryce. Please come back to the office. Never mind how late, I'll be up until two or three. No need to call, just come as soon as you can. It's important. Take a cab." Gina was still in her bike shorts. She listened to the message again and got into the shower.

Although it was twenty minutes before midnight when she got back to the office, Bryce was dressed as if it was just time for lunch. His tie was perfectly knotted and his shirt perfectly pressed. She was glad that she had changed back into an office outfit, although she was aware that her hair was still wet.

"Do sit down." Bryce waved her into a leather chair in front of his desk. "I'm sorry to have called you back so late. I came down to see if you were still there, but you were gone. Can I at least offer you a cup of coffee? I have prevailed upon Rosaria to wait up until your arrival, so I'll have one whether you do or not." Gina declined the coffee. She had not had any plans for the evening other than a bowl of soup, some television, and sleep. Coffee at this hour would ruin the possibility of the latter. She asked for water. She was starving.

"While we are waiting, let me show you one of my favorite possessions." Bryce moved deliberately and beautifully, as if his movements had been designed to show how well his suit was cut. He took a watercolor landscape of a Swiss lake from the wall. It was a small thing that more than held its own against the gilt-framed oils that filled the room. There were mountains in the background, a village below, and a small sailboat crossing the blue-gray water. Flecks of color suggested cows in a meadow.

Bryce drew her attention to a spot of forest on the right-hand side. The artist had scraped the paper—perhaps with his fingernail—and his touch had created the breeze which brought the forest to life and drove the boat across the water. "It is the hand of the artist, in this case J.M.W. Turner," Bryce said, "that brings life to the world. It is the hand of God that Michelangelo painted." He went on talking about the sketch until Rosaria came in with the coffee. Gina was sorry to hear Rosaria say that she would be turning in, but glad that she lived in the building.

"I have been thinking about the future directions of the firm in these sad days. Also thinking of you, of what your role might be," he said. "I have been watching you, you know. Paying attention to the way you go about things. Quite impressive. That was nicely done with the Hassam."

A few weeks earlier Gina had negotiated the sale of a Childe Hassam seascape for much more than anyone in the office had expected. Both the buyer and the seller had professed themselves delighted with the transaction. She had hoped that Bryce would notice; but given the hour, his praise both pleased her and put her on her guard.

"It must have pained you. Hassam is so vulgar. When I saw the thing I almost felt ill. I had a moment of despair; I thought we might have to hang it downstairs for a while. But you did well, my dear, very well. Mr. Ashford called the other day asking that I keep my eye out for any other such. His taste in art is hardly developed, but he admired you. You keep yourself fit. A nice complexion. Beautiful hair. A figure a man like Ashford might admire. He was most complimentary. He requested, in fact, that you take care of any future transactions between Madison Partners and himself. You might let him simmer a bit, but perhaps in a few months a visit to Santa Monica will be in order. Bring along a canvas or two. Dress well, but a bit more Hollywood, you know. Mr. Ashford will appreciate the gesture.

"Now, don't look so shocked. Madison Partners is everything you believe it to be, and, quite frankly, more, but it is also a business. We require the Mr. Ashfords of Santa Monica to purchase the kinds of things they do in order to make all of this possible." His gesture seemed to encompass not only the room in which they were sitting but other realms that were beyond her grasp.

It had been a matter of some pride to Gina that she was able to get such a good price for the Hassam. It was her enthusiasm for the painting, she thought, as well as its beauty, that had convinced Ashford. She was hurt by the suggestion that it was her looks and embarrassed that she might have been guilty of the same weakness of taste as Mr. Ashford. She wondered if Bryce was making fun of her or if he was paying her a compliment she did not deserve. Her sense of discomfort increased. An elaborate clock in the corner of the library chimed midnight.

"Perhaps you feel uncomfortable? But you are young. You have much to learn. It is not all sweetness and light; the path to greatness is not always easy. Or nice," Bryce said. "I watch all the young people I hire. I hire only the best. But I have noticed you above the others. You work very hard, which is the first thing. You still have, if you don't mind my saying so, a young person's appreciation of things, but that will change with time and experience.

"But I did not ask you to come here at this hour to talk about a man from Santa Monica, nor even a small but perfect watercolor, though we shall come back to Turner in due course. I have, as they say, bigger fish to fry.

"There is," Bryce said, "the art history they teach you in school and the paintings one sees in museums. But there are other works, you know, that remain forever in private collections. Most of these are very bad, and they stay where they are for sentimental reasons or because no one wants them, but some are so exquisite they represent a subterranean tradition of excellence that very few are able to appreciate.

"Opportunities to acquire such works come along but rarely. I spent a number of years pursuing a set of drawings by Michelangelo called *The Allegory of Love*. People had been whispering about them forever. They had spent the Second World War in Berlin. From there they had gone to Moscow. An opportunity to acquire them seemed to open up in 1993. The wall had fallen; the Soviet Union had crumbled. History had cracked open and a number of extraordinary pieces had become available, although *The Allegory of Love* was by far the greatest of these. I was hot on the trail, but at the last minute I was outmaneuvered and outspent. As a kind of recompense and in exchange for my silence, I was granted a few minutes' look as they were in transit to Dubai. We were standing in a drafty hangar in Frankfurt. The light was appalling and the crew was impatient to take off. It is a complex allegory of Platonic or Grecian love in which the figure of Plato bears a striking resemblance to Michelangelo himself. Extraordinary lines, shadow beyond imagining. God the father and Socrates are merged into an ideal of perfect masculinity. I saw the transfer of the divine spirit into the ecstatic body of Plato in exquisite anatomical detail. I was in such a fever of despair that I could hardly see, but it was, nonetheless, as profound an experience as I have ever had."

Bryce shuddered as the memory washed over him. Gina sat in silence and waited for him to recover. She saw that he was offering her a glimpse of a world that was greater and more beautiful than the one she lived in. She wondered if she would ever be able to see as clearly and feel as passionately as he did.

"Time has cracked open again; I feel it in my bones. I aim to have that experience once more, but this time I will win. And you, if you are willing, are going to help me and, perhaps, share in it yourself. You have surely heard the story of Turner's estate? When Turner died in 1851, at the age of seventy-six, Ruskin took on the task of cataloguing the large body of work the artist had bequeathed to the National Gallery. In about 1856 he discovered a body of 'obscene' works amongst Turner's remains and, assisted by Ralph Wornum, the keeper of the National Gallery, he burned this material.

"Now, what was this stuff that Ruskin burned?" Bryce went on to say that most scholars assume it was of a piece with the atmospheric and almost abstract oil sketches of copulating couples or those doodles of sexual subjects that survive, but he thought that among the material were some sketches or notebooks related to a lost painting. Bryce handed Gina the leather folder that contained Wyndham's note.

"I believe," Bryce said, "that Ruskin burned material related to the 'infamous painting' mentioned there. Further, I believe that this painting still exists. I have asked you here tonight because I want you to help me find it."

She looked at him quizzically for a moment. Bryce did not seem unduly excited. He was as calm and perfectly groomed as ever. She was flattered by his request, she told him, but she needed to understand more.

She was to move to England, he said; Madison Partners maintained an apartment near Sloane Square that would be turned over to her exclusive use. She would be assigned a number of important British clients. His secondary goal was to give her a broader experience of the business, but her primary task would be to find some evidence of Turner's "infamous" painting.

"One can only learn by doing. An object of the sort I am seeking," Bryce said, "does not pass through the world without leaving traces. You see the wake from that sailboat in Turner's sketch, how it trails behind the stern? Turner understood these matters—he was a great sailor, you know. Each life, each thing, leaves some trace—a wave, a ripple, depending on its size. I firmly believe that traces remain of everything that ever was, of every action ever undertaken. They are merely too small and too faint, too far removed from their first cause, for our weak intellects to comprehend.

"These traces—broken hearts, idle gossip, scraps of paper— can lead us to the thing itself, if it still exists. In this case, of course, the matter is a good deal more complicated because, I suspect, all those involved have made every effort to hide the trail. But those efforts themselves leave traces, the broken twigs, as it were, in the underbrush. You are perhaps too young to understand this, but everything is connected to everything else. This coffee cup I am holding leads back to the pillars of the Temple of Poseidon at Paestum and to the windows of Chartres. Everything is part of a vast network; one needs only to find the thread and follow it carefully back. In theory it is simplicity itself."

He went on to explain that she would receive a significant raise and could look forward to a sizable bonus whenever she made any discovery that seemed to advance his quest. He would give her his private cell phone number, and he expected her to come to New York once or twice a month to provide an update on her progress.

"Are you interested?" he asked.

She understood that if she were to refuse or show any sign of hesitation the door that Bryce was holding open for her would close, never to be opened again.

"Of course," she said. "You're offering me an extraordinary opportunity. I would be a fool to say no."

"Good. I expect to hear that you are settled in London on Monday."

. 9 .

WHEN I RETURNED to the house I inquired about a coach that could take me to London. Urgent family business, I said, required my immediate attention there. I had to admire the way in which Egremont's people remained perfectly composed as I made my request and told my lie. I was sure that word of my disgrace had preceded my arrival.

I went to my room and began to pack; word was brought to me that the coach would not leave until the morning. I debated as to what to do. I could go to the village and spend the night at the inn, although the expense was nothing I had counted on. I could remain in my room and say I had a headache. Going to the village would make it seem that I was slinking away. Pleading a headache was hardly any better, but it seemed somehow preferable.

As the hours passed and I thought about my situation, my head did begin to ache; I consoled myself by considering that I would be telling the truth when I offered my excuse.

I passed a miserable afternoon, perhaps the worst in my life except for that afternoon when I arrived at my father's too late to ask for his forgiveness. As I stood before the window and looked out upon Petworth Park, the colors seemed richer than any I had ever seen, as if Nature had reserved some special pigment for this place only. I felt a mixture of shame and outrage and sorrow that I cannot express. To think that my love for you, the finest feeling in my nature, should be hurled back at me in contempt filled me with sorrow and rage. All my usual complaints welled up in my breast with more than usual force: Why must I be despised for a mode of love honored by the greatest minds of antiquity and sanctified by our affection for each other? Why should I feel shame for the best and truest parts of my nature?

I passed two or three hours in these gloomy cogitations, pacing back and forth in front of the window until my shins ached. I did not know where I would go and how I would live. I did not feel, like Adam, that the world was all before me after my expulsion from Paradise.

I tried to write, I tried to read, but all to no avail. Just after three o'clock there came a deferential knock on the door. It was one of the chief servants. He handed me a folded piece of paper and a sealed envelope. "My lord and Mrs. Spencer send these to you with their compliments." His eyes met mine for a moment before he bowed, and I thought I saw something, either respect or contempt, that I had not seen before.

The note read as follows:

Grant,

   My behaviour this morning was inexcusable. Pray forgive me.

                                  Egremont

I opened the envelope and found a letter in a graceful feminine hand:

My dear Charles,

   Word has come that you are planning to leave us. I have not yet had the opportunity to know you well, but my heart tells me you are a gentleman. As you are a gentleman you had no choice but to make your plans to depart, but I beg you to reconsider your decision in light of Egremont's note of apology. Although you would be well within your rights to do so, please do not bring shame upon an old nobleman by departing prematurely. Egremont forgets himself more often than he did in the past. I hope you will forgive him his outburst and remain here with us so that I may get to know you better. I should very much like us to be friends.

                              Elizabeth Spencer

On first reading these missives I felt overwhelmed by joy, like a man given a reprieve at the foot of the gallows. But then I was half ashamed. I realized that the injury remained in the eyes of the world and that mere words written to my private eye could do nothing to eradicate the calumny. Then I thought further. I am, dear David, what the world calls a sodomite. It is a vile word, used to hurt, but call it what you will, it is one of the words the world uses to describe my nature. By leaving, I reflected, I would say to the world that I was ashamed of my nature.

For about an hour I went back and forth as I tried to look at the thing from all sides. The more I thought, the more of a muddle I found myself in, as my feelings and logic did battle with each other. But every so often we are all blessed by moments of grace. Such a blessing fell upon me that afternoon. I can recall what happened, but I can hardly explain it. I was standing before the window looking out at the view, which had seemed to promise so fair a day in the morning. I was in an agony of confusion. But then the beauty of the place and the vista came over me with an almost palpable force. It poured a living balm into my wounded soul. I felt calm. Hardly knowing what I did, I went to the fireplace and burnt the two notes. I took up my pen and wrote to Egremont.

My honoured lord,
  The fault was entirely mine this morning. Your note was unnecessary, but appreciated. I will remain forever in your debt for the kindness and hospitality you have shown a poor young scholar.

  Your humble servant,
  Charles Grant

And then I wrote to Mrs. Spencer:

Dear Mrs. Spencer,

Thank you for your kind note. The hospitality at Petworth is incomparable, and I will be delighted to remain here for a while longer. As the fault this morning was entirely mine, Lord Egremont was well within his rights when he lost his temper. But I very much appreciate his condescension to a penniless young scholar with no great prospects. I do not know what role you have played in this small matter, but I sense that your kind hand was involved. Thank you from the bottom of my heart.

Hoping to become your friend as well, I remain,

Your servant,

Charles Grant

I put both notes in envelopes and called for a servant, feeling as if a great weight had been lifted from my shoulders. A small voice, it is true, called out that I had been a coward and chided me for allowing myself to be bought by mere promises, but in general I felt at peace.

I went down to dinner at the usual time. At Petworth the custom is to gather just outside the dining room and await the arrival of Egremont. Guests begin to congregate five or ten minutes before the appointed hour. At seven the doors are flung open and Egremont takes Mrs. Spencer's arm and leads her in. Egremont's son and his wife make a great show of going in next, while the rest follow, with those of us, like myself, who are conscious of being outsiders to the ranks of the blessed hanging back and going in last.

As we waited, everyone was most cordial to me. When Egremont and Mrs. Spencer arrived, they paused for a moment before me. I bowed and said my greetings. Egremont took me by the hand and said, in a voice that all could hear, that I was "a damn fine fellow." Mrs. Spencer also took me by the hand and said that she was very glad I was able to prolong my stay. She held my eyes for a moment or two longer than is customary and applied more pressure than is usual. There is a wealth of feeling in her eyes that I have never seen elsewhere. Her eyes, one suspects, have seen much; they express a kind of world-weariness on that account. But there is also an almost childlike sparkle of joy and laughter there, and it was this aspect that predominated as she took my hand. "I am so very glad to know that you will be remaining with us," she said.

Everyone standing around us marked, of course, these exchanges, and I saw that they were intended to let all those assembled know that I was in the good graces of my host and hostess. I found myself seated next to Turner, who had grabbed me by the arm and steered me into a seat next to his. "We are in luck, sir," he said as we sat down. He gave me a conspiratorial wink and nodded behind him. He spoke in a low whisper. "This is the best seat at the table. The steward stands directly behind. One can get a third glass without attracting attention."

As the first glass of wine was poured Mr. Gedding rose and proposed my lord's health in more words than were necessary for the task. But he is, as I might have mentioned earlier, the member for Pulborough and, like most members, is enamored of the sound of his own voice. When at length he sat down, His Lordship rose, somewhat piqued, I thought, at the fulsome praise he had been forced to endure.

"You are too kind, Mr. Gedding, but I thank you for your gracious and eloquent words. Let me propose, in turn, a simple toast: to your health, ladies and gentlemen." He paused for a moment and looked round the table. I fancied he held my eye for a moment longer than those of the others as he offered me a kindly smile. "But no more speechifying! Let us to our meat while it is still piping."

All that was good of field, pond, garden, and vine was placed before us in more than customary abundance, including an enormous roast of venison. There was that usual lull in the conversation as the party commenced with the serious business of eating, but Mrs. Spencer soon worked her magic. She drew Mr. Gedding out on political gossip. From there we were embarked on a lively discussion of some matter of church policy, but when Mr. Sockett was on the verge of becoming heated over something Mr. Gedding said, Mrs. Spencer managed to toss the ball to Turner, who recounted one of his adventures while traveling in the Rhineland. It involved an attractive chambermaid, a pot of mustard, and two drunken Frenchmen. The story had all the table laughing except for Wyndham and his wife, who looked daggers at Mr. Sockett for his failure to support them in their sanctimoniousness.

At one point while the conversation was particularly loud and animated, Turner turned to me. He spoke so softly that no one else could hear. "His Lordship was most cordial to you before we came in."

"He is kind and gracious," I said. "One of the most remarkable men in England."

"He sent you a note, I understand."

I looked at Turner, unable to comprehend how he had come to know of it. "As I said," I replied, "His Lordship is most kind. I burnt it."

Turner looked at me closely with his piercing gray eyes. "Very good, young man. Very good indeed. You will do well." He patted me on the shoulder and gave me a wink, motioning to the steward to fill our glasses.

"Come," he said, "to your health. This is a better vintage than usual. Have you seen His Lordship's cellars? Most interesting. Wine there bottled before I was born, put down by Egremont's father when he was a young man. The likes of us must drink wine like this when it is offered. Drink up, I say, for we pass this way but once."

. 10 .

⟨⟩ ON THE MORNING of July 7, 2003, I woke just as the sun was rising. Mist rose and swirled up from the surface of the lake; the sun was an orange disk framed by golden clouds as it crested the hill on the far shore. Usually I'm not a morning person, but self-pity was waiting just around the corner, and I knew I had to keep it at bay with action. I made a pot of coffee, swallowed half a bowl of cereal, and went straight to the barn.

Once there, I went deeper and deeper into the past. Mostly it was just junk that my father thought might come in handy one day, but there were some old toys of mine, too, the sight of which almost moved me to tears. A paper bag contained wrapped presents for my mother that my father had never given to her. Another contained a filmy black nylon nightgown. I almost got sick thinking about it. There was a suitcase full of clothing that I had worn in high school, and boxes and boxes of my mother's old clothes. As I made my way through the sheer quantity of stuff, I saw that it was a disease, a dry goods addiction equivalent to my father's drinking. I set aside some of the clothes to bring to Goodwill, amused at the thought of the local girls in Tupper Lake walking around in the emblems of my mother's vanity.

By late morning I had reached the previous owners' junk, which was of a different class, more modest and less fraught. I found old electric motors and various unidentifiable machine parts. Almost everything went into the dumpster, but I set aside a few things that might be of interest to the antique shops in Bucks County.

By late afternoon, when the barn was empty, I took a broom and swept out what must have been a hundred years of dirt and dust. The floor was in remarkably good shape, but there were two windows that needed to be cleaned or perhaps replaced. The walls were painted tongue-and-groove boards of the sort that the Mossbachers used in some of their most tasteful renovations.

Deep down, I knew I'd have to take Mossbacher's money, but I gave myself half an hour to indulge in the fantasy that I could make something of myself in this room. Then, as I was considering various locations for my desk, I noticed three small hinges set into the back wall on the left side of a three-by-four-foot rectangle that was formed by an almost imperceptible cut in the wood. This spot had been hidden by an old bedstead that was one of the last things I had taken out of the barn.

I tapped on the center of the rectangle; it sounded about the same as when I tapped elsewhere on the wall. I pressed on the side opposite the hinges. The wood gave slightly; there was a click, and the panel sprang forward.

When I pulled the panel toward me and peered inside, I saw a rectangular bundle wrapped in what appeared to be old sailcloth and tied with coarse twine. I lifted it out of the recess and placed it carefully on the ground. There was no mark or lettering of any kind on the cloth. I undid the twine.

Inside was a painting in an ornate gold frame. As I propped it against the wall and stepped back to get a better look, light poured from the canvas and lit up the barn. I could feel its glow on my face.

I knew at once that it was Helen. And I suddenly knew something of how the world worked. An army of heroes struggled on the vast plain below her window. I could not see the gods, but I knew they moved among the men. Her lover, Paris, was visible on the left, moving toward her as surely as the apple moves toward the earth and each human life moves toward death. There was a brass plate on the painting's gilt frame:

THE CENTER OF THE WORLD

J.M.W. TURNER, R.A.

I don't know how long I sat there. The day turned into evening. As the light in the barn faded and changed, I understood things that had been incomprehensible a moment before, while the certainties of the previous hour were lost. I remembered sensing the presence of the gods, although I knew they were not depicted on the canvas. I wept with rage and frustration at the thought of the feelings I had lost. I sat there until it was quite dark, seeming to see things in the painting long after the light had failed. At last I realized I could hardly see my hand when I held it up before my face.

I made my way back to the house and unplugged the phone. For the first time in longer than I could remember, I didn't feel hungry or in need of a drink. I lay down on the old bed upstairs. There was a cold clarity to the visions which appeared against the pitch dark bedroom ceiling. My mind had never been so full nor my perceptions so acute. I don't know if I slept or not, but if I did there was no difference between waking and dreaming.

. 11 .

꞊꞊ **AS THEY WAITED** for their coffee, Gina and Bryce talked of her upcoming visit to Mr. Ashford. She mentioned that her father's wedding had been put off and described how her mother, forgetting that there was a time difference between New York and London, had called in the middle of the night to read her the article in *The Enquirer* describing Megan's wild night out with the costar of her latest film. Gina managed to turn it all into an amusing story, but her mother's toxic glee at her father's self-induced misfortunes was difficult for her to take. Since she no longer had a place of her own in New York, she had spent the night at her mother and Julia's apartment. There was too much wine with dinner, too many drinks before, and too much yelling. She felt dirty when she woke in the morning, but a long shower had not made her feel as clean as sitting down in Bryce's leather armchair and seeing the beautiful Turner watercolor and Bryce's perfectly knotted tie.

"But there is a kind of glow about you, in spite of your unfortunate family, that I have not seen before," Bryce said once Rosaria had delivered the coffee. "London seems to agree with you."

"I have been lucky with a lot of old letters," she said. "How familiar are you with the painter William Collins?"

"He is uninteresting beyond his friends and his progeny," Bryce said. "A member of the Royal Academy. A friend of Sir David Wilkie, whom he persuaded to be the godfather of his child. The child grew up to be the novelist Wilkie Collins. Small realistic interiors of the worthy poor. Insipid seascapes. Please don't tell me you have discovered a new painting by Collins. There is a market for that sort of thing, but he makes Hassam seem like Matisse."

Gina colored slightly but went on to explain that she had found a letter from Collins to Wilkie that was previously unknown, but which seemed relevant to Bryce's quest.

He raised his eyebrows. "If I recall, both Collins and Wilkie were insufferably moralistic, a tendency that was fatal to Collins's art, less so for Wilkie's. Turner and Wilkie respected and admired each other: one of Turner's most moving seascapes, *Peace—Burial at Sea*, commemorated Wilkie's death off the coast of Gibraltar in, I believe, 1841."

"You are correct, of course." She handed Bryce a folder. "This letter was written in the fall of 1838, when Wilkie was traveling in Ireland. The first page or so deals with some small matters of business having to do with picture frames. But then

he goes on to share some Royal Academy gossip which I think
you will find interesting. Start here."

She pointed to the middle of the second page and waited
patiently as Bryce read.

> *Our mutual friend (or, more precisely, your friend and*
> *my acquaintance) J.M.W.T. has unleashed a* Burning of
> the Houses of Parliament *on an unsuspecting world. I do*
> *not know what the general public will think of it, but our*
> *brother painters will be merely polite in their public utter-*
> *ances. In their private hearts they will feel what I now say*
> *to your private ear: it is hardly a painting so much as a force*
> *of nature and the very hand of God on canvas. He sets all*
> *rules at defiance and flings paint like one gone mad. There*
> *are the usual yellows, of course, and red and lurid orange.*
> *One can almost feel the fire's heat coming off the surface.*
> *The painting brings back that awful night most vividly,*
> *but, and I hardly know how to say this, more in the man-*
> *ner of a nightmare than a recollection. It is as if, seeing it,*
> *I feel those horrors that stem from a disordered digestion*
> *intrude themselves upon my waking mind. And yet—and*
> *this is the queerest part of the whole business—while I still*
> *feel the nightmare quality, it also makes me feel (and I am*
> *almost ashamed to admit this) a kind of devilish joy. As a*
> *Christian gentleman I know this was a terrible event for our*
> *nation, and yet Turner's painting makes me feel a savage*
> *glee in the conflagration, as if I were a heathen Hottentot*
> *dancing about a gruesome idol. It may be that this glee is*

an involuntary response to the mere beauty of the thing that
Turner has made. This makes Turner a dangerous man.
The beauty and passion in his work trump good sense and
plain morality, even in someone who has his wits about him
and knows a little about how Art moves the human heart.

But so much for the public Turner. What follows is a
much more private and delicate matter. I only mention it because I know you have his trust and perhaps his ear; I have
neither of these, but I do have the good name of our brotherhood and our Academy at heart. I therefore take the liberty
of sharing these few words with you and you alone.

Of Turner's private life, aside from the fact that it is
conducted on the most irregular principles, little enough
is known, and the less known the better, for all of us. But
many of our fellow Academicians have noted that ever
since the death of his great patron Lord Egremont, Turner
has grown ever more dissolute. Egremont's son has cut him
most dreadfully and he who once had the run of Petworth
House is now distinctly persona non grata. Some say it is
on account of that familiarity which Lord Egremont encouraged and which young Wyndham can't abide, but others say it is on account of those goings-on a few years before
good Egremont's death, which were much whispered about
in town at the time. It matters not the cause—the result is
that Turner is cut off from his greatest source of advance-
ment, and although he does not need the preferment (and
I speak as one often in that need) he rails against its loss
most bitterly.

Yesterday my boy of all work came to me and said he was troubled in his conscience on account of something he had heard when I sent him over to Macrone's to see about some engravings. When he arrived they were not yet ready and he was instructed to go to the back of the studio and assist in packing them up. My boy reported that Macrone was entertaining Turner with a bottle, even though it was but two o'clock in the afternoon, when three hours of God's good light remained in which a man might do some work.

They were, my boy said, quite merry. Turner spoke familiarly of Egremont and the great days at Petworth, boasting that he had done his best work there, work which the world would never see. Macrone questioned him on this point, and made some rude jests about how the best performance was always done under cover of darkness. At this Turner grew quite angry; my boy told me he feared the two might come to blows, but then, as if to settle the matter, Turner took out a note book and showed Macrone some sketches. At this Macrone (who, between ourselves, is no better than he needs to be) grew even more violent; he cried out that he had never seen anything so shameful and that "Helen be damned, but the mistress of Petworth is nothing more than a damned whore." Turner took great offence and used words that my boy was too ashamed to repeat and I am too decent to write down. He stormed out of the studio, vowing never to see Macrone again.

Now, my boy is a good lad. I cautioned him about telling tales out of school, but he assured me he was so troubled in

*his mind that he needed to unburden himself. He was right
to do so, I said, but on no account must he pass this story
on. And yet I fear that grave damage may already have been
done, for if it has come to me, who knows who else might
hear the same or worse? The plain fact is that Turner needs
to take better care of his reputation. He is, after all, the chief
of our brotherhood, and if a cloud should fall on him, all of
us will be equally under its shadow. Do speak to him when
you return.*

Bryce read the letter twice. "You have done well, my dear,
very well indeed. You are not only beautiful, but resourceful.
I was not mistaken when I chose you for this task. My taste
has never betrayed me yet. People are like paintings, you know,
and not everyone can distinguish the good and the beautiful
from the rest."

He asked her if anyone else knew about her find. She shook
her head.

"Very good. We must keep it that way. If the vultures that
hover over the graduate schools caught wind of this, we might
not be able to keep them away."

They spent the next hour or so discussing the significance
of the letter. They agreed that it was likely that the notebook
Turner had shown Macrone was one of the documents that
Ruskin had burnt. They also agreed that Gina should turn her
attention to the history of Petworth House next.

"It's a well-plowed field, but I think it might be worth your
time. Poke around the edges of things; perhaps you will find

something there. But let me repeat: I am very pleased." Bryce rose from his desk and walked her to the door of the library. He took her hand and raised it to his lips. The dry pressure lasted longer than she had expected it would.

"Good luck with Mr. Ashford. I expect to hear great things. Or at least remunerative things. It is a long flight from L.A. to London," he said, placing his arm around her shoulder. "But you can while away the hours thinking about your next paycheck. I am sorry to see you go, but absence, as they say, makes the heart grow fonder. I look forward to your next visit."

. 12 .

❧ THERE WAS MUSIC and agreeable conversation after dinner, but the ladies soon grew tired. Jones and some of the others went off to play billiards, while I bade them good night and went to the library. It had been a momentous day and I felt that a few solitary moments before the fire would do me good.

There is something wonderful about a great house like Petworth after dinner. It is like an immense living organism. As I sat there in my quiet nook I was aware of the sounds of human activity all around me—the faint noise of the servants preparing the upper rooms, the distant murmur of conversation, the quiet clatter of the dinner things being put away. Gradually the creature seems to come to rest as the greater part of the servants complete their duties. One still hears something occasionally, but it is like the sound a sleeper makes as he dreams.

I heard footsteps approaching. It was Turner. He had a portfolio under his arm. "Ah, there you are, you young dog. You have found the coziest spot with the nicest fire. I had been coming to this house for five years before I had settled on this as my favorite place, and here you are after less than five days." He pulled a chair up closer to the fire. "Always loved warmth. Cat for an ancestor, I suppose. But it is harder and harder to stay warm as I grow older. A sad business."

I mentioned that he still had the energy of a younger man and that I had seen him go out as the sun rose.

"No, sir. You did not know me when I was younger. When I was younger I would have been waiting on the sun, not running after him like a schoolboy late for his lessons. I was so vexed with myself for my sloth today that I could hardly do the work I meant to do. It is a hard world we live in, sir, and it won't do to lie in bed while the fight goes on about you."

"I greatly admired the view as the sun rose this morning," I said. "It was wonderful in the way the various shades of green appeared out of the gray. I suppose you went up there to do some sketches. I would be very much interested in seeing them."

Turner seemed somewhat taken aback by my request and I myself was surprised by my boldness. At length he shrugged. "No harm in that, I suppose. Generally I keep my sketches to myself. Thinking in one's small clothes, you know. Best done alone. But here, turn up the lamp."

Turner had been sitting on top of the hill. On the first page I saw he had been looking down on the pond and at the rising sun beyond. It was evident he had been working with some sort of soft crayon or chalk. The page was a sea of color, swirling about as if the world were not yet fully formed and matter and light were just emerging from the chaos. I recognized the lake and the hills beyond; the sun was doubled in water and sky; some trees and low shrubs were fighting to be born out of the darkness.

"It looks nothing like," I said, "but somehow more true. I hardly know what else to say, but you have put the truth of this morning on the page."

Turner smiled like a delighted child. "You are too kind. But I see that you speak from your heart. That is a good thing, even if your eyes are not up to the task you set yourself. There is much that is wanting here. Turn the page. You will see that I warmed to my task as I worked. Here I was still annoyed at my tardiness. It is a picture of my indolence, not of the light I saw."

I turned the page as instructed. The next drawing was more finished, as befitted a day that was already an hour old. The colors still swirled and the shapes were indistinct, but I could clearly recognize the contours of the pond. I could see the deer that had come down to the water's edge to drink, and the cattle in one of the distant fields.

"That is a most beautiful drawing," I said. "But I hope you will not think me rude if I say that I prefer the first. The world, I am sure, will admire the second more but the first feels more like the morning, if I can be allowed that. There is less likeness there, but more feeling."

There were a few more pages of drawings, each done in a rapid and confident way. The most magical of them conjured up the view and the feeling of the morning out of only a few lines and splashes of color. It seemed like alchemy.

As I turned the last page I noticed a little drawing in one corner. It was the kind of crude sketch a naughty schoolboy might make. I thought of myself, David, when I am down on my knees before you in your glory. I wondered if Turner had allowed me to see the notebook because he was hoping to make an overture. He is not, as I have said, a handsome man, and you have no reason to fear on that account. His eyes met mine for a moment and I think he saw that I had noticed the sketch.

We were saved from any further discussion, however, by the sound of footsteps. It was Lord Egremont. Turner and I both rose to greet him, but Egremont waved us down. I moved an additional chair up close to the fire. "I knew this was Turner's favorite spot, but I didn't think that he would be so willing to share it."

"Sharing had nothing to do with it," Turner said. "The young dog is a dog of sense; he found it on his own."

A servant entered, carrying a tray with glasses and a bottle. "I thought I might enjoy a glass before I retired," said Lord Egremont. "I would be most gratified if you would join me. At my age it won't do to drink alone."

"To your health, my lord," Turner proposed. He let the wine linger in his mouth before he swallowed it. "This is most fine, sir. I've never had anything like it—this must be, what is that stuff, Grant?—ambrosia, sir. The stuff of the gods, the very light in Apollo's chalice."

Egremont took another small sip before responding. "Glad you like it. This was laid down in the cellar half a century ago. Old Hartley, bless his soul, chose it. He was a man who knew his business. Not two dozen bottles left. I am getting to an age where it won't do to save them. But I have put away enough young wine so that the youngsters shall have their share of fifty-year-old port when they reach my age."

He turned to me with a smile. "You are silent, Mr. Grant. Do you not approve of the wine?" His kindness sparked a pounding in my chest as I remembered how he had addressed me this morning in the field.

"I am speechless," I managed to reply. "I thought I had tasted port before, but this is a different order of thing altogether. I thank you for the privilege of drinking it."

Lord Egremont nodded with satisfaction and then spoke to Turner. "The other night you said something that I have been puzzling over ever since."

Turner held out his glass and watched as Egremont filled it. "Indeed?"

"Yes. You said that there was more truth between a woman's legs than between Homer's ears. You went on to say that the truth is what matters and that I would understand. I think, Turner, I do understand—but how did you know that?"

Turner's manner changed abruptly. He seemed to look inward and spoke to himself, as if neither Lord Egremont nor I was in the room. "Passion, sir. Sensual delight." He took another sip of port and savored it thoughtfully. "I have devoted my life to my art. Other men may have had greater genius than I. But no man has worked harder. The hours in the studio. The days and weeks upon the road. Sleeping in the most god-awful places, sir. Risking life and limb in the Alps. Getting poisoned by innkeepers. Nearly having my throat cut by Italian thieves. Having myself tied to the mast so that I might see the play of the gale upon the waves. All for my art, sir. I never took a wife. The obligations of home and family would have prevented me from devoting the full measure.

"But there have been times when the urgency of my sensual feelings has been such that I have risked much—money, health, position—in order to satisfy them. And when I think back on my career thus far—all the honors I have received, my early membership in the Academy, your patronage and hospitality, my lord, the esteem of my fellow artists—I doubt that much of it is as memorable to me as a night I spent in a country inn—Lord, it must have been twenty years ago—with one of the maidservants."

Turner paused and a faint smile flickered over his face. Egremont smiled as well. The two of them seemed to have forgotten that I was there.

"Lord, yes. Before you were born, Turner, there was a lass that was the daughter of one of my tenants. She was a fine-looking girl. Clever as a whip. Lively. I had her in the house as a kitchen maid. I taught her some tricks I learned from the London whores. She was an apt pupil and took to them with a right good will. The hours I spent with her will live in my mind until I die."

"So what became of her?" Turner asked.

"I married her off to another of my tenants. When the young man weighed her lack of virtue against the size of the dowry I provided, he took her. When on their wedding night he found what she could do, he saw he had made a most excellent bargain. She died about eight months after the wedding, bless her soul. The brat died too, but I don't think it was mine.

"I am eighty years old. My teeth are better than yours, Turner. I can still walk, ride, shoot. My hearing is not what it once was, but if I sit close to the harpsichord I can hear Mrs. Spencer sing well enough. She is not such a wonderful singer, but the heaving of her bosom still affords me pleasure. The will is still there, Turner, after all these years, the will is still there. But the ability to perform is quite extinguished. I have consulted with my physician about the matter. The young puppy appeared quite surprised it was still a matter of concern to me. He is good enough in his line, I suppose, but he seemed to think that a man of four score ought to put aside that sort of thing and be grateful that he is still breathing. I wonder if he will be humming that tune when he is my age."

"I confess, my lord, that what you describe has always been my greatest fear. But I imagined the desire would simply fade away like the light at close of day."

"No. That's the damn pity. There are times when I look at Mrs. Spencer, when she is reading to me or when she is gracing some buffoon with that lustrous smile of hers, and I feel the heat of it quite as if I was a young buck. But then, when we are upstairs, nothing comes of it, although the burning remains. It's damn peculiar."

Egremont suddenly looked at me, as if he had just recollected that I was in the room. "A young fellow like you," he said. "You have no conception of what we are talking about, we old men who half live in the shadows. But you will, mark my words, you will." He smiled at me quite kindly, as if our encounter that morning had never been. "Youth is a gift, young man. Do not waste it."

"I've always thought of it as light, not burning," Turner said. Turner reached for the bottle and filled his glass again as if our host was not present. The wine was potent stuff, but it did not seem to have any effect on him. I drank mine very slowly. I felt I was sailing upon deep waters and that it would not do to lose my way.

"Stands to reason you would," Egremont replied. "But what do you mean by it?"

Turner took another sip of wine. He held his free hand out before him, like a man reaching for something in the dark, as he often did when he was trying to describe a difficult concept.

"Light. It is what makes the world. Without light: no clouds, no sky, no reflection on the water. This most excellent port? It would not be. Light is the prime force, creating all. Light drives us. Light, in all its aspects, is the motive of the world."

We were all silent for a moment. I could hear the distant sounds of the great house settling into sleep. Turner went on, "That, you see, is what matters. Homer understood—rosy-fingered dawn and all that fuss—what was it about? A cunt, my lord, begging your pardon, a cunt. The Greek fellow wanted to fuck her and so did the Trojan fellow. We all would if we could see her, even young Grant here. And so a thousand heroes died, each death more bloody than the last. The very gods poking about in human affairs. Zeus himself having to set things to rights. All on account of that cunt. Even Homer could only hint at it, but that is the light that makes us be."

"As I said this afternoon, you must paint that," Egremont said, adding as he nodded in my direction, "and make use of Grant now that he is staying with us."

Turner snorted. "You are a man of the world. I am a respectable member of the Royal Academy. You must understand that even if I could paint such a painting, which I don't believe I can, I would never be allowed to show it in Somerset House, nor any public place. Indeed, if the painting were true, I could never show myself in respectable society again. There are worse fates, I suppose. But understand, sir, my father was a barber. You are a man of genius and sympathetic understanding, but I think, with all due respect, that like most men of noble birth you cannot understand how damn difficult mere respectability is. Neither my father nor Grant's, I suspect, would have dreamed of sitting in this most noble of English houses, the seat of the Percys in Shakespeare's day, with you, my lord, one of the greatest men in England, drinking a wine that could only be purchased with half a year's labor."

Turner smiled and tasted the wine again. "I hesitate to think how many greasy scalps he would have had to touch for each sip. But he was a good man, my father. I owe everything to him, God rest his soul."

I was astounded at the liberties Turner had just taken with Lord Egremont. I sensed that Egremont himself was taken aback by the frankness of Turner's speech, but I also saw that he relished Turner's honesty. A man like Egremont only hears flattery, and it must be a tonic to hear plain speaking.

"I dare say you are right. There is that in my blood and breeding which makes me what I am and limits, I suppose, my perspective. But you would see things that way: being a painter you always have to trouble yourself about point of view. I don't. I'm Lord Egremont. I see things as I see them.

"Enough of this. It is time for bed. Up we go, the three of us. I thank you both for your company and your conversation. But I repeat my point: you should paint it. Good night!"

. 13 .

IT WAS RHINEBECK'S NATURE to hide more than he revealed. Since his marriage he had had affairs with perhaps half a dozen women; one of them he had almost loved. His wife, he knew, suspected, but they had never spoken of the matter, just as they had not spoken about her little fling with Mr. Preston in Newport. His business dealings were also conducted on the principle that only those who needed to would be told. Only fools and buffoons said more than necessary.

But of all of his secrets, none was more important to him than his Turner. He hardly knew why. It was a shocking painting, to be sure, which the world would condemn. But Rhinebeck had stood up to senators and union bullies and he knew he had nothing to fear from ignorant puritans. He was what the world calls a brave man, but he also knew that he was afraid of others, especially his wife, seeing his Turner. He feared somehow that it would give her the key to his soul; once she saw it he would be at her mercy.

It was all nonsense. He shook his head and lit a new cigar. All the preparations were complete. The ladies would arrive at any minute. He was suspicious of Lottie's new friend, Mrs. Overstreet. He hadn't met her, but the suddenness of her warm attachment to his wife and the fact that she worked for an art gallery gave him pause. He had heard rumors over the years of a Turner unlike all others; he himself had been asked ever so casually over brandy and cigars if he had ever heard of such a painting. He wondered if Mrs. Overstreet had heard similar rumors.

He looked at the Renoir. She annoyed him. There was a time in his life, he knew, when he would have wanted a woman like that, but now he found her unpleasantly pneumatic. She was the sort of woman who would take hours to get dressed, who would feel an obscure and heartfelt hurt as he grew impatient with her comments about the weather and her friend's dresses. After dinner she would question the waiter gravely about the relative merits of the napoleon and the éclair. Lottie had her faults, but she was much better than that.

There was a commotion downstairs, signaling that the women had arrived. He greeted his wife with a polite kiss on the cheek. He shook hands with Mrs. Overstreet. The trip from New York had been dreadful; the hotel in Albany a disgrace; the train stopped for ever so long without a word of explanation.

"But thank goodness for Maria," Lottie said. "She never lost her nerve; she always knew what to do. She found blankets when there were none to be had. I don't know what I would have done without her."

Rhinebeck thanked Mrs. Overstreet for her assistance. He did not like the look of her. She was pretty, but somehow too pretty; charming, but too charming. A button, or perhaps two, had been negligently fastened and a good deal of her attractive bosom was on display.

He showed them into the main room and led them out onto the balcony.

"You have come at just the right time," Rhinebeck said. "Look out across the lake to the island there." The three of them stared at the green island and the blue water. Suddenly the island seemed almost on fire with color, the various shades of green more vivid and living than anything either of the women had seen before. They both gasped.

"Happens every evening when the sun goes down, if the weather is fine," Rhinebeck explained. Tears formed in his wife's eyes.

"I have never seen anything so beautiful. It quite takes one's breath away. I can see," she said, "why you intend to keep this all to yourself. It is not kind, but I understand."

At supper the conversation was indifferent. The glass eyes of the various creatures that decorated the room sparkled in the firelight.

"I did not know," Mrs. Overstreet remarked, "that you were such a huntsman."

Rhinebeck shrugged. "I confess to very little of the actual murder. I have a man who sees to these things."

"Does not the sight of all these poor creatures on the wall take away your appetite?"

"No, it doesn't. Nor does it, I observe, take away yours. My appetite depends on how active I have been and how good the food. Today I had nothing but a piece of cheese and a hunk of bread at midday. I have been active about the place since then and, for my taste at least, the venison is excellent."

"But there is something a trifle gruesome, don't you think, about seeing on the wall the creatures as they looked before they became the meat upon your plate?"

"Nonsense and humbug. It seems a deal more honest to acknowledge what you are about than not to do so." Rhinebeck cut his meat and stabbed a piece of it with his fork. He held it up to the ladies. "The last time I saw this fellow was a week ago. Kircum and I had gone out in the early morning while it was still dark. For about an hour we waited by a meadow not too far from here. He came into the clearing, a fine six-pointer, unaware of his fate. He heard me raise my gun. His eyes met mine for half a moment as he tried to make up his mind to run away. But it was too late. I fired, and my aim was true. He staggered for about twenty feet before he fell to the ground."

Rhinebeck put the piece of meat in his mouth and chewed it. "He was a beautiful fellow in his life and a tasty morsel in his death. If I think back I can see the spasm that wracked his body as his knees buckled."

"Cornelius," his wife interrupted. "There is no reason to be so horrid."

"But that is my point. I keep the animals on my walls, Mrs. Overstreet, to remind me of the truth of the wilderness. We are not in Manhattan. If given half a chance that mountain lion that you see up there would have pounced upon you and enjoyed your delicate flesh as much as you are enjoying that of this deer."

Mrs. Overstreet smiled archly and placed a large piece of meat in her mouth. She chewed with obvious pleasure.

"But surely the canyons of Wall Street are filled with more dangerous creatures than your forest?"

"There you have me, Mrs. Overstreet. But it is a different kind of danger—your stockjobber will smile as he hands you the pen, while your panther will roar and snarl as he fastens his teeth on your throat. And although I have made my fortune in the company of the first, I prefer the second. It is the honesty I admire. As I grow older I find the truth of things more and more important to me."

When they finished dessert Rhinebeck said, "Come now. We will take our coffee upstairs. And although you are women, I will treat you to a glass of port and show you the final mystery of Birch Lodge."

He showed them the small door and led the way. "Be careful. These steps are steep. Watch your head as you go through the door. This is my Snuggery."

The response of the two ladies was everything that Rhinebeck could have wished for. They gasped with pleasure and wonder. The room was illuminated by a fire in the large fireplace and by two candelabra of deer antlers that hung from the ceiling. The silver reflection of the full moon shimmered on the water; the trees on the opposite shore showed blue-green and almost black.

Rhinebeck saw the sorrow that was mixed with the wonder in his wife's face. He hoped that the tears which he could see forming in the corner of her eyes were not the preface to an outburst. But she made an effort, and before she spoke again she brought herself under control. Lottie, he reminded himself, had her virtues.

Rhinebeck settled them down in front of the cabinet that he had built for his Turner. He handed his wife and Mrs. Overstreet each a glass of port.

"You men," Mrs. Overstreet said, "are such beasts. It is rare that we ladies are ever offered port, but I have never tasted a beverage as delicious as this. This is what the gods drank when they were still among us."

"Yes. It is fine stuff." Rhinebeck went on to explain the various features of the room. Mrs. Overstreet was most enthusiastic.

"This room is both cunning and cozy. Your architect is a very brilliant fellow. It is quite wonderful how that narrow mean staircase opens up into this most marvelous and expansive room. The staircase is, I see now, deliberately shoddy; I confess that my heart sank as you led us up. What could this be? I was prepared for something rough-and-tumble and rude. But this is too wonderful. There is a childlike sense of delight in this room that is quite enchanting. I commend you, Mr. Rhinebeck."

"And you, Lottie. What do you think?" her husband asked. "You seem less enthusiastic than your charming friend."

She paused for a moment before speaking. When he was younger, Rhinebeck found the time she spent gathering her thoughts an affront to their collective mortality, but his Turner had somehow taught him to value the care with which she spoke.

"It is, as Maria says, a most marvelous room," she offered at length. "And I see the qualities of play and delight that Maria has mentioned. But there is something sad about it as well. I see that the room has been designed so as to accommodate many of your friends, but I mostly see you here, Cornelius, by yourself. It seems somehow a solitary room."

Rhinebeck shrugged. "There is something to what you say. I had the room built to suit my own fancies. But the chief mystery of the place is not yet revealed. I have promised that I would show you, even though you are ladies, all there is to see of Birch Lodge." He stood up and moved to the cabinet. As he opened the door Rhinebeck felt a moment of unease as he recognized in his gesture the flourish with which Stokes had opened the curtain when he revealed the Turner.

The two ladies looked at the painting for a moment. "She is naughty, very naughty," Mrs. Overstreet said. "I understand now why you wish to keep her for your gentleman friends."

Rhinebeck turned to his wife. "What do you think of her?"

Again there was that pause. "Oh, I worry for her. I think she might catch her death of cold."

"Should I cover her up again, so that she will be warm?" he replied, returning her smile.

"No. She is very pleasant to look at. She reminds me of myself during some long August afternoons in the house on Nantucket many years ago. I was a young woman then, more a girl, really, but old enough to plead a headache on certain afternoons when the grown-ups and the younger children were about to embark on some tedious march along the beach. I would be all by myself in that big old house with the warm sea breeze blowing through the open windows. I look back on those afternoons as some of the happiest times of my life. But it was so many years ago now."

There was a long silence.

"I don't know about you two," Mrs. Overstreet said, "but I am very tired. The journey was exhausting. Thank you so much for your kind hospitality, Mr. Rhinebeck. If you both do not mind, I will bid you good night."

. 14 .

I CAN LOOK at a calendar and see that I found the painting on the afternoon of Monday, July 7, 2003, and that I drove home on Sunday, July 13, but the days, hours, and moments between the first event and the second are a blur of sensation and feeling. I cannot distinguish what I saw when I was awake and what I dreamt when I was asleep. I am not a romantic character. I am not a person who needs medication. I am a middle-aged American male who works for a small charitable foundation. I read grant applications for a living. My colleagues consider me a steady and reliable worker. But this is my truth.

I recall being in bed—this was probably the first day after I found the painting—and being overwhelmed by the fear that I had left it propped up against the barn wall. I seemed to see Mossbacher coming back to make a concrete offer for the house. I saw him step through the open barn door and take what was mine. But then I was sitting in front of it on the barn floor before the sun had quite crested the hill. The world was coming into being with the brightening daylight, but I could not tell if the light came from the sky or from Turner's canvas.

I saw Helen's lyre leaning against the corner of her dressing table, the strings still vibrating, as if she had just put it down. There were times during those days when I could hear its beautiful music, although it was so faint that it was more like the idea of music than music itself. It was the saddest music I had ever heard or imagined, the tone as delicate as the mist which rose from the surface of the lake at sunrise. And at the far limits of my perception, fainter than the sound of the still-vibrating lyre, I thought I could detect the sound of Helen's voice as well. It was difficult to make out, but I knew it was a song of yearning and that I was its object. I stared and stared at the painting, trying vainly to make out the words that were always just beyond my grasp.

Susan remembers that it was three days after she left that I finally called her. I remember our conversation, but I can't place it within the chronology of those first days. I know that when I came into the house and saw that the phone was unplugged, I felt angry at the intrusion of the quotidian world into the newly beautiful one.

She picked up on the first ring. "I've been calling and calling. I was so worried I was just about to call the police. I kept seeing you face down in the lake."

"I'm sorry. The phone was unplugged and I didn't realize it. I must have knocked it out when I was vacuuming in the living room." For a few moments we went back and forth about how worried she was and how inconsiderate it was of me not to have called. She didn't believe what I said about the vacuum and the phone, and I wished I had thought of something better. I had no choice but to lie. In those days immediately following my discovery of the painting, I hadn't thought about what I was going to do. My only reality had been Helen. But as I listened to Susan reproach me about not calling, I realized that I could no more tell her about my discovery than Paris could resist Helen.

"So what have you been doing all this time?" she asked. Although she was right not to trust me, I felt unreasonably offended. Her voice sounded ugly in my ears.

I told her that cleaning out the barn had taken longer than I'd thought and that I wasn't quite done. I tried to make her feel sorry for me because I was working so hard on my vacation. I didn't consider myself a happy person, but I had mostly thought of myself as happily married. It is so much easier to be married than not to be married: having someone to talk to and have children with, the more or less regular sex, the extra income, and the companionship and support through the slog of everyday life. It wasn't always that way. As I listened to Susan's voice, I found myself tuning out what she was actually saying and drifting off into a reverie about what it had once been like. We had been passionate young people in our day, and what I had seen in the curve of Helen's breast and in Helen's thigh, I had once seen in Susan. But now I saw someone who had put on some weight (although not thirty pounds, as I had) and who had breast-fed two children. There were lines on her forehead and an extra fold of skin beneath her chin that seemed of a piece with the way she complained about my behavior. If I hadn't looked so unappetizing myself I might have thought I was entitled to someone better.

That phone call was my entry into the world of duplicity, the beginning of my double life. On the one hand there was my wife and the disappointing world, on the other there was Helen and everything that was possible. I knew, however resentfully, which one was my fate, but I yearned to get back to the other. After I promised not to leave the phone unplugged again, and to call every night before I went to bed, Susan said I love you. I said I loved her too, but the words rang hollow even as I spoke them. As soon as the call was over I went back to the barn.

As my days at the lake came to an end, the world in which I had to live came into sharper focus. I was able to see that the painting was an object in that world rather than a world itself. It was a piece of canvas in a gilded frame, a thing I had to figure out what to do with. I knew, of course, that if it was a real Turner it was an object of immense value. If I sold it I would be able to tell Mossbacher to take his money and stuff it, to tell the Nassau Foundation thanks very much for twenty-three years of paychecks, but I'm done. I would be able to do pretty much whatever I wanted.

The painting was mine, and mine alone; I could not bring myself even to think of sharing it with anyone—my wife, perhaps not surprisingly, most of all. I could only think about selling it in the most abstract and theoretical way. I felt that I had found out what life was and that to give up the painting—for no matter how much money—would be to die. After what seemed like endless agonizing, I decided to leave it in the Adirondacks. On Sunday, July 12, I carefully wrapped it up in the old sailcloth and retied the cord. I put it back in the wall where I had found it, and placed the old bedstead and some of the other stuff that I had been planning to sell to antique shops in front of the compartment.

Leaving the painting behind was as difficult as anything I'd ever done, and it was quite late by the time I left. What with the weekend traffic, it wasn't until 11:57 by the Volvo's digital clock that I pulled into the driveway. I had called Susan on the way to tell her that I was going to be late and not to wait up for me, but the lights were still on.

"Howdy, stranger," she said as she opened the door. She was wearing the linen nightshirt that I had bought her when we went to Montreal to celebrate our twentieth anniversary. She put her arms around me before I had my bag down. Her lips found mine and I felt her tongue seek mine in the familiar way.

"What's the matter? Aren't you happy to see me?"

"Don't be silly," I said. "It was a long drive. Tons of traffic around Albany and a huge backup before the tolls. And I have to piss. I drank a lot of coffee to keep myself awake." When I got back from the bathroom, I found she had set out a plate of cold cuts, some cheese, and a glass of beer. "I found some of that Spanish ham you like."

"That's sweet of you," I said. "But I thought I wasn't supposed to eat this stuff. I was very good about eating while I was up there." The fact was that I had hardly eaten since I found the painting. Food had seemed irrelevant and alcohol unnecessary.

I didn't want to hurt her feelings, so I picked at what she had laid out. I told her about some of the other things I had found in the barn.

"Let's go to bed. I have to catch the seven-twenty tomorrow, to be at a nine o'clock meeting," she said. "You must be exhausted from all that driving. Come upstairs."

I puttered around in the kitchen until I thought she would be asleep. When I went upstairs, I let my clothes fall to the floor and slipped into bed. As she turned over toward me, I hoped it was nothing more than one of those automatic habits of the long-married, but she said, "I thought you'd never get here."

She propped herself up on her elbow and kissed me. Her hand worked its way into my shorts. There should have been nothing more familiar and comfortable, but I felt a shudder of distaste.

"Come on," she said. "You've been gone for a week."

I told her I was tired and that I just wanted to go to sleep. "Good night," I said. "Thanks for making me such a nice snack."

"This is something new. Welcome home." She turned over with emphasis and settled down on her side of the bed as far away from me as possible.

I lay on my back like a dead person and listened to her breathing. Eventually she fell asleep. Helen's eyes seemed to meet mine in the darkness. Aphrodite herself was woven into the transparent cloth which caressed her perfect shoulders. In the far distance the beautiful ships crossed the sparkling ocean. An eagle, who was Zeus, looked down on the world of men.

. 15 .

GINA CALLED BRYCE from London to tell him that she had found something of interest, something extraordinary, but he silenced her before she could say anything further. "Whatever it is," he said, "I'd rather hear about it from you in person. Our people will have you on the next flight out. There will be a driver at JFK. It will be a joy to see you, since a happy errand will no doubt do wonders for your complexion. Not a word more."

Bryce put down the receiver and sat perfectly still. He allowed himself a moment to wonder what she had found. It had been months since she discovered the Collins letter. The last few times he'd seen her, he had detected signs of stress and overwork that threatened to mar her beauty. She had lost a few pounds, which was, in his opinion, to the good, but there had been something haggard about her eyes which, in combination with her brisk and professional demeanor, gave her the unappealing air of a newly fledged McKinsey consultant. But she was doing very well. Mr. Ashford had been delighted with her visit and had purchased both the Soutine and the Cassatt, a transaction that was both aesthetically and financially rewarding.

Gina, on the other end of the line, was glad to be returning to New York, and not only because she looked forward to seeing Bryce's reaction as he grasped the importance of what she had found. Lately there had been too many incoherent late-night calls from her mother, which made Gina anxious to find out what was going on. Julia had been living with her mother for about five years, ever since her mother had hired her to redo the apartment in honor of her second divorce. Gina liked Julia well enough, but there was something going on between the two of them, something that seemed to involve more alcohol than usual. It occurred to Gina that she was trying to grow up as hard as she could while both of her parents were succeeding in doing the opposite.

Thanks to the first-class ticket, she had been able to nap on the plane, so she felt quite rested when she arrived at Madison Partners at lunchtime. Bryce betrayed his eagerness to see her by calling her up to the library before she'd even had a chance to put her suitcase down and say hello to her colleagues.

He was dressed, Gina thought, with unusual care, his red-and-blue silk tie so extraordinarily rich and fine that she found herself staring. A salad and a plate of cheese and cured meat was waiting on the sideboard of the library. Bryce asked if she wanted a snack.

"I do," she said, "but I can eat while you read. You will have noticed that I've been spending your money on various shady characters and unemployed graduate students who have been scouring the Sussex countryside on your behalf. One of them hit pay dirt in a used bookstore in the village of Kirdford, which is just outside of Petworth.

"Do you remember our friend George Wyndham, the bastard heir of Lord Egremont, Turner's great patron? You once described him as one of 'those angry vulgarians upon whom aristocracy is wasted.' The phrase stuck with me and I determined to find out what I could about him."

Wyndham, she explained, was born in 1787 and spent his entire career being furious at his illegitimacy. He served briefly in the Guards but primarily passed his time as an inconsequential hanger-on at Petworth. He lived there with his wife and children, but he was never part of the company of artists and intellectuals who were his father's guests.

When his father died in 1837, he inherited one of the greatest estates in England, but he was so bitter about being unable to inherit his father's title that he devoted most of his energy to an unrelenting assertion of the privileges he felt were his due. While the father had been loose and easy in his relations with others, the son was comically strict and formal. He banished the artists and painters from Petworth. He kept the property up in a conservative way, he hunted, and he engaged in a series of petty quarrels over the demarcation of his hunting grounds.

"His wife, Mary," Gina went on, "was a pious woman, with a strong Evangelical streak. She set the tone that prevailed at Petworth in the years following Egremont's death. She and her husband both worried that the 'sins of the father' would be visited upon the son.

"It's with this background that you need to read the document that I'm about to give you. Sometime in the early 1840s, when Wyndham was in his mid-fifties, he had a kind of conversion experience and was tempted to write one of those spiritual biographies that were popular in Evangelical circles at the time. He never completed it, but the manuscript turned up in that used bookshop, in an old register book detailing the proceedings of the Sussex hounds." Gina opened her portfolio and gave Bryce a stack of yellowing manuscript papers, covered in an awkward hand. She turned her attention to the salad and the cheese; Bryce ordered more coffee and began to read.

I was born into the curse of illegitimacy on the fifth of June 1787, my father being George O'Brien Wyndham, 3rd Earl of Egremont of Petworth House, Sussex, and my mother being Elizabeth Iliffe of Westminster. My mother and father were married in 1801, too late to cleanse me of that stain which attended my birth.

My father was avowed to be during his lifetime one of the greatest men in all of England, celebrated for his enlightened view of Agriculture to which he made many improvements, including advances in the breeding of swine. He was also known as a man of taste and fashion due to his wonderful collection of paintings and statues. He was much given to Immorality of the flesh. I was the oldest of the nine children that he had with my mother, and to this I owe my position and property, for which I am grateful. But the Countryside was filled with Rumours as to his carryings on with the daughters of his tenants as well as ladies and girls of fashion both here and in London, and only God knows what the true number of my brothers and sisters is.

My mother was a jolly woman and most kind but hard worn out by my father's Irregularities. In her youth she was no better than she needed to be, coming to Petworth without the benefit of matrimony when she was but fifteen years old and eighteen years younger than my father. She tried for many years to become a decent woman and do what she could to make amends for the sins of her past and to confer some decency on her children. Well do I recall the fierce quarrels they had on this subject when I was young. At last my father gave in to the pleas of decency and common sense and married her when I was already fourteen years of age.

But Matrimony and advancing age did not confer Morality upon my father and he continued with his irregular ways, often bringing his whores to Petworth and carrying on most shamefully. My mother bore all with good humour and the patience of a Saint, but at times his outrages provoked her to leave. He thought no more of it than a sixpence and carried on as before, knowing she would always return to him, as she was dependent on him for Income.

My mother died in 1822, done to death by my father's Sinfulness. At that time I was returned to Petworth, married to my beloved Mary and attempting to live a life of sense and decency amidst all the licence of artists and so forth who surrounded my father and mother. My father had been truly fond of my mother and was sorrowful for her. I had hopes that her Death would be a Lesson to him and he would live out his days as a decent old Widower, for he was an old man now of seventy-one.

After she died my father went to London for a month or two. When he came back he had with him Mrs. Spencer, who took my mother's place before the sod had fairly sprouted on her grave. He had her carve, and installed her at the head of the table where by all rights my wife should have been. Mrs. Spencer was known in London for a beauty and had fine gold hair and good teeth. When we first met she held out her hand to me but I refused it, knowing that she was taking shameful advantage of an old man's lechery. During the course of my father's lifetime I had known many of his amours and liaisons and always made an effort to be civil to them if it was needed for form's sake. But Mrs. Spencer I could not abide because she was younger than I was and because she showed no deference to those of a higher station. Once when my father was travelling to some distant estates Mrs. Spencer and I quarrelled most fiercely. My temper got the better of me and I said that she was no more than one of my father's whores. She stayed as cool as could be and said we were too alike to quarrel as I was merely one of my father's bastards.

From that time on we never spoke unless we were required to for decency's sake in front of my father or company. Not wishing to expose my own children and Mary to the licence and uproar of the house, I retired as much as possible during that time to our quarters and only mingled with them when required to for the sake of form.

At around this time Turner was much in attendance and had become a great favourite of my father and Mrs. Spencer. Turner was an ill-formed little man with a great nose, black teeth, and a dirty coat, but Mrs. Spencer favoured him above all the other artists and pushed him forward towards my father. She spent more time with him alone than a decent woman would but she was not a decent woman. Her Vanity was such that she convinced Turner and my father that Turner should paint her portrait. He did and the result was a poor likeness called "Jessica," after the character in Shakespeare, that was much mocked and scorned, with one clever fellow saying it looked like the woman had just climbed out of a mustard pot.

I knew privately from my father that he was displeased with the painting and that he had half a mind not to pay for it, but in the end he did, no doubt because of Mrs. Spencer's pleading and her taking advantage of his weaknesses.

My father's lechery continued unabated with Mrs. Spencer and with others when she was away in town which was a great miracle in a man of seventy-four. The house was full with a most disagreeable Miscellany of artists and other worthless fellows who ate and drank each one like two Guardsmen who had no care for the estate. The conversation at dinner was most indiscriminate with no recognition that there were those present such as Mary who had no desire to have their ears sullied by Scandal and Impiety. Over all this Riot Mrs. Spencer presided using her wiles and her smile to encourage the conversation whenever it threatened to flag and approach Decency.

One day I noticed that carriages had been called for and a number of the party departed. The next day the same thing occurred and no new arrivals came to take their place. I had the strange Fancy that reason had prevailed and that my father had seen the error of his ways. But I was much abashed and annoyed when the next day my father called me into his study. At first the conversation was indifferent and concerned with matters of the estate. Then my father suggested that it might be pleasant for me to go to London at this time and that he had need of me to look after some matters there. I protested that I did not enjoy London at this time of year, that the matters he wanted attending to could surely wait until a better season, that the Cost of living in London was high and for reasons of Economy it seemed more reasonable for me to stay at Petworth with my family. As soon as I had uttered these words I could see that I had displeased him. All we Wyndhams have a temper; his was the hardest to provoke but when provoked it was the most fierce. He had a look of anger I had feared since I was a small boy. This look he directed at me and slammed his Fist upon the desk so hard that I feared for the Greek vase he prized so much. He insulted my Intelligence, saying that he had offered me a decent pretence, but that I was too much a Sheep to see it for what it was and as for Economy I would go to China at his expense if that was his desire. Wrath was also one of his sins in addition to Lechery.

I was, in short, to vacate Petworth on the morrow and remain in London attending to that business he wished me to take care of until such time as I should be recalled. I knew

there was no gainsaying him when he was in such a mood so I
said that I should be willing to oblige him and took my leave.
As I made my way to my apartments to give the orders for our
departure, I could see more carriages waiting to take guests
away. Mrs. Spencer was there bidding adieu to the guests, as
was Turner and a young fellow whose name I have forgotten.
I thought it odd that these three should be saying good-bye to
all the others, but I didn't devote much attention to it as I had
other matters on my mind.

That night when we came down to dinner, I saw that
the Party was much reduced, viz. only Turner and the young
fellow plus Mrs. Spencer and my father. Dinner passed tolerably, although my father was in a vile temper and chastised
me for not replying to one of Mrs. Spencer's jests. Most of the
conversation was between Mrs. Spencer and the young fellow;
Turner kept his face close to his plate and drank a good deal of
wine as was his wont.

The next morning there was much ado as we prepared to
depart. The carriage was full with Mary and the children and
the nursemaids, as was the cart and another carriage to take
servants that would accompany us. Others had gone on before
to prepare things. I knew that Mary would be displeased by
the disorder we would find when we got there, but there was
nothing to be done for it since we had been ordered out so
suddenly. My father came out from his study to bid us adieu
and a few steps behind him was Mrs. Spencer. She put her arm
through his and stood beside him as he gave me some final instructions on the matter he wished me to attend to in London.

Mrs. Spencer was as gracious as could be, saving especially kind words for Mary and the children and wishing us all a safe and pleasant journey in her very best manner. But I knew that she was doing it to spite and aggrieve me for she knew that I could say nothing in front of my father. As the carriage pulled away she stayed on the walk a moment after my father had already turned to go inside and I could see that there was a wicked smile of Triumph on her face.

What her scheme was and why we had been bundled off to London I could not guess, although I was sure that there was some debauchery in it. What, I wondered, would those four be doing in such a great house all by themselves and with most of the servants gone too?

I did not find out the answer until a few years after we returned and it proved that my father's great sins of Lechery had gone on unabated until he had reached a very old age indeed. He was doing quite poorly—this was about '32 or '33, five or six years before he was finally carried off—and I had gone up to his chambers to inquire after him. I was much concerned at this time that Mrs. Spencer would take advantage of my father in what might be his final illness. I also feared she might take as her own certain properties that rightly belonged to the estate.

In those years that he was with Mrs. Spencer my father was most particular that no one ever enter his chambers without his specific permission. The door was ajar and I tapped on it to signal my arrival. There being no answer and being concerned that perhaps he had been carried off or was in his last throes, I entered. He was lying in the great bed with the covers all disordered. I could see at once that he was in a fever, for the dew stood on his forehead and he was quite red. He mumbled something I could not make out, so I approached the bed. As I did so I saw that the new cabinet he had ordered was open. There was a picture of a woman there, but so Obscene as to make me gasp and stand stock still at the Depravity of it. It was just at that moment Mrs. Spencer entered from the other door, carrying a basin of water and a towel. She gave a gasp and closed the cabinet doors as she came toward the bed, but not before I could see that it was a painting of her and could guess that Turner had painted it, because there were Greek columns in it and sunlight. I understood now that it was only to make this Abomination that all the company had been expelled from Petworth.

Whereas another woman might have cowered in shame if someone had seen such a picture of her, she drew herself up to her full height. Rage glowed from her eyes. She ordered me out of the room and said it was like me to be sneaking about just at the moment of Crisis. She said I was to call for the Doctor and do it quickly. She gave me a look that quelled my complaints and I am ashamed to say that I did as she bade me. She never gave me another thought but bent over my father and tended to him with the water and the towel.

The Doctor stayed with my father for two hours and came out looking very grey. He said that my father had a ferocious fever and that if it were any other man his age he would give up hope, but my father was remarkable for his Animal power and there was no telling but that he might survive. He gave orders that no one but he, the nurse, and Mrs. Spencer was to come into the bedroom. I objected that I would like to see my own father and comfort him in his sickness, but the Doctor said I would do so on my own responsibility as my father had been quite particular as to who was to come in and who was to stay out. The Doctor said that rest was the only medicine that could help, and he would not answer for it if my father were to be crossed and enraged.

Mrs. Spencer never left my father's side for two weeks. She took what rest she did in his chamber and all her meals likewise. I stayed outside the door constantly, leaving only for meals, sleeping, and going with the hounds. Business of the estate I carried out at the desk I had brought into the hallway and so as not to disturb my father I conducted all business in a very low tone of voice. I saw Mrs. Spencer only occasionally when she put her head out to give some command to the servants that I had ordered to be constantly there. Her face was drawn and the very lustre had vanished from her hair. Her eyes had become large and sunken in her skull and there were new networks of lines and wrinkles on her neck. She was most distressed because she knew that her days of Ease and Luxury were soon to come to an end.

But then the Doctor came out to me one day and said that my father was a good deal better and that he wished to speak to me. I went in and saw my father sitting up in the great bed, having his breakfast of an egg and toasted bread and tea. He looked worn. He had been cleaned and shaved, and there was *a tolerable colour about him. Mrs. Spencer stood by his side. The new cabinet was closed. I enquired as to his health. He said he was not yet ready for a ride round the estate, but that he was better than he had been. He thanked me for my devoted attendance and said that it was no longer required. He said he would call me in once a day to give me instructions as to the management of the estate and other matters.*

At first when I came the most he could do was sit up in his bed while Mrs. Spencer sat off on the side reading. He got stronger as the weeks passed and soon he was sitting at his small desk, going over the papers and accounts. He began to take a keen interest in the affairs of the estate and I knew he was healed and ready to come downstairs when he called me a blockhead for not knowing the weight of the prize bull that had been sold.

Mrs. Spencer had not been away from his side the whole time of his illness. One day as my father was discussing estate matters with me he encouraged her to go out and get some air. She acknowledged that the air would do her good. As soon as the door was closed my father put on that tone he had for serious matters of business. He said he knew that I did not love Mrs. Spencer and that she did not love me. There was nothing to be done about that and he had no Desire to remedy it at his time of life. But I was to remember that Mrs. Spencer had been a good friend to him since the death of my mother, and that it would displease him greatly if I was to quarrel with her or show that contempt which he knew I felt. He had, he said, no intention of altering his instructions regarding the disposition of the estate, but I was to remember that I had more than one brother and numerous cousins. He hoped, he said, that even my Understanding was sufficient to comprehend what he meant. I told him that my Behavior would be all that he could desire.

He went on to say that his recent illness had taught him that he could no longer be certain that there were many years left to him. I ventured to suggest that perhaps it was time to seek Spiritual Counsel and to take care of his Immortal Soul. It is a salve to my Conscience that I reminded him of this, even though his response was harsh. He waved his hand as if he was brushing away an Insect, and said that it was always a wonder to him that I, who had not the Wit to reckon the number of Swine that could be sustained upon an acre of land, could claim Understanding of the deepest of mysteries. He said he had no wish to speak to me on this subject and if I wished to remain in his good graces I would refrain from mentioning it in the future. He knew full well, he said, that he could not trust me to make a decent and humane provision for Mrs. Spencer, as virtuous and pious as I might be. He had, therefore, called in his legal man to adjust his Will so as to make a modest and reasonable provision for her. He advised me that more than sufficient remained and I would not miss her small legacy, but that if I Objected I would miss all.

Although it pained me to give silent assent to his Lechery, I said that I would honour his wishes in these matters as in all others. There was one other matter which he wished to speak to me about. He was aware that I had seen the painting in the cabinet. He was sorry that I had seen it, but there was nothing to be done for it now except to remind me that he did not wish me or anyone else sneaking about and entering his chamber without his permission or Mrs. Spencer's. His feelings about this painting were most particular and he wished to have no single word of conversation about it with me. On this he was most adamant and he wished me to understand that if I so much as mentioned it to him again, or if he was ever to learn that I had spoken of it with another living soul, he would take those steps that would please my brother. Our last word on the subject was that upon his death, as I was a Christian gentleman, I was to make sure that Mrs. Spencer got it. I had no recourse but to give my consent, but it was a powerful lesson to me about the shame that sinners feel over repeated Sin.

We had reached this stage in our conversation when there was a knock on the door. It was Mrs. Spencer, and my father bade her enter. I greeted her cordially because I knew my father was watching. It was always a Wonder to me that she could look me in the eye without colouring after I had seen that picture, but she was brazen if she was nothing else. The walk had done her good, she said, and indeed it showed. She put her hand on my father's shoulder and I could see from the look he gave her that neither age nor illness had dampened his tendency towards Sin.

. 16 .

⟨⊛⟩ I TRIED TO GET back into my life in New Jersey, but the knowledge of the painting gnawed at me like an ulcer. I felt foolish for having abandoned the greatest happiness I had ever known, and I woke most nights in a fever sweat at the thought of something happening to it. Though I tried to console myself with the thought that it had been hidden where I left it since the days when Rhinebeck owned the property, I became obsessed with the notion that Mossbacher or one of his people might find it. It was an irrational thought, but nothing, including my mind, was as it had been before.

The hardest thing to convey is how unreal the world in which I found myself seemed. Everything I knew and cared about—my wife, my children, my job, my finances—seemed like a pale reflection of a dream. I felt as though I was walking through a world of shadows. All the while, however, I was tormented with the certainty that the real world—or at least the world that was true and meaningful—was on the canvas that was hidden in my barn in the Adirondacks. I don't think I was really mad, but I am not sure a psychiatrist would agree with me.

So I floated uneasily through those last days of July, hoping that with time my life would click into focus. Susan kept on trying to engage me in a conversation about what was wrong. She claimed I was detached and disengaged, that I seemed depressed, that I was hiding something, that I wasn't "there for her." All of this was certainly true, but she, through no fault of her own, wasn't there for me either, in the sense that she no longer seemed adequate to the truths of the world as I had come to understand them. I knew she was trying and I knew she had done nothing wrong, but I had felt the power that fires all poetry and moves the world. I had seen Helen of Troy. I knew the truth of her like no one who is now alive, like no one who has been alive for a hundred years. I tried to be polite, to say that I was fine, that I was just worried about money or just thinking too much about turning fifty, but we had been married too long for her to believe me. Naturally enough, she would retreat in hurt and anger, but after a few days she took a deep breath and tried to reach me again. Looking back, I can see that it was a measure of her affection and decency that she stayed with me as long as she did.

My birthday, August 7, was on a Thursday. Susan made reservations for dinner in New York; there was something so sad and so hopeful about the way she told me of her plan that I tried as hard as I could to pretend it pleased me. Neither of us could afford to take a day off from work, so we agreed that we would meet at a restaurant in the Village.

It turned out to be a wonderful day for early August in New York. Not too hot, not too humid, and a nice breeze. As part of making an effort, I had put on my favorite summer suit and a tie. When she saw me at the restaurant I wanted her to know that I was trying.

I hadn't been in the city very often since the attack on the World Trade Center, and I was still shocked by the absence of that ugly but familiar landmark. Washington Square Park was filled with young people; they all seemed to be flirting with one another, as if they had all been given permission at once to go on with the business of living. There was an air of gaiety and yearning about them; they seemed bathed in Helen's light.

A young couple walked toward me. He was very hand-some, like a young Marlon Brando. She was tall and African American. She was wearing jeans, high heels, and a thin red camisole. I don't think I had ever seen anyone so beautiful just walking down the street.

Her arms were around him, but just as they approached me, she turned and, in response to something he said, broke into a beautiful smile. She said something in his ear; he laughed and kissed her. Then they passed me and were gone. I walked on for a few more steps and a sentence formed in my mind: *I will never sleep with anyone as beautiful as that, but it's okay.* And then, quite mysteriously, after a few more steps, I thought: *It is okay to die.* It just sort of hit me: *It's okay to die. There is nothing to be afraid of.* And I felt, for a moment, that a cloud had lifted or a curtain had opened. I am not sure, to this day, exactly what happened or the precise meaning of what had occurred, but I became convinced, somehow, that it was Helen speaking to me. These were the words, I thought, that I had been struggling to hear as I looked at the painting.

I think I smiled for the first time since I had left the painting in the mountains. I had a hint that whatever it was that Helen meant was not entirely dependent on being in her presence, that she could live in my mind even when I was away from her. As it turned out, this lesson—if it was a lesson—didn't stick. The moment of brightness made the darkness that followed so much the darker.

But for the moment at least I was happy to see Susan when I got to the restaurant and happy to be alive in the moment that we had. We had a lovely dinner; we talked about what the children were doing; we traded gossip about our jobs. She said that she noticed that I had lost some weight and that I looked good.

"Five pounds so far," I said. "I've been watching what I've been eating since you left the mountains. Nothing crazy: sensible choices and no seconds."

I told her that she looked good too, and it was true. She seemed more beautiful to me than she had at any time since I found the painting.

We left the restaurant and walked up the street holding hands. "This has been a lovely evening," she said. "I'm glad you made an effort. We are worth it, you know."

When we got to a corner, Susan hailed a cab. "I have a surprise for you," she said. She had taken a nice room at the

Park Lane overlooking Central Park. There was a half bottle of champagne in a cooler and a pretty little cake with a candle on the table in front of the window.

"No wonder you wouldn't let me get any dessert," I said. "This is all too much, you know."

"Happy birthday. You only get to get old once." She went to the closet and took out two nicely wrapped presents. She opened the champagne and lit the candle. We sat next to each other and looked out over the dark green park ringed by the sparkling city.

I opened my presents, a handsome shirt with French cuffs and a pair of cuff links made out of blue stones. "These are really nice," I said. I leaned over and gave her a kiss. "But are you trying to make us go bankrupt?"

She explained that she had just gotten a big bonus. "But mostly I want you to know that I love you. I want you to be happy. I want us to be happy."

I thanked her and touched my glass to hers, apologizing for having been so gloomy. I didn't know what it was, I said. This would have been the moment to tell her about the painting, and the words to do so started to form in my mind. But I just couldn't do it: it was mine and mine alone. "I love you too," I managed to say.

We undressed and got into the big bed with its luxurious sheets. I let her get on top and do all the work. I thought of the young couple I had seen in the park earlier that day. I thought of Helen and the way the diaphanous cloth caressed her thighs.

I thought of the beautifully articulated muscles on Paris's back. I closed my eyes and saw the sea beyond the field of battle. There were ships in the far distance. Argosies, I remember thinking, is the word. I could see hope and fear on the mariners' faces. I could see the treasure they were carrying and the distant lands to which they were bound.

. 17 .

:<>: I REALLY WISH, David, that you could see this place. Its wonders are almost wasted on me. Your superior taste and discernment would find even more to admire than I do. Yesterday Egremont took his son and daughter-in-law up to London to see to some business. A number of guests had departed. It seemed as if the living being that is Petworth House was resting. I was sitting outside on the Portico with writing implements, trying to make some sense of the notes I had taken in the North Gallery, but mostly just looking out over the pond. Turner was off sketching somewhere. The beauty of the place and the peculiar fact that I had the freedom of the house rendered me almost idiotic with happiness.

Mrs. Spencer approached and said that she had been looking for me. After inquiring about my health and comfort she asked if I could do her a service. I naturally told her that I was hers to command.

"You must put down your pen and ink and come with me," she said. "It is a fine September day. Days like this do not come often to the south of England. You are a young man and need to bestir yourself; I am in want of air and a cavalier. So you will accompany me on an excursion. You have not yet seen the Rotunda, have you? It will please you." With that she commanded me to change into a costume suitable "for tramping."

Before this time I had only seen Mrs. Spencer when she was surrounded by others or in the company of Lord Egremont. She dressed in the more voluptuous style of the last century. At dinner she wore fine gowns that showed off her figure and displayed a good deal of bosom. It was amusing to see her next to Egremont's prim and pinched daughter-in-law. When she came out to me she was wearing a dress such as a prosperous farmer's wife might wear, but even though the stuff was simple and the cut was plain, she looked more like a duchess than any duchess I have ever seen.

Mrs. Spencer led the way. We walked over groomed paths, rough roads, and forest ways. "You mustn't think," she said, "that I am going to take you to our destination by the shortest route." As we walked she talked to me about the history of Petworth, particularly of the park and gardens, which had been designed by Capability Brown in the 1750s. It was a massive undertaking during which, she told me, "no expense was spared to make nature more perfect than nature." We had reached perhaps the most charming spot I have seen so far in the park, a bit of grass at the edge of a stand of fine trees, with a small brook running by.

"Let us sit here for a moment and rest." She led me to a small stone bench half hidden by the banks of the brook. I commented on how sweet and charming a spot it was.

"Yes," she said. "It is most sweet and charming. And false, you know. All this sweet nature was made by the hand of man. There was no brook here, no grass. This is as real as a canvas by Turner. Old Capability Brown bent the brook so he could make a perfect setting for this rustic seat. This is one of my favorite spots at Petworth," she said as she settled herself, "but I sometimes think it is too much like certain charming ladies. Quite delightful as far as appearances go, but all rather contrived." She turned to me and smiled, but I could see a sadness too deep for words in her eyes.

She quickly redirected the conversation, and we chatted for a while on a variety of subjects. She has an extraordinary gift for speaking easily and winningly on almost any topic. I found myself, to my surprise, saying interesting things on topics I had never thought about before. It is the way she listens that is the secret, and I can see why an old man like Egremont would find it so easy to be in love with her. Hers is a receptive genius; everything she hears comes back to the speaker burnished and ennobled.

I don't know how long we sat in that pleasant spot, but at length she suggested that we move on. We walked another half hour or so, going by various twisty and pleasant ways, mostly through forest, until we emerged on a green field and began to climb a beautifully manicured hill.

"Look!" she said. Her face had been transformed by an expression of childlike radiance and joy. "I am always overcome with happiness when I first see it." She pointed to the top of the hill. Eight Ionic columns supported an open ring of weather-worn marble. I too broke into a smile. It was as if some giant child had made a Greek temple in a living playground, or as if we had stumbled on some relic from youthful Arcadia, when life was simple pleasure and our worship was our joy.

We scrambled up the hill like two delirious children. I gained the top first, and then held out my hand to assist her. Her face glowed with delight and exercise. Leading me into the charmed circle of the little temple, she directed my attention to the magnificent view of the Sussex countryside that lay stretched out before me like a vision. I had not realized how high we had climbed in our rambling walk, but we had reached the highest point on Egremont's estate.

It is a glorious view. Mrs. Spencer named the villages and farms below us and pointed out, in the far middle distance, the silver thread of the river that marked the border of Egremont's possessions.

There is something delightful about a prospect, and some-thing more delightful still about the feeling of having the high vantage point to oneself. I felt a keen pleasure in imagining that I was the lord of all I surveyed, or that I was a worshipper of one of the minor gods to whom the temple was dedicated. These pleasing musings were interrupted, however, when I saw a pony cart coming up the hill. Mrs. Spencer saw the look of disappointment that crossed my face. She broke out in a wonderful laugh and assured me that our visitors would not be with us long.

The cart drove up to the Rotunda, and I recognized the figures who were walking beside it as two of the house servants. Mrs. Spencer gave instructions and they quickly set up a table and two chairs. The cloth was laid, and a large hamper was set down beside one of the chairs. Mrs. Spencer bade the servants be on their way.

As we watched the pony cart disappear Mrs. Spencer said, "You did not think that I would ask you to walk all this way without offering you some refreshment?" She directed me to sit down. A wonderful meal was soon before us: cold chicken, cheese, bread warm from the oven, pickles, and a cucumber salad. A bottle of rosé wine still cool from the cellars completed our repast.

She raised her glass and wished me health. She asked me how I found the wine.

"I am but a mendicant scholar," I said. "The wines I have had at Petworth have been a revelation; the wine I drink at home is so poor I am half ashamed to drink it at all."

"You must not be ashamed," she said. "We must have our wine, no matter how poor. Wine lifts us out of ourselves and infuses some gaiety into our lives. I remember a night many years ago. I was in a low inn outside Florence. The wine was execrable, but I was young and my companions were kind and beautiful. I have never been so happy, and the vile wine was no small part of that happiness."

As she was speaking she cut a slice of bread and piled cheese upon it. She ate with grace, but with an unladylike appetite.

"It is curious," she said, "how often and at what length we expatiate on the virtues of wine, but how rarely we speak of the humble foods like cheese. This cheese is made on the estate; when he was younger His Lordship made quite a study of cheese, and his dairies produce some of the finest cheeses in all of Sussex. He once brought over monks from France to teach the farmers how it should be done. Do try some; it is most wholesome and delicious."

I did as she bade me. "You have been," I said, "most generous and kind to me. This day—this view, this lovely meal, your company—will always live in my mind."

"But it is I who owe thanks," she said. "I know how kind and brave you were in that matter of the stag."

I felt the world begin to spin under my feet. My expression must have indicated my confusion.

"Lord Egremont," she said, "is old. He has wealth and power. You gave him the opportunity to exercise his heart and his feelings."

"He certainly exercised his feelings out in the field. His Lordship heaped upon me such a stream of abuse that I was half afraid he would exhaust himself."

Mrs. Spencer smiled and drank some wine. "A lesser man than yourself would have stomped off in a pique of righteous indignation. There would have been a quarrel. You would have departed. My lord would have found his old heart grown so much harder. But as the case turned out, he was able to reflect, to apologize, and we all have the benefit of a few more days of your company."

She then went on to tell me that she believed that Lord Egremont was secretly grateful to me because I had given him an excuse not to kill the stag. Egremont had half confessed; it seemed that the reason he had missed his shot was his sympathy for the creature. The stag, she said, was, like Egremont, old and noble; he spared it out of tenderness for himself. Yet he could not admit these things in front of his people because his position required him to act in certain ways. "You can little appreciate," she said, "how a man like Egremont is bound by the rules of his position."

"But his position did not require that he write me an apology. Indeed," I said, "it would seem to require that he not do so. Did not Lord Egremont find it unseemly that he, one of the great lords of England, should condescend to apologize to someone as mean as myself?"

Mrs. Spencer took another swallow of wine. "So it would appear. But my lord was with Turner when he wrote the note. That makes all the difference. Turner is a remarkable man. What do you think of him?"

"He has been," I said, "most kind to me. I feel that he is another order of being. His genius is such that we mortals cannot quite comprehend it. Do you know him well?"

She grew more thoughtful and her smile disappeared. She poured herself more wine. I saw a brightness in her eyes that I had not noticed before.

"He is a frequent guest here, so I have come to know him. My lord, indeed, suggested that I should get to know him better still. Do you find Mr. Turner handsome?"

I was taken aback by this question. Turner is short and stocky, with a large nose. His fingers are always dirty with paint. He has bad teeth, which you can often smell, but thick, sensuous lips.

"No, Mrs. Spencer," I replied. "I do not."

"Nor do I," she said. "But he is a man of strong sensual leanings. He has never married, but he is rumored to have fathered a pair of brats with an elderly woman who runs a boardinghouse somewhere. He is fond of rambling about the harbor, you know."

We spoke about the view and the delightful weather, as she helped me to some chicken and filled our glasses again.

"Tell me, Mr. Grant," she said. "How do you live?" She had put down her glass and was looking at me most earnestly. I had never been asked that most important of questions before. If anyone else had asked I would have felt it a terrible impertinence, but from Mrs. Spencer's lips it seemed most natural. "Come," she added, "you and I must be able to understand each other. You have nothing to be afraid of. How do you live?"

There was nothing for it, so I plunged in. I hope you will not be annoyed. As I looked into her lovely face, I felt a great weight lifting from my shoulders. Living as I have been in a great house like Petworth, a small voice has always whispered my shame and imposture. It was a relief to tell her of my modest inheritance, the occasional payment for a review article, the visits to country houses. When she spoke again, it was clear that she had been doing sums in her head.

"Is that all, Mr. Grant? It hardly seems sufficient for a man of your taste."

I confess that I blushed at this. I told her that although I attempted to keep up a good appearance my needs were quite modest, but that I also had a dear friend in Cambridge who was sometimes so kind as to give me gifts that allowed me to make ends meet.

She reached over and grabbed my hand. Her smile was radiant. "I knew we could understand each other!" she said. "At least you have the small income and whatever comes in from your articles; then, too, you must hope that you will someday write books that will bring in money. And I suppose, since you are clever and agreeable and handsome, you might take a position in the city, assisting some merchant or banker with accounts and correspondence. Or you might work on Fleet Street writing for one of the publications."

She took another deep swallow of wine and then filled our two glasses again. "What is hard, I find, are the gifts. The stays in country houses can be easy if the host is genial. You are aware you are a mere guest, but you are also aware that you don't have to pay for your supper and your wine. It must have been no small part of your feelings yesterday when you suddenly realized that you would have to find some other way to fill your belly for those days that you had counted on being here."

I felt uneasy and began to protest, although the fact was that she had hit very near the mark. "Oh, Mr. Grant," she said. "There is no dishonor in that. You and I, as I said, have nothing to fear from each other. We are kindred spirits. But what I really wanted to ask," she went on, "was about the gifts. How do you feel about them?"

Something about Mrs. Spencer's frank gaze undid me.
I hope you can forgive me, David, when I tell you that I was
soon unburdening myself of thoughts I hardly knew I had.
I told her how much I appreciated your dear gifts. But I also
confessed, which I have never mentioned to you, how I sometimes feel myself to be a mercenary wretch and how (and it
pains me to write this) I don't quite express my true feelings
because I am afraid of offending you. When, for example, you
say something unkind, or something with which I disagree, I
sometimes refrain from commenting because I am anxious not
to cut off those gifts which are so necessary for my survival. It
is hard, I told her, when mercenary considerations prevent one
from being honest.

"Ah," she said, "but at least you have your small income and
your cleverness to fall back on. What have I? Mr. Spencer was
an error of my youth; he provides me with nothing except for
the occasional blackmailing letter and the inability to marry. I
have no way of earning money. I have no family. I have, at present, the kindness of Lord Egremont. In the past I have had the
generosity of other gentlemen. But this comes with unspoken
expectations: that I act the charming hostess, that I play after
dinner, and so forth."

She touched my hand again and drank some more of the
wine. "It is, don't you think, the fact that so much is unspoken
that makes it all so hard. And yet, if it were spoken, we should
die of shame, should we not? Since we do not speak of these
matters we are always in danger of offending; we are always
unsure if we need to do more or do less in order to maintain

that upon which we so much depend. But the silence is what allows us to go on. Were it not for that, we would see it all as a most common and sordid transaction. Let us raise our glasses, Mr. Grant, to the silence."

She held up her glass and the crystal sparkled in the sunlight. Her face was flushed with wine, but she seemed more radiant and beautiful than ever. "Do not fear me, Mr. Grant."

I raised my glass as well. She touched hers to mine. "You are young and handsome. Your youth will pass and your beauty will fade, just as mine has done. You will, however, have your wits and your small income to see you through those dark days. I, on the other hand, will have only the ruin of my beauty. Perhaps I will become one of those horrible creatures of paint and horsehair. I will frighten small children when I walk by."

"Mrs. Spencer," I said, "you will grow older, to be sure, but your beauty will merely become beauty of another sort. Your charm will not desert you."

She smiled at my weak gallantry. "It is most good of you to say so. And most contemptible of me to place you in a position where decency requires that you pay me a compliment. But you will forgive me, for you are most kind." She emptied her glass and we both took a few more bites in silence.

"But you are not kind to Mr. Turner," she said with a smile.

"I admire him above all other painters," I said. "His conversation, too, is droll and ingenious."

"You said he was not handsome."

"He is not," I repeated.

"True," she said. "But there are worse fates." We had finished our meal. Mrs. Spencer rose from her chair and leaned against one of the pillars. I stood by her side and together we admired the view. "You must give me your arm as we walk home. I have had too much wine. We will go now, if you don't mind. The servants will be here in less than an hour. You must amuse me and make sure that I do not turn my ankle. Come."

. 18 .

SHE WAS SITTING UP in bed, reading, when he came in. There was a shawl thrown over her nightgown. Her hair was down. She had added a few logs to the fire, and the room was warm and inviting. Twenty years ago, Rhinebeck had married her for her looks and her family connections. Time, the children, and the life he had given her had taken their toll. She was tired around the eyes and thicker around the waist, but still attractive enough to turn heads when she got herself up in an evening gown. When he thought about the last young woman who had been in that bed, he felt a moment of regret. He tried to recall her name—was it Julie or Jenny?

She peered over her reading glasses. He had noticed the gray in her hair before, but somehow, in the firelight, there seemed more of it. Perhaps there *was* more of it. It had been a month since they had seen each other.

"You look very well. I'm glad to see you," he said.

"And it's good to see you as well. Birch Lodge is much more beautiful than I had imagined. From your descriptions, I expected something very rough, like a Viking fortress. But everything is charming and oddly delicate. Your Snuggery is the most marvelous room. This is a lovely room as well—the birch bark wall coverings look wonderful in the firelight. I am only sad that you intend to keep all this from me."

"Men require some place where they can be alone with other men. We have had this discussion before, but perhaps we can revisit it. Where did you find your new friend?"

"Do you like her?"

"I asked where you found her."

"At the Cranleys'. There was a tea. Ladies interested in the arts, you know. She said she had always wanted to meet me, so I invited her over. More tea. She has written a monograph on Constable—she has something to do with one of the galleries. She is very agreeable, and I wanted company. I believe she is rather hard up. She only protests a bit at my offers to pay, but she doesn't seem too greedy. Not like Miss Danvers. I like her very much. Do you?"

"Is there a Mr. Overstreet?"

"He exists, but they are separated. She doesn't like to speak of him, but she hints at drink and gambling debts."

"You must tell me which gallery. I know all those people; I will make inquiries."

"So you don't like her?"

"She is certainly attractive. But she was making love to me during dinner. I am not so vain these days as to think that my personal charms are enough to make a woman lose her sense of propriety."

"You are still a handsome man. But that is just her way. She's always trying to be agreeable. Sometimes, perhaps, she tries too hard."

"Perhaps she could try a bit harder to keep her buttons fastened."

Rhinebeck had changed into his pajamas and was sitting on the side of the bed. They paused to listen to a loon's cry echo across the water.

"So tell me. The boys. Are they well?"

"I received a letter from Tom last week. He's enjoyed Yellowstone and California. Hollywood in particular. Some of his Triangle Club friends provided him with introductions, I'm afraid mostly to so-called actresses. I hope he's careful. His father's name is not unknown. I wouldn't want them to take advantage of him."

"I would worry more about his taking advantage of them. He's a cool customer. Perhaps too cool. He will make his way in the world. And Herman? How is he?"

"He wasn't happy in Canada. He said the place we sent him to was beastly. No hot water. Endless marches through the wilderness. Sleeping in the cold and rain."

"But good for him. Toughen him up."

"Oh, don't sound like a typical masculine fool. It's too stupid."

Rhinebeck acknowledged the wisdom of her remarks by kissing her gently on the forehead. "But you must admit he needs it."

"I do not. He isn't like other boys. He is half a poet."

"He is a kitten that has just seen a bulldog. He always appears to be frightened of something."

"Don't you think it might be you?"

Rhinebeck looked at his wife. She went on. "You're always so gruff with him. Always disappointed. Whereas Tom can do no wrong in your eyes, Herman is conscious that everything he does displeases you."

"I wish he would be more forthright. I admit that I lose my patience with the boy. But if he would only look me in the eye and not sneak about so, it would be much easier."

"If you didn't glare at him as soon as he walks into the room, he might not cower so. You know that your glance can bring some of the most powerful men in America to their knees; you must understand what it can do to a fifteen-year-old boy."

Rhinebeck was silent for a moment. "I'll try to do better," he said. "Perhaps I'll bring him up here. I will keep my pretty Renoir locked up so as not to give him any ideas. How did you like her?"

"You should think better of me, Cornelius. Come to bed."

Rhinebeck got under the covers. She reached over and touched him. "It's been a long time since we've been together. I'm not such an old lady yet that I will be offended by a pink young thing, even if she reveals the hair between her legs."

He responded to her familiar but unexpected touch and returned her kisses. She sat up and pulled off her nightdress. Orange firelight flickered on the walls. She smiled at him as her face emerged from the white cotton. The gray of her hair almost glistened in the firelight. Her breasts were full and pendulous, there was a fold of flesh around her stomach, but he felt the same heat and urgency that he had felt for her younger body, a body he could not even remember.

She kissed him again and pushed the covers back before touching him once more and turning over on her stomach. She raised her hips into the air.

"Come," she said.

Rhinebeck pulled off his pajamas and positioned himself behind her. He saw her raised and parted thighs glow golden in the firelight, a gift from the gods. He looked at the smooth skin of her back and her rump. The place where their bodies joined disappeared in the darkness. He felt that he was seeing certain things for the first time. There was a beauty in the animal foolishness of the whole business—the pumping in, the pumping out—that he had never quite recognized before. His wife, the mother of his children, was as beautiful as Helen. He would bring her back to Birch Lodge the next time he came; he would show her the Turner. Together they would decide who would inherit it.

As he drifted off to sleep he wondered why none of the other thighs he had parted, nor any of the other kisses he had received, had ever been so profoundly connected to the heart of things.

. 19 .

WITHIN HALF AN HOUR of our arrival at the Millers'
party, I'd had too much wine. It was a pretty good setup—there
was wine out on the patio and wine inside in the dining room.
I walked back and forth between the two stations and figured
that, worst case, someone might notice that I'd filled up a second time. There was no excuse for it really, but as soon as we got
there Susan attached herself to some friends for what I assumed
would be some girl talk. I had been doing pretty well with the
drinking, but I needed a serious cushion to get through the afternoon. It was Labor Day and I hadn't seen the painting since
mid-July; the blessing was starting to wear off. It was the kind of
Princeton crowd that we hung out with: lower-level university
administrators, folks from the foundation, local lawyers, spouses.
There were a few faculty members, but none of the heavy hit-
ters—they had better invitations. But there were enough of those
young tenure-track types on the make to remind me of what I
had wanted when I was younger. Hence the wine.

Usually we go up to the mountains for the last week of the summer, but I had told Susan I had a lot to do at the office. That wasn't true, of course—I never really have a lot to do—but I still couldn't tell her about the painting.

Although things had been a bit better between us since my birthday, the time we spent together felt hollow. There were long silences in which we neither asked the questions that needed to be asked nor gave the answers that needed to be given. She felt, naturally enough, that I was holding back and hiding something, while I felt I was always being interrogated and backed into a corner. The party seemed like an acceptable way to kill the afternoon, which is a stupid goal when you are a human being doomed to die, but it was all I could muster at the time.

Halfway through my fifth glass of wine, I realized that if I didn't get something into my stomach I would be in serious trouble. Looking back, I think it was at about this time that I started thinking and acting like someone who was drunk. I don't think I ever got to the stage where people would look at me and say, "Henry is acting the way his father used to act," but the fact is that I did some things I wouldn't have done if I'd been sober.

I made my way over to the food and loaded up a plate. A cluster of people were standing around the shrimp bowl listening to Clive Richmond go on and on.

Richmond was in the art history department and had only been there for two years, but he seemed like one of those guys who were almost guaranteed to get tenure, unless there was some unpleasantness involving attractive undergraduates or somebody's wife. He had already published a couple of books, he dressed well, he was handsome, and he had enough of an English accent to make us Princeton people swoon.

He was holding forth on the relationship between the art markets in New York and London and the value of art in post-modern America. "Money," he said, "is the signifier par excellence; money is that by which we value things and find them beautiful. If a man sees a woman walking down the street and knows that the designer dress she's wearing cost five or six thousand dollars, she will be—not just seem—more beautiful than if she had been wearing one of those Princeton outfits they sell at Talbots. Similarly with paintings. Just the other day, for example, at Sotheby's, a Cézanne landscape went for about sixteen million—two million more than the estimate. I heard someone say that the sale showed that the wounds of September 11 were starting to heal. Imagine that! We all knew that nothing was beautiful on September 12. We could look into our hearts and we knew. But now we look at the size of a pile of money and we can tell that beauty has returned. That's the only way we have of assigning value, but, oddly, the values we assign are true." He paused to take a sip of his wine. "Or at least as true as any others."

"But okay," I said. I wasn't really a part of the conversation and should have kept my mouth shut. I had the sensation of hearing my own voice as if it came from the other side of the room. "There is this Cézanne. We can all agree that it's a beautiful thing. But why do you say it has become more beautiful? Why not just say that whoever had the big check-book was feeling a little bit more optimistic about the way the market was tending? Or maybe he felt just a little safer and didn't have the same need to put his money into lead underwear futures or wherever it is you put your money when you're feeling nervous. His feelings didn't change the way the painting looked."

Richmond smiled at me. It was one of those smiles that I get more and more from young people. "But I think they did, you see. His feelings prompted him to open his checkbook as wide as he did. The price he paid is now, for better or worse, as much a part of the painting as the canvas on which the paint is smeared. It's what people see when they look at it. And it doesn't make much sense to talk about the way a painting looks if that's something different from what people see."

I wanted to grab him by the collar and shake him. You have no idea, I wanted to say, no fucking idea of what you're talking about. The painting is the thing itself. There is beauty and meaning beyond measure on the canvas. It exists in your mind and your body; it gives you a soul. But I just shook my head and said something lame about how I was too stupid for all that postmodernist stuff.

I wandered away and refilled my wineglass. Susan was on the other side of the room, engaged in what looked like serious conversation. She caught my eye and waved; I waved back but didn't join her. I was afraid she'd recognize that I'd had too much to drink if I got close.

Eventually I settled in with some folks from the foundation

and we traded office gossip. When my glass was empty, I went to refill it. Richmond was helping himself to another glass as well; the crowd around him had disappeared. I had reached that stage of drunkenness where I didn't realize I was drunk.

"I got so involved in the conversation," Richmond said, "that I never got a chance to get something to eat. Fortunately, there's a lot of good stuff left."

I smiled at him. "In situations like this I always make it a point to deal with my physical needs before attending to the intellectual ones. I was interested in what you were saying back there, although I have to admit it bugged me. I guess I'm old enough or naive enough to think that the value of something beautiful is independent of the thing's cost, but the more I thought about what you said, the more I could see that you have a point."

"Well, I was, perhaps, overstating things a bit—that's what one does at parties."

"But let's say, just for argument's sake," I went on, "that I'm upstairs cleaning out my grandmother's attic and I find this old bundle up there." I was so drunk that I felt clever for using the phrase "for argument's sake" and for making it *my grandmother's attic*. "And I open it up and there is a painting in there that I find very beautiful. I guess you'd say it has no value, because there is just my opinion and I may like a black velvet Elvis better than I like a Botticelli or a Vermeer. And that makes sense because this painting doesn't exist in the world, only in my mind. But let's say, further, again for argument's sake, that I see that there's a brass plaque on the frame that says Turner or maybe Constable. And let's say that it's not a forgery, but the real deal, and that I'm a person of reasonably good, or even educated taste. What is the value of the painting under these conditions?"

Richmond chewed on a piece of bread and cheese and thought for a moment. It occurred to me that even at Princeton it might be something of a struggle to live on an assistant professor's salary. Getting a free meal at a party might be nothing to sneeze at. I started to feel better, almost paternal, about Richmond.

"Theoretically, of course, it would be exactly the same as in the case of the black velvet Elvis. The painting's only value would be that which you assigned to it. But if you are like most people the brass plaque will have had an effect. Since you are a person of educated taste, the painting will be more valuable in your own estimation to the extent that you consider it the work of Constable or Turner, because you know who those guys are. But practically, of course, it's a different matter. It seems to me highly unlikely that you'd be able to leave yourself in doubt as to whether you had something worth perhaps millions and millions of dollars. So you would take the bundle to Sotheby's. There would ensue a series of technical processes that would result in some statement of authenticity. Then it would be put up for auction and the result would be exactly like the one I described earlier."

"But let's say it was a Turner. How much would it be worth on the auction market?"

Richmond laughed. "That's every art collector's dream. It's impossible to say, although it would be some very large sum of money; it would depend on the quality, the condition, the certainty of the authentication. The Tate has all this North Sea oil money and a stated policy of going after everything by Turner. So the money would get very serious very quickly. Twenty-five, thirty million dollars? That wouldn't be crazy."

The number hit me in the head like a hammer blow. I had known, of course, that if my painting was a real Turner, it would be worth a great deal, but I had never allowed myself to consider what that might mean. Even if Richmond was off by fifty percent, I realized that I could do whatever I wanted. Like most people who work for a living, I had allowed my sense of what was possible to be determined by my income. Suddenly beautiful vistas opened before me, which promised, like the sea behind Helen's tower, to take me to unimaginable lands.

I gave Richmond a weak smile. "Well, I guess I'm lucky that I don't have that sort of problem."

"I can't imagine a better problem to have," he said.

"Me too, but, like I said, it's not a problem I have." I was drunk enough that I thought it important to remind him. I told him that I'd enjoyed our conversation and went off to look for Susan.

. 20 .

THE WEATHER HAD TURNED cold and wet. Egremont had sent word that his business in London would detain him for a few days more. I asked that a fire be made up in the Carved Room and decided to pass the morning with my book and more tea than I would normally allow myself.

Of all the wonderful rooms at Petworth, the Carved Room is perhaps the most wonderful. It is long and narrow, more like a gallery than a common room. Some of Egremont's finest paintings are here, including four views of Petworth Park that Turner completed just two years ago. It is a testament to the esteem in which Lord Egremont holds Turner that these paintings keep company with two magnificent Van Dycks and an imposing portrait of Henry VIII by Holbein.

But the glory of the Carved Room is the walls themselves. Imagine the carving on the most elaborate and elegant picture frame you have ever seen. Now imagine a whole room covered with these carvings and, further, that the carving is not in vulgar gold, but natural wood so supple that the wooden leaves and garlands seem to flutter in the breeze, and you begin to get the idea.

I had been settled there for about half an hour when I heard footsteps. It was Turner, carrying his sketchbook and wearing a disgruntled look.

"Ah. There you are. Not your usual place, I see, but a fine one, nonetheless. Damn rain." Turner sat down and pulled his chair closer to the fire. He poured a cup of tea. "Don't mind if I do," he said. "I had planned to go out toward the edge of the estate. There is some fine scenery there, half wild. When I was younger I often sketched in worse weather, but now I am too old. My bones hurt, my teeth ache."

I commiserated with him on the state of the weather. I said that I had been looking forward to taking a ramble of some sort, but that I had decided to make the best of it through the generous application of fire and tea.

"Not a foolish notion, young man." I went back to my book. Turner pulled himself up a few inches closer to the fire. He seemed nervous and slightly uneasy. "Damn weather," he repeated. "You'd think I had never seen rain before. I went to bed thinking of today's sketching expedition. Got myself pleased at the prospect. Good work to be done, death approaching, candle against the darkness and so forth. And now nothing but a reminder of my age and weakness."

"But surely," I said, "there must be indoor subjects that could absorb your attention until the sun comes out again?"

"Certainly. I learned to draw indoors. The plaster casts at the Academy. The hours I spent in that cold and dusty room, good Lord, that was my youth, young man. But there are finer things to be studied here—the greatest collection of classical sculpture in all of England, I dare say. It is the hope blasted, not the actuality. Funny creatures, we men."

I went back to my book again, but was very much aware of his piercing eyes. He took out his sketch pad and his box of chalks.

"Do you mind?" he said. I shook my head and he began to draw.

"Must I do anything special?" I asked.

"No. The best thing for it is just to keep reading. Don't mind me. As if such a thing were possible! That's why I prefer landscape: a mountain doesn't change the way it looks just because a poor fool sits before it with his sketch pad."

I tried to get back to Homer, but I found it difficult to concentrate on anything but the sound of Turner's pencil.

"Come now," he said, "you look as if you suspect that your host's wife is about to confess to her husband how she has passed the afternoon. If you cannot read, then you must talk to me. So, are you still at your Homer?"

"Yes," I said.

"Are you a master of the ancient tongues?"

I said that I was a passable Latinist, but confessed that my Greek was not all that it could be.

"I envy you," he said. "As we were saying the other night. Were the ancients smarter than the likes of us or just the first ones up in the morning?" Turner's pencil never stopped moving as he spoke; it was as if his hand belonged to some other being. "Never could decide, but they come to me as an echo's echo through the dim mists of time. Ancient tongue to modern. Still, more wisdom than I can comprehend." He worked in silence for a few minutes as I listened to the sound of his pencil.

"You are born for it, sir," said Turner, "now that you have relaxed a bit. 'Tis a pity you are not rich, for if you were I might break my resolution and paint your portrait if the price were right."

"If I were rich," I said, "I would surely be less agreeable. I am not sure that I would be willing to part with my ill-gotten wealth on a portrait by Turner. If Reynolds were still alive he would be more to my liking. And on a horse—I would insist on the horse, you know. Leading a charge against foes foreign and mythological."

"It would cost you a deal extra." Turner laughed. "Once you get a horse involved it's a damn bad business. Not many of my brethren can do a horse to satisfaction. Stubbs, of course, and Landseer, but it doesn't seem worth the trouble. Gentlemen are very particular about their horses. Make the wife a bit prettier than she is, put the child's nose in the middle of his face, you shall have no complaints. But make the forelock too short and there's hell to pay. I make it a rule to stay away from the damn creatures."

I felt as if he was drawing my soul from my body, and it gave me, in ways that I can hardly bring myself to think of, an intense feeling of pleasure. His serious attention was gratifying to my vanity, of course, but it was more than that: his attention was like a caress that appealed to the more noble aspects of my being.

"So tell me," he said, "what did Helen look like?"

"No one knows. Homer is too subtle for mere description. The old men on the walls of Troy say she is worth fighting for, but how you would recognize her if she were walking down the Strand is unknown. All we can be sure of, I think, is that all of us would turn to stare at her. Some of us would do things we did not think ourselves capable of."

"Always fancied her a blonde. Some days a redhead."

"She is the common type of her time and place, but perfected," I said. "She is an idea that always lies just beyond our grasp."

"But what about 'the face that launched a thousand ships' and all that? She surely must have looked like something."

"But that is Marlowe, not Homer. And Marlowe put it as a question. What Faustus saw before him was a boy actor smeared with paint and covered with horsehair. 'Was this the face that launched a thousand ships?' I think not. Shakespeare came closer to the mark when he has Ulysses describe her as 'a theme of honor and renown.' He understood that she was not flesh so much as an idea."

"So you don't think she can be painted?"

"You would know, not I. But think of all the Eves you have seen. She too was the perfected woman, and painters have often dared to represent her."

"But Helen," Turner said. "Another order of being altogether. The Bible and Homer are wholly different. Queer when you think of it, but Helen is much harder to imagine. More beautiful. Eve always partakes of the fall. No fall about Helen, although the world falls about her."

His hands stopped moving and he looked intently at his drawing. I suddenly ceased to exist for him. He said something to himself that I could not catch, and then gave a shrug. He took his half-empty teacup and dipped a brush in it. He worked the liquid into the paper and then took out paints and began applying them, working in silence. I went back to my book. I was aware that he took occasional glances at me but I also knew that he did not want to talk now. Somehow reading became easier and the sound of Turner working almost seemed like soft music accompanying the battles of the heroes.

I do not know how long we sat there, but at length Turner put down his tools and looked at his handiwork.

"I suppose," he said, "that you want to see it."

Before I had a chance to reply, he held the pad toward me. The paper was glistening with moisture, a living thing, almost. When I was young we kept a cat, and I recalled a time when the cat had left a baby rabbit on our steps. The poor creature couldn't have been more than a few hours old, small enough, as I recall, to fit into my child's hand. I picked it up and saw the still-beating heart through the open wound and as I watched, I saw the heart cease to beat and the quick flesh take on the grayness of death. As I looked at Turner's drawing I saw a similar transformation. When he first showed the drawing I felt that I could see my soul shimmering in the light that infused my portrait. As I watched, however, it began to fade and soon it was gone altogether. I felt as if I had witnessed my own death.

Turner half-smiled at the horror that was written on my face. "It is always so," he said. "One of the great rewards of my art is that I am the only one to see the living painting. Paint is cruel. That is why I do so much work on Varnishing Day at the Academy. I know that many say I do it for show or out of laziness, but I do it so that the public can, for a moment, see my work as I do. A painting is like a woman. Never quite the same pitch of perfection as in the first blush of youth."

I studied the drawing more closely. I had been captured in three-quarters profile. The outline of the room was visible in the background. The light came both from the fire behind me and the windows toward which I was facing. I have always been dissatisfied with my face. I confess that I have spent hours in front of a glass looking at it, trying to see who I was and trying to comprehend what others, especially you, dear David, could find attractive in a countenance that seems entirely wanting in grace and balance. I have always felt that my chin is too weak and that my eyes lack character. As I looked at Turner's sketch I saw myself for the first time and understood that I had hardly known myself before. And although some part of me had vanished as the painting dried, there was still more of my character on view than I usually allowed myself to acknowledge. Turner understood the man who lived below the appearances and I wondered, David (and I write these words with great sorrow), if you have ever seen me half so clearly. In Turner's sketch I could see all those doubts and fears about my future and my mode of living that you are so kind as to ignore.

"This is wonderful," I said. "But it is nothing that I would give to my mother, if I could. It would break her heart."

"She would see that?"

"She is not an educated woman. But she has an understanding heart, a mother's heart. That is, in some sense, her only possession now that my father is gone. So yes—she might not be able to tell you why the drawing gives her sorrow, but she would certainly feel it."

"And you?" he asked, his voice quite serious.

"It is the truth," I said. "You have captured those fears and doubts which I hide from myself and from the world. You have not made me more handsome than I am, but you have honored my face by depicting it as it is. I don't think the mirror has ever reflected me so faithfully."

We were both silent for a space. I handed the sketch pad back to Turner. He studied his work for a moment, and then he began to put his paints and pencils away. "I am not done with this yet," he said, "but perhaps you shall have it someday. You see more in it than I do, and I honor you for your vision."

"I would be most appreciative," I said. "But only if it suits you."

"We shall see," he said. "You and I, we will have much to talk about in the days to come. But now look—the sun is breaking through the clouds. I must be off to see what can be salvaged from the morning's light. Until dinner."

. 21 .

SUSAN WAS STILL INVOLVED in a conversation that didn't seem to need me, so I spoke to a few more people and probably had another glass of wine before I wound up in a corner talking to Ruth Carpenter. She was married to Bob, who works in my office, but she was at the party alone because Bob was off in Paris trying to find himself.

What happened next was my fault, but it felt as inevitable to me as Paris's approach to Helen. It was really just a combination of alcohol and the sense that I was worth maybe thirty million dollars. Fuck you, Mossbacher, I remember thinking, I don't need you; I don't need anything but my painting. I felt full of strength and possibility; it was time for me to break the bonds that had been holding me back from the world of pleasure and fulfillment that was rightly mine. And Ruth was drunk too, and sad. The whole thing was so pathetic in a middle-aged suburban way that I still cringe when I think about it.

Ruth is an attractive woman, maybe a few years younger than I am, but once I figured out that she was available, I saw things in her that I don't think her husband saw when they were first married. It's hard for me to explain, and difficult to remember because of all the wine. Although I can't say that I mistook her for Helen or even that I saw some Helen in her, her lips were ripe and inviting and her bosom seemed like paradise. That sounds awful, I know, but that's the way it felt.

She talked about how unhappy she was; she talked about what a jerk Bob was being, how she thought he might be having an affair, how unjust it all was. I think I was the one who suggested we go outside for air.

The Millers have a big yard with nice flowerbeds and a pond out back, so it was okay to go out and look at them. We wandered away from the crowd around the patio. There was a little bench tucked away in a corner of the yard, in front of the pond, which had big gold and silver fish swimming around in it. I think it was Ruth who wanted to sit down and look at the fish. She said it was pretentious of the Millers to have a koi pond. I said the fish were interesting and it was a nice place to sit. She agreed it was a nice place to sit and looked at me. That's when we started kissing.

It was pathetic. I had been given an extraordinary gift, a vision of Helen. I had seen the truth, and yet the best I could do to make it real in my life was a drunken embrace with a woman I didn't particularly care for. As I kissed her, however, the thought of Helen's smooth shoulders lent a sense of urgency to my tongue and guided my hand to the clasp of her brassiere.

"I'm sorry to interrupt, but I want to go home. From the look of things, neither of you should be driving, so unless you want to come with me, and it's fine with me if you don't, I'll tell the Millers to call a cab."

Ruth and I had jumped apart at the sound of Susan's voice, and I was aware of Ruth trying to stuff her blouse back into her slacks. When I saw the pale flash of skin at her midriff I became nauseous. All thoughts of Helen vanished.

"Gosh, I'm really sorry," I said to no one in particular, "I've had way too much to drink." Ruth looked up at me and burst into tears. She ran off toward the house with Susan in close pursuit. Susan wanted to make sure that Ruth didn't try to drive home. It was a good thing she did, because, Susan told me later, Ruth threw a fit like something out of a bad television show. Joe Miller had to pry the keys out of her hand, and his wife had to sit with her as she sobbed hysterically in the extra bedroom. I'm glad I never found out what Ruth said about me.

I stood outside by the pond for a few minutes, listening to all the commotion in the house. It's all fuzzy because of the alcohol, but I thought I could make out Ruth's wails and a low chorus of voices who all seemed to be saying I was an asshole. I felt bile rise toward the back of my throat. I thought about my father, and what a sad and lonely drunk he'd been in his final days. Helen wouldn't come to me, no matter how hard I tried to conjure her up. It was only when I realized that she had deserted me that I began to weep.

. 22 .

BRYCE PUT THE LAST page of the manuscript down and looked at Gina with admiration. "Extraordinary," was all he could muster. He thumbed back through the pages and read aloud, his voice hushed and reverential: "'I could see that it was a painting of her and could guess that Turner had painted it, because there were Greek columns in it and sunlight.'" He looked up again. "We are vouchsafed few such moments; it is as if a window to the past has opened up and I am able to see what no one has seen before. He is an ass, of course. But still."

After they spent an hour or so talking about the implications of the document, and considering next steps, Bryce changed the subject. "I'd like to take the opportunity of your being here to introduce you to another aspect of the work of Madison Partners.

"Not everything we do is glamorous. Not everything we do, for want of a better word, is clean." Bryce regarded her very seriously for a moment. "Nothing that I am about to propose, when rightly considered, is unethical, although it might, I suppose, appear that way. As I think about your future with the firm—and I am being perfectly frank here—I need to know how far you will extend yourself for beauty. Sometimes this work is not for the faint of heart. Are you willing to take the next step with me?"

"I don't know, of course, what you're talking about. But I have moved halfway around the world on your behalf. And although I didn't think it worth mentioning, the bookseller in Kirdford was not made aware of the existence of the document you've just read within the register book she sold me, if you're concerned that I might be too scrupulous." Gina paused for a moment as she searched for the right word. "But I think you have no reason to question my gratitude or my *devotion* to you and your work."

Bryce nodded. "I recently received a call," he said, "from a professor of my acquaintance at Princeton. Someone had asked him a 'hypothetical question' about the value of a Turner on the open market. I have a number of such contacts in the academic world. People find things—in flea markets, in their attics. They suspect them to be of value. They make inquiries at the local college or university. The fact of the inquiry is made known to me. Considerations are exchanged. Most often it is nothing more than a bad copy of a mediocre painting or some amateur working in the style of so and so, but occasionally it is something worthwhile. Sometimes it is possible to intercept the work on its way to the open market. Such transactions can be highly profitable."

"Does that mean we steal them?" she asked. Bryce was pleased at her use of "we," but proceeded with caution nonetheless.

"The question is a fair one, but premature. First we find out if the object in question is worth acquiring. Only then do we consider the means. Most often I find a way to purchase it in such a way that the owner feels they have gotten more for a piece of worthless junk than they could have expected, while I have acquired something world-class for a trifle. It is, as they say, a win-win."

"And when you can't?"

Bryce shrugged. "It depends on the context. What is at stake. The moral and the practical risks. My sense of the greater good. Are you still with me?"

Gina nodded.

"You will work with our usual people. You will need to wear comfortable shoes; it's not all first-class air travel. But come, you must be exhausted. We will make arrangements in the morning."

Two days later, having spent two depressing and exhausting evenings at her mother's house, Gina found herself sitting in a booth at a diner on Route 1, just outside Princeton. She had never met a private detective before and she had been hoping for something more interesting than George.

He was in his mid-forties, thinning light brown hair, an unfortunate mustache, and thick aviator-style glasses. He looked her over carefully. It was not, she felt, the sexually charged gaze that she associated with men of his sort; rather, it was a perfectly neutral professional scrutiny. He had told her how she was to dress on the telephone, and she had followed his instructions as best she could: old running shoes, a loose-fitting shirt under a sweatshirt, unremarkable jeans. "If you're a good-looking woman," he'd said, "don't make a big deal of it. And no perfume or fancy smelling soap. You are coming to New Jersey to break into someone's house and nobody should notice that you've been here."

He waited until the waitress had taken her order. "You can follow instructions. The last one seemed to think she was coming to an opening. A white shirt, tight black pants, and a black jacket. But you'll do. Listen: the guy's not very interesting, but who is?"

George took a sheet of paper from his pocket and consulted it as he spoke. "His name is Henry Leiden. He's married twenty-six years, two grown kids. Wife seems to be the brains and the looks in the organization. She works in New York, partner in a midsized law firm. About the time he got in touch with the professor rumors started going around that the marriage was in trouble: he was sleeping with somebody else, so was she, maybe. But they're still together. He works for something called the Nassau Foundation. Small outfit, staff of about ten. They distribute maybe ten million dollars a year in small grants, mostly in the arts and education. He reads grant applications, travels a bit to tell folks about the foundation. It's one of those strictly nine-to-five jobs, not too stressful. Pay's okay for what it is, but no way to be a millionaire. She's the one that brings in the cash. Summer place upstate; been there and checked it out. Nice lake view, but nothing special." George's cell phone rang and he listened for a few moments before putting it back in his pocket.

"Okay, we're good to go. She's in New York and he just got to the office. Finish your coffee." As they were driving toward Princeton, George handed her a clipboard. "This should be pretty easy: no pets, no alarms, no help. We're going to park on the street about a block from the house. If anybody sees us they'll think we're insurance adjusters. Something about a clipboard—it makes you look official."

Hawthorne Avenue was lined with modest split-levels that looked as if they had been built in the fifties or early sixties. Gina had expected something grander from Princeton. She followed George up the driveway to the back. He took a ring of picks from his pocket and crouched down in front of the door. In thirty seconds it was open. He smiled with contempt. "Try not to touch anything and make sure your shoes are clean before we go in there." He handed her a pair of thin cotton gloves and put on a pair himself.

The first thing she noticed was the smell; the second was the silence. The smell of burnt toast and coffee was so powerful she thought she would need a shower to get it out of her hair. The odor seemed amplified by the same trick that made the fall of her feet sound like thunder. She could hear the blood pounding in her temples and the air rushing into her nostrils. There was a copy of the *Times* on the kitchen table: "Iraqi Looters Tear Up Archaeological Sites." There was a stack of junk mail on the counter. A shopping list stuck to the refrigerator. Just normal people whose lives were being violated. She felt both sorry for them and excited in a way that surprised and disturbed her.

It was a modest place, like the Wisconsin home of her freshman roommate at Sarah Lawrence. Everything seemed a little worn around the edges, but it looked comfortable enough. She thought about how miserable her mother was in spite of all the money, about how little her own money contributed to happiness.

George went through the house systematically and with quiet efficiency. "People like this," he said, "are not very sophisticated—unless looking unsophisticated is part of the act. So we have to look in the obvious places: in closets, under beds, in the attic, leaning against a wall, in the garage."

When George went up to the attic, she stayed behind and looked around the bedroom, trying to get a sense of these people by looking at the photographs on the bureau: babies, a boy and a girl playing catch, college kids at a picnic table, wedding pictures, a middle-aged couple having drinks on a wooden dock with blue water in the background. She was a good-looking woman, whereas age had shown more on him. She picked up a picture in which he was looking up from a computer. He was smiling and making an effort, but nothing could disguise the thinning hair, the unhealthy fleshiness of his face, and something defeated around the eyes. He reminded her of the guy her father was trying so desperately not to become.

Hearing George on the attic stairs, she set the photograph carefully back in its place. She hurried to the unmade bed and looked under it.

"Anything under there?"

"Just dust," she said. "And a sock. And a pair of his underpants. Any luck upstairs?"

"No." George bent down and looked under the bed. "You missed the bra," he said. "Let's get out of here."

They had been in the house for less than half an hour. Once they got to the car George called someone on his cell phone and told them he was done. Then he turned to her. "There's nothing here. You can tell your boss I said so. Just the same old same old. Middle age and all that shit. Some day it will bite you in the ass too. Just you wait. I'll drive you to the station."

. 23 .

"TIME," TURNER SAID, "is the great subject." He handed me a glass of sherry and took one for himself. "It will do you good."

We were up in his studio. The morning light streamed in from the east. There was a great fire in the fireplace. "The passage of the past to the present, of youth to age, of the golden age to the dismal one, the rise of empires and their fall. Most fellows don't think of it as they paint, but one must, since it takes so damn long to execute a painting and nothing is as it was when you started.

"Queer how some of those old Italian fellows went about it. Birth of saint in the upper right-hand corner. Pious education upper middle, first miracle upper left, gruesome death front and center, further miracles over on the left. Seems damn clumsy if you ask me, but it has a certain charm. I always try to get a hint of time in one way or another: a ruin or a twisted tree; something about to happen. Otherwise there is no interest.

Time is the only thing we care about. How long before we die is the only question."

He put his glass down. "But come. Time is passing. This light will only be with us for so long. You are a fine-looking young man, but before long you will be like me and knocking on death's door."

He directed me to get up and stand on a small platform that was in the center of the room. He asked me to take my shirt off.

"I will give you a pose," he said, "and ask you to hold it for about five minutes by my watch. And then another, and so forth." He took his watch out of his waistcoat pocket and placed it on the ledge of his easel. I took my shirt off as he bade. Although Turner had taken pains to make the room as warm as possible, I felt goose bumps form on my flesh. I looked down at Turner and was relieved to see that he was not staring at me, but still setting up his materials.

"Ah, there you are," he said after a few moments. I felt him look me over critically. "You will do." He gave me a kind smile. "Are you comfortable? Warm enough? Not sure what I can do to make it warmer, so I hope the heat will suffice."

I assured him that I was warm enough, but confessed to being a little uncomfortable.

"Most natural thing in the world. But you could make a career of this. Not that I would recommend it. As you shall see, it is tedious work. And I am a reasonable man, while many of my brethren are tight-fisted reprobates. Now, turn your back to me and clasp your hands behind your neck. Good. Shift your weight so that you place most of it on your left side. Now keep very still. You may amuse yourself with the thought that you are a pagan youth awaiting a visitation from the gods."

I did what I could to banish the incongruity of my position from my thoughts by looking out onto the park. A herd of deer was grazing in the middle distance, bending their heads down to the horse chestnuts. Traces of yellow and red were starting to appear in the trees. Formations of geese wheeled through the sky. I could hear the sound of Turner's pencil scraping against the paper.

"Good. Now put your hands down. Rest a moment. You have lovely muscles on your back. Not so bulky as the Horse Guards I used to sketch at the Academy, but nicely articulated. You will not do for a hero, but you will make an excellent Athenian youth. Or perhaps one of those poor blokes the gods are always falling in love with. Doomed, of course. Or, if I was in that line, a first-rate Saint Sebastian."

I put my hands in my pockets for warmth. I felt vaguely foolish looking down on him, as if I were going out for a stroll and had simply forgotten my shirt. But I also felt flattered by his remarks. "I don't fancy being Saint Sebastian," I said.

"You would not get the point of it, would you?" Turner asked. He broke into a hearty laugh. I smiled as best I could, more at the sight of his laughter than at the humor of the thing.

He wiped his eyes. "We must get back to work, although it does a soul good to laugh. Let us try another. Face me, and now turn a bit to the side. Turn your head also to the side. Raise your left hand and point to something outside the window there." I did as I was told.

"This will be harder for you, but I'll try to be quick." Turner worked steadily for a moment or two, his eyes moving rapidly between me and his work. He muttered to himself as he worked, seeming more and more agitated about something. At last he cried out, "Damn," and threw a piece of chalk to the ground. "Those trousers," he said, "do you mind?"

I broke the pose and looked at him.

"I cannot leave the nineteenth century. Lord Egremont has asked me to do a classical composition. I wanted to do these sketches of you to help me in my thinking. But those trousers. It is impossible." He gave me the most pathetic look.

Knowing that if I thought about it for more than a moment I would be lost, I took the plunge into unknown waters. I sat down on the edge of the platform and quickly divested myself of my trousers, stood up, and resumed the pose.

Turner went back to his drawing. In the moments that followed, something remarkable occurred. I cannot do justice to it, but I will try.

I concentrated on the place in the distance at which my finger pointed, trying to see whatever was there with all of my being. Turner and the sound of his pencil disappeared; my sense of my ridiculous position quite faded away. It seemed to me that I had left this world of steam trains and parliamentary debates. I was one of Cortés's men in Keats's poem, standing high above some unknown world and about to see something no man had seen before. And then it seemed that I had become the Greek youth in the painting that Turner was creating. I looked out at the far trees of Petworth Park, at the very reach of my vision. I saw what I can only describe as a bright shadow on the physical world, and I knew in the depths of my heart that a goddess was making her appearance. I cannot say now what she looked like. No images remain in my mind. But I still have a sense of a beauty beyond all beauty that I had ever seen or imagined. My heart, I know, began to beat faster, and my body grew moist, as if I had been anointed with precious oils. I felt myself quiver with joy and worship.

But then I heard Turner gasp and the spell was broken. The goddess or the vision or whatever it was disappeared. It was if I had awakened from a dream and into a nightmare in which I was stark naked and in a most embarrassing state of excitement in front of a queer old painter in his drafty studio. I broke the pose in a panic, and looked about for something to cover my nakedness. Before I could speak Turner tossed me a robe, which I quickly donned. I sat down on the edge of the platform, still breathing hard. Turner handed me another glass of sherry, which I accepted gratefully.

There was something tender and solicitous about Turner's aspect that touched my heart. "How long," I asked, "had I been holding that pose?"

Turner consulted his watch and then his sketch pad. A look of amazement passed over his face. "Seemed more than five minutes' work. We were both gone. Seventeen minutes by this watch. Is not your arm sore?"

I had not thought about my arm, as my mind was full with the wonder of what had just happened and with the vain attempt to capture the vision before it fled. But I realized that it was indeed quite sore and that it hung like a dead thing at my side. I explained to Turner what had happened.

"Rum," he said. "From my side it started out plain enough. But then the frenzy came over me. That's what I call it. Happens rarely enough. The work seems to make itself, as though I'm a mere medium for some other power. Wish it would happen more often. But your body seemed almost to glow with light. Something in my mind, I suppose. Inspiration and so forth. Sweat, most likely. But that is enough for today. Enough. You should get dressed. Perhaps, if you would be so kind, we could try again. You and I, perhaps we can take a ramble in the park now."

I gathered up my clothing and went behind the screen to get dressed. I could hear Turner putting away his materials.

"Funny about the gods. They're a damn hard business. They are long gone in this miserable nineteenth century of ours. The groves are empty and so forth. Still, I sometimes imagine I catch a glimpse of them. Or see what they might be if they existed, if you follow me. You can walk about the park all you like. See deer. Foxes. Flocks of fowl. Most wonderful songbirds. Marvelous light. Color. Shades between shades never seen before. But no gods. They are gone. Decamped to who knows where. Railways and machines took their place. Who knows? But sometimes, when I look about me, I sense that they were here, that they have just departed. It is hard to explain. They leave behind a scent in the light. As though an attractive woman's been in the room. Only her scent remains. But in light. The residue of their glory in the world. An odd business."

. 24 .

SUSAN DIDN'T SAY ANYTHING on the ride home,
except that she was going to sleep in the guest bedroom and
she didn't want to have a serious conversation with a drunk. It
was the first time we'd had this kind of issue in our marriage,
and neither of us quite knew what to do. The days following
were a miserable round of fruitless arguments. She was hurt
and angry; I was abject and embarrassed. I am a weak and inconsiderate person, I said. I'm sorry. There's nothing between
Ruth and me; there never was anything between Ruth and
me; I don't even like her particularly. I had drunk too much
wine because all those university people reminded me that I
had failed in what I wanted to make of my life; I had kissed
her because her willingness to kiss me made me feel special at
a moment when I felt like shit. I wouldn't have given in to the
temptation if it hadn't been for the wine.

All this was true enough, but it didn't make Susan less
angry; nor was it, of course, the real truth. I couldn't bring

myself to tell Susan about the painting, so I couldn't explain what I had been seeking in Ruth Carpenter's lips.

Eight days after the party Susan announced that there was a weekend meeting in Cleveland that she had to attend. She told me that she would be leaving from the office on Friday and coming back on Monday.

"Cleveland on the weekend?" I said. "That's sort of odd."

She explained that her firm was working on an acquisition for a drug company and that the weekend was the only time they could get everyone involved together. There was a lot of money at stake, she said, so no wasn't really an option, but I felt that she was still so angry that she would have jumped at any chance to get away from me for a few days.

As we were having breakfast on Friday, I saw how right I was. She pointed to a slip of paper that was stuck to the refrigerator. "I left Ruth's number up there, so you don't have to look it up."

There was nothing to say that hadn't been said already. I tossed the slip of paper into the trash.

"Look," I said. "I know I deserve it. I've said I'm sorry a hundred times. I'll say it again, if you want. But I'm going to the mountains while you're gone; I was happy up there by myself. I made an appointment to talk to Eddy about the repairs."

I woke at three on Saturday morning and drove up through the dawn. After all the unpleasantness of the previous week, I took comfort in the way that Helen seemed projected against the sky as I drove. The highway only existed to lead to her.

Looking back, I suppose I was crazy. When the sun rose over the Berkshires, I saw it was a poor copy of the sun in my painting. I thought of Helen and remembered a night when Susan and I had stopped at a cheap motel on the side of the highway. When I came in from my shower she was lying naked on the bed, opened up like a hundred other women who had slept there before her. But she was mine and I was hers, and we went at each other with a mixture of tenderness and passion that made sense of my life. Only an ass would throw all that away for Ruth Carpenter's needy kisses.

But then it occurred to me how odd Susan's weekend business trip was. I tried to recall if anything like this had ever happened before and couldn't. In retrospect, I see that I was trying to justify my own bad behavior and, perhaps, pave the way for some that was to come, but I suddenly knew with a horrible clarity that as revenge for those soggy kisses and the humiliation she'd endured in front of her Princeton friends, she had gone to Cleveland to have an affair. Maybe she'd been having one all along, I thought. She wouldn't let go of Ruth Carpenter because she needed to justify her own cheating.

At any rate, I decided, there probably was a meeting; it was just that he was going to be there too. It was no doubt some guy from the office. They each had a room at the Marriott, just two colleagues in line to check in. They rode up in the elevator together, and he got off first to drop off his suitcase. She had slipped him the extra key to her room and when he came in, she was naked and waiting, just as she had been for me so many years before.

I drove on in a fever compounded of my fantasies of what
Susan was doing and my fear that the painting might be gone,
or that it might be some pale imitation of what it had become
in my imagination. By the time I got to the lake my hands were
shaking, and it was with great difficulty that I opened the door
to the barn.

The bundle was still where I had left it. I unwrapped it
carefully and placed the painting against the wall. The plaque
still read *The Center of the World*, J.M.W. Turner.

My memories were inadequate to what I saw. That is the
paradox of the story I am trying to tell: no words of mine nor
even my memories are adequate to the thing itself. Every time
I saw the painting I was overwhelmed by the sense that I had
not really seen it before. Every time I try to recall it, I am aware
that my memory is a poor shadow. Paris, I saw, had the body of a
hero, but there was a hint of feminine softness which suggested
that his inevitable union with Helen was nothing less than the
fated rejoining of flesh that had been sundered. The muscula-
ture of his back was so beautifully rendered that I could read
his desire in his flesh. But the desire I saw inscribed there was
also my own, and I understood that I had never known desire
before.

Waves of yearning and sorrow and beauty washed over
me, just as the sea in the painting washed up on the shore. I
heard Helen's music again, strange tunes in an unfamiliar scale
that sounded like red and golden leaves falling from the trees.
Helen had been playing her lyre as she awaited Paris's arrival.
It was this music, floating through the halls of the tower, that

drowned out the clash and roar of combat on the field; it was this music that had called Paris to her chamber. She had leaned the lyre against the side of her table. I could see that the strings were still vibrating.

Sensation after sensation broke over me. I was possessed and ravaged, mastered, overcome, coaxed, and beaten. It was everything I had ever wanted.

Not until late afternoon did I finally come back into myself. I walked back to the house, my knees weak. I made some coffee. I went down to the lake with the steaming mug and sat on the dock. The sky had clouded over; it looked like rain. The sky was the same gray as the water; the color was drained out of the trees on the far shore. It was perfectly quiet. My mind was empty. I had no fears and no desires.

. 25 .

To: arthur@madisonpartners.com
From: gbolton@madisonpartners.com
Subject: Petworth

I went down to Petworth yesterday to visit Mrs. Spencer. I spent some time in London looking through all the
standard material on Turner and Egremont to see if I
could find any references to her, but no luck. She seems
like a remarkable person—I am half in love with her—
but she is a blank as far as history is concerned.

She's hanging on the west end of the central corridor in
the picture gallery. The only other time I went to Petworth I didn't pay any particular attention to *Jessica*, but
I was familiar with the image from reproductions. It's an
odd painting. I stood in front of it for an hour, trying to
get past the various things I knew about it to get to the

moment where I could finally "see the thing itself for what it is," as you say. It was difficult.

The inescapable fact about *Jessica* is that it is the only large-scale oil painting in Turner's enormous oeuvre whose subject is a human figure. It's a passive picture in a way, but I could feel his struggle with Rembrandt as I stood before it, and it wasn't pretty. The great Turners are effortless encounters with the painters he admires. Claude survives, not greater than the Turner, but somehow elevated as well.

But that isn't the case with *Jessica*. She is looking, as you know, out of the window, the extravagance of gold paint behind her. She is decorated with jewels and lace, as if she was in a Rembrandt or a Hals, but Turner can't or doesn't care to compete with the Dutchmen the way that he competes with the light, the landscape, and the architectural space in Claude. He is not in love with things. He loves light and nature and the sweep of history. As Jessica leans forward, the lace mantilla she wears hangs over the window frame. We see through it and are meant (or, perhaps, *think* we are meant) to admire the painterly skill that allows him to represent transparent lace, but Turner doesn't love lace well enough to paint it perfectly and I half suspect he wanted us to know it.

The real struggle is with the body. The standard line is that Turner couldn't do bodies; the human figures in his paintings seem oddly boneless and one-dimensional. In *Jessica*, for example, her arms are mere tubes of flesh and the hand that reaches out toward the cord on the window is so badly foreshortened that it almost looks like a Thalidomide baby's flipper. But he was a fine draftsman and we can see from his academic figure studies that he was able to represent the male and the female nude in a competent Old Master style. The bodies in those studies are fleshy, articulated, and expressive.

There is a sketchbook in the Tate where Turner lays out the composition for *Jessica*; on the same page is a quick pencil sketch of a reclining nude; she is not rendered in much detail, but I assume she is Mrs. Spencer. There are at least two questions here: What was the mistress of one of the wealthiest and most powerful men in England doing posing nude for Turner, and Why did he represent her body as he did?

I think Turner was having an affair with her. Wyndham describes her as a woman who wasn't bound by conventional notions of morality and who spent more time with Turner than was decent. Egremont was a very old man. And Turner—we know from those stories of his bastard children—was devoted to the flesh.

I think there is a private joke built into *Jessica*, which no one has been able to notice because they didn't know about Mrs. Spencer. The painting was exhibited with the inscription "Shylock—Jessica shut the window, I say." It's been pointed out that there is no such line in Shakespeare. "Shylock" equals Egremont, the man of wealth. His command to shut the window is an expression of a rich man's possessiveness. Jessica/Mrs. Spencer is being shut in *and* being told to keep her legs together. We can also now make better sense of the famous yellow background. We know the old story of the after-dinner conversation during which someone said that Turner's yellows were fine enough for landscapes, but they wouldn't do for portraits. Turner rose (or failed to rise, as many would argue) to the challenge by producing *Jessica* and was rewarded with the famous line about the "lady climbing out of a large mustard pot." But it is not mustard that frames the lady—it is gold: gold that symbolizes Egremont's wealth and, quite literally, the gold paint that is Turner's signature. Jessica is embraced by Turner's signature gold/yellow. *Jessica* is a sly memorial of an affair between the artist and his model.

This also explains, I think, her body, and the fact that *Jessica* was not, according to Wyndham, a good likeness. As I tried to see Jessica's body beneath her dress, I felt that the painting was almost aggressive in refusing that view. The tubelike arms direct the viewer toward the large and illuminated (but oddly flat) expanse of bosom and the pensive face above. The corsetlike dress binds

the body in a row of horizontal bands and encrusts it in
a vertical row of jeweled buttons. There is some small
sense of volume and depth, but mostly the shape of the
body is indicated by the cinched waist and the width of
her hips and shoulders. As Turner lays out the composition in his sketchbook, Mrs. Spencer is shown with a
waist reduced to almost waspish proportions by a tightly
laced corset. She is not yet wearing the lace mantilla, and
her voluminous bosom is on display. One gets a strong
sense of the body beneath the garment, with the flesh
almost spilling out at the top of the dress. In the painting
Turner has repressed the body in order to hide his carnal
knowledge of his patron's mistress.

So instead of a body, we have a rack on which Egremont's wealth is displayed—the heavy earrings, the
necklace, the jewel-encrusted dress. One of the early
reviews of the painting said that it provided "roundabout proof that Turner was a great man; for it seems to
me that none but a great man dare have painted anything so bad." I think there is a particular way in which
this might be true of *Jessica*. Turner was great enough to
be able to afford to hide Mrs. Spencer's looks in order to
protect their secret affair.

Having some sense of what the thing we are looking for
might be like gives me hope. I can't quite form an image
of Mrs. Spencer/Jessica as Venus bathed in Turner's

light, but there is something in my mind now that is more than a mere abstraction.

I don't know if I was just looking at everything through the light of Wyndham's testimonial, but it struck me that the collection at Petworth, particularly the works added by Egremont, is remarkably sensual. There is, for example, a not very good nude by Hoppner called *Sleeping Nymph with Cupid*. It is also, and this is somewhat suggestive given our current concerns, known as *Sleeping Venus with Cupid*. It is charming in a porno-kitsch way, polite but slightly naughty, although the Petworth House guide tells us that Hoppner considered it his masterpiece (which seems surprising, since I only know of him as a portrait painter). The nymph is an attractive young woman; she is lying on her back with her arms behind her head, wearing nothing but an aggressively coy bit of drapery. A plump winged baby Cupid covers his eyes with his hands as he flies above her. (One fears that he might crash into a tree.) Wonderful brushwork, a murky forest background. Egremont purchased it in 1827 from the estate of his friend Sir John Leicester. It is said that Turner accompanied him to the sale and advised him to make the purchase. Not sure what to make of that.

It was a lovely day, so I took a walk toward the far end of the estate where there is a marvelous structure, half gazebo, half Greek temple. It sits perched on what I had been told is the highest point on the estate and provides a glorious view of what seems like most of Sussex. The structure itself is charming, classically proportioned but playful as well.

On my way back to the house I climbed the rise behind the building and sat on the bench beneath one of the ancient chestnut trees, looking down on Petworth House and the pond. It occurred to me that Turner and the remarkable Mrs. Spencer had sat on this very spot under this very tree and looked down on the house of their lord and patron. I wondered what Turner saw, what Mrs. Spencer saw, and what they had to say to each other.

Sorry to have gone on for so long—it's just that my mind is so full. London was colorless and dreary by the time I got back, but I felt energized. I think this thing you are looking for exists. I half believe that we will find it. Thank you for letting me join you in your quest.

I hope Hong Kong is treating you well.

. 26 .

LORD EGREMONT RETURNED a week ago, but I was surprised last night when I discovered that all the guests are leaving, except for Turner and myself. Even Egremont's son and his family are departing. This morning there was a carriage and a wagon at the door, laden with a mountain of luggage, including an easy chair and what looked like enough kitchen equipment to meet the needs of a small army. I was told that His lordship's son and heir was going up to London to look after some family business. I came downstairs to wish Wyndham and his wife a bon voyage, but they seemed severely out of sorts and were hardly civil to me. It was plain that my presence was not welcome, so I bade my adieus quickly. I went back to my room to write, but I was, I confess, aware that I was so situated that I could hear everything that went on by the front door just below me.

Wyndham's temper did not improve with my absence, and for so pious a man, he used a good deal of rough language with the servants. In general he needs more done for him than most men, and none of it is done to his satisfaction. This was certainly the case today. Dozens of things had been forgotten, and for each one the servants were roundly abused. A roil of confusion seemed to last for about an hour, building to a furious pitch just before ten, when I could hear Wyndham damn any number of eyes as the possibility of arriving in London after dark loomed.

At last the family was assembled and the ponderous wagon about to embark; Lord Egremont was summoned and from my room I could hear that deferential silence that always follows his appearance.

"So. You are ready at last?"

"Yes, my lord," his son replied. "In a manner of speaking. What with the suddenness of the command, I am not sure that we have quite got everything we need. But we shall make do, my lord. We shall make do."

"And what is in that wagon?"

"Why, just some small manner of things we require."

Egremont let out a furious oath which I will not repeat here, but which provoked an audible gasp from his virtuous daughter-in-law. "I have sent you to London—not the Antipodes. Do you not recollect that my house in London is well equipped with chairs?"

"But you know how Maria suffers—this chair affords her some relief. We shall bring it back, of course."

Egremont swore again. He made some particular suggestions as to that part of his daughter-in-law's anatomy that most often comes in contact with a chair. Again I could hear an audible gasp. Her husband began to remonstrate with his father, but Egremont silenced him with another oath. He said that he had no desire for further conversation and especially no desire that his son should keep the carriage waiting. But then his tone became quite cordial, as if he had made a great and successful effort to control himself.

"Godspeed, my son. I much appreciate your willingness to assist us with our affairs in London." By this time, I confess, I had moved to the window. I was so positioned that I could see Wyndham, his family, and all their equipage. I could not see Lord Egremont, who was standing in the doorway just beneath my window. Wyndham and his wife were almost completely undone by Egremont's change of tone; they could do nothing but bow.

I now heard Mrs. Spencer's voice. Her tone seemed particularly clear and ringing. "I hope you have a safe journey and a good stay in London. We shall miss you here, of course, but there is so much to do in London at this season. You shall be content."

As Wyndham looked up at her, his self-possession deserted him completely. His face contorted with hatred. If he had been a wittier man he might have said something cutting at this point, but all he could produce was, "The only thing that will make us content is not being with you!"

Egremont's tone of cordiality vanished. "Get in that carriage, you puppy. If you tarry longer I shall drive you to London myself. Godspeed and good day, sir. Be off! Come, my dear."

I heard the shuffle of the servants' feet as the door was held open for Egremont and Mrs. Spencer. Wyndham and his party mounted the carriage amid much ado and shouting by the servants, although Wyndham himself was beet-faced and tight-lipped. I felt, I confess, almost sorry for the man, as I thought about his rage trying to break through his dullness.

Later that afternoon I took my book outside and found the bench under the cluster of chestnut trees that overlooks the house and pond. Petworth House is not a beautiful building, although there are many, I suppose, who might confuse its massive grandeur with beauty. The house sits in the landscape as an emblem of power. Petworth House does not need to be beautiful—it is above that. Solidity and mass signal its potency and its dominion over those who dwell in its shadow. It is always to me something of a shock that such a heavy building should contain so much exalted art. But then the sheer mass of the artworks, the profusion of Claudes, Van Dycks, and Turners also speaks to the truth that the lords of Petworth are peers of the realm, no more like the rest of us than the sun is like a candle flame.

I was engaged in these thoughts when I saw Mrs. Spencer emerge from the house and go into the park. It was late afternoon, that time when His Lordship usually betakes himself to his bedroom and Turner secretes himself in his studio to take advantage of the last good light of the day. She seemed to be scanning the horizon. When I waved she saw me and headed up the hill.

She was slightly out of breath when she reached me; her face flushed with laughter. "Is the mere sight of me so amusing?" I asked.

"No. You are a delightful vision. I was thinking of Wyndham's face as he bid his adieus. You did not see it, but he was purple with vexation. I pity him, to be sure, and I do not wish upon him the apoplexy that is his due, but I will confess that the sight of his impotent rage did me good."

As she sat down beside me I told her what I had seen and heard this morning. Had she, I asked, intended to provoke him?

"It was, perhaps, wicked of me. I know that if I had kept silent we might have been spared his outburst. But I did not intend to provoke him, although, if I am honest with myself, I was not unwilling to give him an opportunity to embarrass himself. Which, to the delight of my evil heart, he did."

We sat in silence for a few moments, admiring the view. "So how," she asked me, "has your work with Turner been progressing?"

"I was just trying to determine which of the windows is his studio."

"It is there, on the left, on the second story—count three windows over from the side of the house. It is a most interesting room."

"Yes. Most interesting. The first time it was odd. I was, I suppose, uncomfortable and nervous. But we have settled down. Turner flatters my vanity by telling me that I make an excellent model."

"Yes. When I sat for *Jessica*, he was most flattering."

"Do you mean that yellow painting in the gallery?" I looked hard at Mrs. Spencer's face. "I suppose," I said, "that there is a resemblance, but it had never occurred to me before. You are, and I only state the fact, a much more attractive woman, although, perhaps, a few years older."

She turned away from me. "I saw the painting before it was completed. It looked a great deal more like me then. But Turner was very unhappy with it. He was in a vile humor for almost a month. He had Egremont's people construct a window frame up there on a platform. I spent hours and hours leaning through it, staring at Turner as he stared at me. He is usually a most sweet man, but he quite forgot himself in his vexation. I heard language that would have made me blush had I not been acquainted with Mr. Spencer.

"But then he took it up to London a few weeks before the Academy show last fall. It was quite altered. My face was transformed from a tolerable likeness to what you see now. The yellow had been there from the beginning but now it looked as if the pigment had been pressed into the canvas with anger. The lace had been added and the architecture around the edges, which had been plain, is what you see now. Almost the only thing that remained unchanged was the jewels. Egremont was most particular that he wanted those jewels in the portrait, and they, if you care about that sort of thing, are done to perfection. His Lordship was quite upset when he saw it. He had half a mind not to purchase it, and in private agreed with those who abused the painting in the press. But his respect for Turner—both as a man and as an artist—allowed him to overcome those scruples. Now that he has had the painting in the house for almost a year, I believe he regrets his purchase less and less."

The afternoon was winding down, and the sandstone surface of Petworth seemed of a richer hue than it had earlier. "His Lordship and Turner, you know, have been discussing a new painting. I am to go to the studio tomorrow morning."

"Ah," I said. "Now I understand why my services will not be required."

"His Lordship told me the painting was to be a classical composition." She paused for a moment. "*Jessica* was not classical. So I was able to keep my dignity."

"When I first started to pose, Turner asked me to take my shirt off. I did so, but at length he exclaimed that my trousers were too much of the nineteenth century, so off they went."

She placed her hand on my leg and patted me as if I were a child or a new puppy. "I am so sorry. Were you ashamed?"

I shrugged. "Yes. I feared mostly that my claims to being a gentleman were at risk. He would never have asked it of a true gentleman, the son of one of the neighboring landowners, or a young man of affairs in London. But I could be asked. I understand that. And yet, at the same time, I was flattered; it was a great sop to my vanity. I am afraid I am all too human."

She touched my leg again. Her smile was still radiant, but there was a tincture of sadness around her eyes. "We are all too human," she said. "Even my Lord Egremont." She waved her arm in a gesture that encompassed the grand house, the lake, the pleasure grounds, and large swaths of the Sussex countryside. "All of this is his. The rules and conventions by which other men are bound do not bind him. I can be his 'special friend' and the world must bow to me and treat me with respect. If, however, Dr. Phillips, a young and handsome widower down in the village there, were so much as suspected of keeping company with a woman of easy virtue, he would be a ruined man. But even Egremont's ability to ride roughshod over convention has its limits. All the other guests have been sent away, as have many of the servants, except for the oldest and most trusted amongst them."

I looked at her blankly. "Don't you see?" she said. "Egremont desires that you and I should be part of Mr. Turner's classical composition. So I shall pay him a visit tomorrow morning."

"And will you do what he requests of you?" I asked.

"I am past that. We must live, you and I. If you do not know that, I must teach you." She rose from the bench. "Give me your arm and take me down to the house. I could do with a cup of tea, or perhaps something stronger. We shall do well enough in the end. Come."

. 27 .

WHEN I WOKE my first instinct was to go look at the painting, but I realized I needed to be in this world when Eddy came. Just to make things worse, there was no hot water. There was an inch of water on the basement floor and a steady rain falling from the ceiling. The floor joists on the north side of the house were all pretty far gone, Eddy explained when he arrived, and one of them, under the piano, had given way. "See how it landed on that pipe there? That's where your water is coming from. There's no water coming to the heater, but you were going to have to replace that heater anyway. It's all rusted out and it's only a matter of time before it goes. But your water heater is the least of it. You never know with rot how much you got until you peel it back."

My father hadn't put any money into the house in years, and the house was rotting away from the inside out. Eddy pointed his flashlight at thick beams that were so soft he could stick a pencil into them. When I asked him what was involved he said it was a big deal: basically raise the whole house up and replace the understructure. Lower it back down. Install French drains and new gutters so it wouldn't happen again. He wasn't prepared to give me an estimate yet, but thirty to fifty thousand wouldn't surprise him.

Susan called just after Eddy left, and I told her what he'd said. She sounded cold and angry, more interested in talking about how things were going in Cleveland. She didn't seem to care one way or the other about our house. She asked me if I enjoyed being alone in a way that suggested I had better get used to it. Then she told me to drive safely; I told her to have a good flight.

My whole life, I saw, was coming apart. Susan and I had been married for over twenty years. We had had our ups and downs, but for the most part we'd always been happy to come home to each other. I suddenly felt myself about to take a step, or be pushed out, into the void.

I took refuge in the painting. For most of the morning I just looked at Helen; every moment seemed to reveal some new beauty. Soon I no longer saw her image. She was simply present to me, while the itchy bundle of anxieties that was me disappeared. From Helen it was a smooth transition to the heroes on the battlefield beyond. I could feel the carnage of the battle in my bones; the suffering of the soldiers seemed my own. I could also feel, however, the presence of the gods who walked among them. They were there, just beyond the limits of my perception. I couldn't see them delineated in paint on canvas, but I knew that divine fingers guided the flight of each arrow and divine hands protected each hero's breast. As the afternoon passed, the battle's chaos and confusion resolved itself. Soldiers cried, horses reared, and the great war chariots rumbled across the plain, but eventually I could see as the father of the gods sees and the pattern of the action was revealed.

I left the painting in the mountains again. If Susan found out about it she would surely do the sensible thing and run off with her share of thirty million dollars. And although I was tempted by the prospect of all that money, I could not imagine parting from it when it was in front of me. Only when I was away from it did the thought that I might be able to repair the life I was living stand a chance against the images in my mind. We could both retire, the kids would be set up for life, the repair bill would be trivial, and Mossbacher's offer laughable.

As I drove back to New Jersey, things seemed to make less and less sense. I was quite literally putting distance between myself and what mattered. I tried to distract myself with NPR and the Yankees, but I couldn't concentrate. I tried to think about the painting, but the farther south I got, the more the thought of Susan's infidelity took up whatever space there was in my brain.

I got home a little before nine and wandered around the house where I had raised my children and lived out fifteen years of married life, wondering how long I could go on living in it.

The car service dropped Susan off just before one. I heard her move about in the kitchen and then come quietly upstairs. I pretended to be asleep as she took a shower. I imagined that she was washing off the residue of her lover's caresses, scrubbing the traces of his saliva from her breasts. She set the alarm and got into bed, taking care not to disturb me. If I had reached over and put my hand inside her it would have come out coated with another man's sperm. I listened to her settle into sleep.

I stared into the darkness, knowing I was on the edge of something. If I fell, there was only darkness and an endless plunge on either side. Or light. I thought about Helen's eyes. "The face that launched a thousand ships" was half hidden from the viewer, and only revealed in the mirror at the foot of the bed. Helen was like the sun, so dangerous that she could not be looked at directly. The source of her power, of her ability to move men and launch ships, was not her face but her body. But her eyes showed her soul and were the window into her intentions. I remembered the way she seemed to look at me. Her eyes met mine in the darkness. What message or command could she have for the likes of me?

When I awoke my wife was gone.

. 28 .

OCTOBER 25, 1929

SPECIAL TO THE NEW YORK TIMES

CORNELIUS RHINEBECK DIES AT 56

The financier, industrialist and noted art collector Cornelius Rhinebeck died yesterday when the car in which he was traveling with three others plunged off the road into the cold waters of a small pond just outside of Saranac Lake, New York.

All the passengers in the vehicle perished.

Mr. Rhinebeck was traveling from his camp, Birch Lodge, to Lake Placid in order to catch the train back to New York City. Interviews with staff members at Birch Lodge reveal that Mr. Rhinebeck had left slightly later than planned. Police speculate that the driver of the car may have been going too fast for the weather conditions.

A light rain had fallen the night before and temperatures were near the freezing mark. The place where the car left the road was particularly exposed, and it is not uncommon for ice to form there, according to local police.

Mr. Rhinebeck's holdings and interests were large and varied, being primarily in steel, shipping and banking. After the war Mr. Rhinebeck traveled extensively in Europe, pursuing both business interests and his passion for art. He is known to have purchased works by Rembrandt, Titian and other old masters. He also took a strong interest in the French school, buying works by Degas, Renoir and Sisley.

The other passengers in the car were Mr. Rhinebeck's wife, Charlotte; Mrs. Maria Overstreet, a family friend; and Mr. William Kircum, the driver. Mrs. Rhinebeck was born Charlotte St. Clair in Boston, Massachusetts. Her father was active in banking and philanthropy. Mrs. Rhinebeck continued his philanthropic work, being active in various charities in the city. Two years ago she was a member of the Ladies' Committee for the New York Hospital Ball.

Mrs. Overstreet was a graduate of Mt. Holyoke College and an expert on English art who had published monographs on Constable, Stubbs and Turner. A resident of New York, she was employed by the Oswald T. Mitchell Gallery. She is survived by her husband, Colonel William Overstreet, of Hoboken, New Jersey.

Mr. Kircum was a longtime employee of Mr. Rhinebeck's and served as the manager of Birch Lodge. Mr.

Kircum served with distinction in the Great War and received a Purple Heart as well as a number of decorations for valor. He is survived by his wife, Constance.

Mr. Rhinebeck is survived by his two sons, Thomas, age 19, and Herman, age 15. He is also survived by a brother, Rupert, who will take over management of the family enterprises.

. 29 .

IT IS ALL MIXED up now, my life in the painting, those days at Petworth, my time with Grant and Turner. Hannah brings my tea and then for a moment I know myself to be here in London: my skin is covered with wrinkles, the flesh of my arm sags downward when I lift the teacup. The sound of the omnibus comes to ears that feel as if they were stuffed with cotton. And when Hannah leaves I open the cabinet door, and there is Helen, and I see him approaching me as he never did, though there were many others who did so. How many were there? It doesn't matter now.

He was the most beautiful man I ever saw. Turner said so too. More of a boy really. When he first sat down at the dining table I felt like a schoolgirl. I was afraid he would see me staring, but he was too nervous to look up toward the head of the table. He was chatting with one of Egremont's painters and looking about him shyly. I could tell that he had never been in a room like this before. I don't think he saw me staring. He wasn't sure which fork to use. I saw him wait to see what others did, but noticed he had the sense not to follow Turner's lead.

He was sweet-tempered and well-spoken. I offered him my hand after dinner. I still remember how cool and soft his was the first time I touched him. His eyes met mine and held them; they did not stray to my bosom as so many men's did in those days. I could see kindness in his eyes, and sweetness, and passion, but not lust. Later, when I got to know him better, we walked through the grounds of the park. Sometimes I wanted to cover his face with kisses. Sometimes I wanted him to throw me to the grass and take me, the way that Egremont did when I was first at Petworth, the way Spencer did, the way that Frenchman did when I was at Königsberg. How many were there?

But he never did. He was too kind. It was not in his nature. At first, before I got to know him, I almost felt it an insult that he made no effort to seduce me. I took great pleasure when I saw desire in the eyes of Egremont's guests. I took pleasure in their lust, watching them weigh the consequences of making love to me. There were only a few—the artists mostly—who had the courage to risk Egremont's wrath, although, if they had understood Egremont better, they would not have been afraid.

He was old, but in those first days that I was with him he could still perform like a younger man. We understood each other. I could smell the other women on him, taste them sometimes; I knew they had sapped his ability. He said he was tired, but I knew. When he went away I was free. And although there were handsome boys about the stables, I never touched them, even though Egremont took his liberties with every pretty chambermaid and farmer's daughter. But he was the lord of Petworth and I was only his mistress. Once, when Egremont had gone up to London, he had left some young cousin of his behind—he was a pretty boy too, but nothing like Grant. He had no conversation in him. Richard was his name, I think. I invited him up to my boudoir for tea and we passed a pleasant afternoon together. He was not good for much else. I intimated that it would be best if he never visited again. He never did.

When Egremont returned I think we both fancied the thought of our sinning, because there was an extra relish to our exertions that first night. He was wonderful for an old man that way, but it was not to last. I had been at Petworth for three years, I had posed for *Jessica*, when Egremont's preternatural abilities began to fail. On some days it became difficult for him to pass water as well. Oh, how he raged. He was a man of temper and unused to being disappointed, particularly in himself. He raged at his physician, he raged at me. He was a terror to anyone who came near him for a time. He was most cruel, and said things to me that I shudder to remember. He said my looks were gone, that the problem was that I was no longer young and pretty. He went up to London to see a renowned physician, but neither the physician nor the young girls at Mrs. Bolcolm's establishment could cure what ailed him. Indeed, when he came back, he acknowledged that if he could perform at all, which was rarely, it was only on account of my patience and coaxing. I think it was only then that he abjured all others.

Such was his temper when young Grant arrived. He told me as we went to bed that he had taken a liking to our new guest because he knew that I would not be able win him over with my whorish ways. He could be most cruel. I had given up protesting his usage because I knew the cause was in him and not me. And I knew that he was fond of me despite his words.

One afternoon he came into the White Room after the shooting party had returned from culling the herd as I was having tea with Turner. He threw his gloves down on the sideboard. He poured a cup of tea and sat down without greeting us. I could tell he was in a vile humor and that he wished I would inquire as to the cause. I resolved to let him stir his tea for a few minutes before gratifying him.

"So, Mr. Turner," I said, "are you content to be idle for so long and to partake of Petworth's poor country pleasures? Don't you miss the excitements of your work and the city?"

It was, I suppose, my evil angel that prompted me to speak thus. Why else would I contrive to have two angry men in the room when I already had one?

Turner responded as I knew he would. He almost spat out his tea as he assured me that he was up at dawn every day, that he had filled ever so many sketchbooks, that he had laid the foundation for ever so many paintings and that he had nearly completed an oil landscape. He began one of his tiresome tirades about the sacrifices he made for his Art and how he had once had himself tied to the mast so as to observe the waves break over the bow. When I interrupted him to ask His

Lordship how the shooting had gone, I took, I will confess, some pleasure in observing Turner splutter to a halt.

Egremont looked at me sternly for a moment to let me know he was displeased, but he was so keen to inform me of his hurts that he could not keep silent very long. He told a tedious tale of the day's events—his memory was wonderful for a man his age—and I was treated to every sight they saw on the way to the shooting grounds and how he had showed the younger men how to clear a hedge. As the tale was nearing its end, Egremont grew more and more angry, working himself up into a spitting fury as he recalled how poor Grant had cried out and saved the life of some poor stag that Egremont was about to murder.

"I let him know my opinion of him, the damned pederast," Egremont said. "If it had not done me so much good, I would be half ashamed of the language I used. But at least we will be rid of him: if he is a gentleman he will not be able to remain here after hearing what he heard."

I looked at him coldly, and then at Turner. The violence of Egremont's outburst had cooled Turner's annoyance. "So," I said to Egremont, "are you pleased with yourself?"

"Of course not. My temper does me no credit, although it affords me relief. But, as I said, we will be rid of him. Petworth will not miss a no-account scribbler—no matter how handsome he is."

"Was the stag the one you call Old Thunder?" Turner asked.

"Yes. Magnificent creature. Old, but stately. Fast as lightning. Wisest of the herd, for otherwise how would he have survived for so long? I have only caught glimpses of him these last few years, but there he was, plain as day. And I'd have got him, if it weren't for that young puppy."

"Don't you think he did you a service?" I asked.

Egremont glared at me and was about to speak, but Turner, bless him, came to my rescue. "Like yourself, you know. Lord of the manor. First among equals. You will forgive me, my lord, but you are too good a shot to have missed on account of a mere sneeze."

"What do you mean, sir?"

"You are the steadiest hand in all of Sussex. You have hit your mark at a hundred paces while the tempest blew like the last trump. Must be some reason beyond Grant's feeble sneeze that your shot miscarried. Inward sympathy, you know."

Egremont looked at Turner; I, who knew him so well, thought I detected some softening about his eyes.

"Sounds as if you are making poor excuses for the two of us."

"No excuses, my lord," I offered. "Certainly none for young Grant—although it is hard to fault a city boy for being appalled at such slaughter. And none for you either. But can it not be that your better nature played you a trick unawares?"

Egremont seemed to consider for a moment. Although he was a brusque and masterful man, he had a capacity for self-reflection far greater than that of others of his type. "Perhaps there is something in what you say," he admitted at last. "But the damage, if damage it is, is done. I have said what I have said and he will no doubt leave us."

We all sat silent for a few minutes, until Turner spoke. "More's the pity. I had fancied he would make a first-rate

Paris in a classical composition. Grecian form, you know; fine features. Good muscles under his shirt, from the look of things."

This was the first time I had heard any talk of the painting. Looking back after all these years, I see that I was standing unconscious on the edge of a precipice.

"You mean a painting of that truth you mentioned last night?" Egremont said.

"Just laying it out in my mind," Turner replied. He poured himself more tea. "Put Helen in a room and she is nothing. Place her against all those Greeks, or just one, you have the Trojan War. A great beauty, begging your pardon, madam, is nothing until a man sets eyes on her. He loses his head. Towers burn; heroes die."

"Odd joke to make Paris a fellow who wouldn't raise a finger for Helen."

"Yes but no," Turner said. "Private joke between us, true. But private truth between us as well. We are speaking of Helen, you know. She causes men to act in ways that Mrs. Spencer, for all her beauty, cannot. Again, begging your pardon, madam. Grant's nature is one thing, Helen's power another." Turner stopped. He nodded toward me and then spoke to Egremont in a lowered tone. "Not so damn awkward. Regular fellow will act like a regular man, in the situation I am thinking of. Fellow like Grant, not. Stick to the idea of the thing, you know."

Had I not been so used to being the kind of woman I was, my heart might have broken at Turner's words. But my heart had been wounded so often, a scab had formed around it that mere words could not penetrate. Besides, I appreciated what he was trying to do.

"I am not so bad as all that," I observed.

"I have no fears on your account, madam." Turner said. "Masculine nature is what I fear. I know something of it myself."

We were all silent for a moment. I thought of poor Grant, humiliated as he had been in front of all the company, sitting in his room and making plans for his departure.

"Go see about supper, will you?" said Egremont, looking at me. I could not tell if there was tenderness or contempt in his eyes. "We owe our guests a good meal. See what John can do. Not overmuch, mind you, but a deal better than last night. Be off. I wish to discuss this painting that Turner is thinking of with him alone."

. 30 .

THERE WAS A NOTE beside her empty cereal bowl. She hoped to be on her usual train, but she would call if she got stuck at the office. I arrived late to work, but found some good news. There was a conference in London on the role of philanthropy in the twenty-first century, and I had been invited to give a short talk about the work of the Nassau Foundation. At first the thought of putting so many miles between me and the painting gave me pause, but then I realized that it wouldn't be a bad thing to get out of the house for a while. My painting would be safe where it was, and it would be interesting to take a few days off and look at some Turners.

When I got home that evening I made a nice dinner. I tried to remind myself that I had no evidence she was having an affair. I had done a foolish thing, but we were grown-ups. These things happen—it was not the end of the world.

I gave her a kiss on the cheek when she came in. I guess she had been thinking too, because she returned it with a little bit of interest. She looked at herself in the hallway mirror. "Jesus," she said. "I look like a wreck. I fell asleep on the train and almost missed my stop. Let me get changed and make myself presentable."

While she was upstairs I took out a bottle of wine and put out a plate of cheese and crackers.

"Looks like company's coming," she said. She had changed into jeans and a T-shirt. She looked a lot better than Ruth Carpenter could ever dream of looking. She took a piece of cheese. "It feels good to be wearing something other than a suit. I'm exhausted, though, so don't try to keep me up all night. Cleveland was brutal. But we got it done, and Richard gave us all nice pats on the back this morning. With any luck, we'll all get a cookie at the end of the year."

As we drank our wine and waited for the salmon we settled into the kind of conversation that had been the norm before I discovered the painting, though it wasn't quite as comfortable as it used to be. We were both aware that my kiss with Ruth Carpenter was lurking just beyond the boundaries of our talk, while for me the painting and my thoughts about Susan and her putative lover also threatened to breach the dike. But we skated along on the war and the weather and the neighbors, and things seemed pretty good.

I told her about the trip to England, and that I thought I might take a few extra days to look around London.

"That's a good idea. How long will you be gone altogether?" About a week, I said. She paused for a moment before she answered. "That will be nice for you. Congratulations." It occurred to me that she was thinking through the possibilities for seeing her lover that my absence would open up, but I let it go.

Dinner was pleasant. "Let's do the dishes tomorrow," she said. "I want to go to bed."

She was on top of me right away. It was the first time we had made love since the Millers' party. "Don't move," she said. "I'll do it." I watched her concentrate. She seemed to go to that place deep inside herself where I could never follow. I wondered how she was with the other guy.

She came with a gasp and her body relented. She climbed off me and got onto her hands and knees. "Okay," she said, "your turn."

I listened to the slap of middle-aged flesh against middle-aged flesh. I thought of her in the hotel room in Cleveland. Surely it had been more interesting and more exotic than this? But the thought of her there was oddly exciting, and I went into her with more energy and enthusiasm than usual. I thought of Helen and the mystery between her legs. I thought of the command in her eyes and the transparent fabric that draped over her shoulders and her breasts. I came with a grunt that would have woken the children if they had been home.

She laughed.

"Not bad for old guys," she said. "We are worth keeping, you know." She kissed me sweetly on the forehead. "Good night."

"Good night." We both fell asleep.

. 31 .

IN THE DAYS FOLLOWING Gina's visit to Petworth she attacked her work with renewed enthusiasm, but she was young, and, as Bryce observed, she found it difficult to accept that progress can be slow or imperceptible. The enthusiasm that had followed her discovery of Wyndham's memoir and her subsequent visit to Petworth soon gave way to something like despair. It didn't help that her mother sounded drunk even in the morning and that her father threatened to "pop over the pond" for a weekend so he could introduce Gina to his latest fiancée. She worked harder than ever, but her growing frustration revealed itself in her emails and her phone calls with Bryce.

"I'm not producing results," she said. "You have entrusted me with a great and important responsibility and I feel that I'm failing you." Bryce was touched by her devotion, but also worried that she might be falling apart.

"Nonsense, dear," he said. "You are doing splendid work. If this was easy, someone would have done it already—or I would have done it—and you would have nothing to do. What we are attempting is just this side of impossible. Despair is the greatest obstacle to any great achievement. We must not give in to it, you and I."

And so she resumed her systematic trawl through overlooked archives that might contain something related to Turner. A few weeks later she sent a note saying that she would be taking the next day's flight.

"Have you ever," she asked as she stepped into the library, "heard of Reginald St. Germaine?" Bryce had not. "St. Germaine," she said, "was a curious character active in London in the early 1930s. He had a small inheritance and set himself up as an all-purpose literary man. He published a few book reviews in small magazines and a few poems in even smaller magazines which he seems to have subsidized, but his major project was a proposed book on nineteenth-century sexual mores. He seems to have fancied himself a kind of Henry Mayhew of early twentieth-century sexuality, although he could be more accurately described as a pornographer or a plain ordinary creep. He was never able to interest anyone respectable in his activities, but St. Germaine conducted over forty interviews, which he transcribed and catalogued, before the project was abandoned."

She opened her attaché case and took out a folder containing a number of sheets of yellowing paper.

PLACE: LONDON

DATE: OCTOBER 23, 1935

SUBJECT: MRS. (?) ELIZABETH (BETTY) HULFISH

INTERVIEW AND TRANSCRIPTION: MR. ST. GERMAINE

AGE: 39

WITNESSES: MISS JONES AND MRS. CORTELYOU

Lord, sir, it was a wicked picture, a very wicked
picture, and he was a wicked man that owned it. It was
an odd and wicked business altogether, conducted on the
hush-hush. As far as I know it was only me and Margaret
that knew of it and we was paid handsome to keep our
mouths shut and threatened with awful consequences if
we didn't. But, Lord, everyone but me is dead now and
there can't be no harm in telling after all these years.

It was in that time when all the boys had just come
back from Flanders. I used to see them on the streets
looking so sad. I was nineteen then and I could pass for
genteel if I kept my mouth shut and had a nice dress on.
My friend Margaret, who had been in the trade with
me, come up to me one day and asked me if I was up
for something a bit unusual. She said it only involved
gentlemen and that the money was more than handsome. But she said it wouldn't do to be too particular
about scruples and what I would do and wouldn't do,
if you understand me. After I said I was game Margaret gave me fifty pounds—fifty pounds, sir, that was
a world of money in those days—and said I would get

another fifty and maybe more if the gentlemen liked me. Lord, in those days I would have done a dozen Turks for a hundred pounds, so I didn't have to think about it long at all.

I was to buy a respectable dress such as a prosperous tradesman's daughter might wear. I was to meet her at six o'clock on a Saturday on Curzon Street.

I remember the dress, sir. It was beautiful stuff, a dark lavender-like color. I wore that dress many times and I would have had it for years, it was so well made, if I hadn't been forced to sell it on account of getting down on my luck again.

An old butler-like gentleman met us at the door. He asked if we wanted a cup of tea. While he was fetching the tea we was to look into the wardrobes and choose something to wear that would please our fancy and make us agreeable to the gentlemen. There were silk robes and silk dresses that were hardly dresses at all.

When he come back with the tea he told us that his master would be needing us in about an hour's time and that we was to spend that time getting dressed so as to show ourselves off to our best advantage. He said it all like it was the most natural thing in the world and he was just a nice old gentleman, but he was nothing but a nasty old man is what he was.

But we was wicked too in those days and Margaret and me had a deal of fun trying on those scandalous things. We was like two little girls playing at dress-up, though a good deal more shameless than any two girls had a right to be.

Margaret settled on a satin corset which she had me lace up tight from behind. She looked so sweet that I kissed her in fun. Margaret was a sweet girl and we always got on so nice; it's ever so sad that she come to such a bad end. I chose a cream-coloured gown that was so fine you could almost see through it. I covered my shoulder with a pretty shawl. Margaret said it made me look like a young innocent girl that was up to tricks, which is, you know, the sort of thing many gentlemen wanted, especially those what had daughters of their own.

When Mr. Stokes come in he didn't say his name was Stokes. He told us his name was Lord Randolph or some such rot, but Margaret had seen him about town and she known who he was. He looked us over most coldly and allowed that we would do, as if that was a great compliment coming from him. But he was very liberal with his money, sir, and being what we was I had no right to get high and mighty on account of him taking on airs.

He told us that in a few minutes we was going into the library. There would be just two gentlemen, himself and Mr. Smith. Mr. Smith was a special friend of his from America and he would make it worth our while if we was to do our utmost to gratify Mr. Smith in any way. Mr. Stokes said that he might join in the fun too, but the primary one we was to attend on was Mr. Smith.

The library was a fine old room with high ceilings
and fine furniture and paintings that were ever so old.
There was oysters and other fine things on the sideboard, as well as bottles of spirits and bottles of champagne on ice. Mr. Smith was sitting on the couch; he was
a fat man with a beard and a moustache and I could tell
that he'd already had a good deal to drink. Mr. Stokes
settled Margaret on one side and me on the other. He
was a laughing sort of man, but in a mean way. I remember thinking that perhaps we wouldn't have much to
do, because it is well known how liquor makes a man
willing but it don't make him able.

The two gentlemen did most of the talking, mostly
about horses and such like, but also sneaking questions
about what we might like to do. Margaret and me was
most attentive to Mr. Smith, hugging and kissing him
and touching him, and we was all quite merry. There
was a fire in the hearth and after a space Mr. Stokes
said it was getting warm in the room and suggested that
we ladies, as he was so kind as to call us, might be more
comfortable if we was to undress. Mr. Smith laughed
most disagreeably and said that as a gentleman he had to
insist. So we did it showlike, with me undoing Margaret's laces and she undoing the buttons on my gown
and pulling it off real slow. Mr. Smith looked at the two
of us all bug-eyed and when Margaret started rubbing
herself up against me, he took another drink of whiskey
and wiped his mouth with the back of his hand.

Margaret and me undid his trousers and his linens and soon we was a kissing him and touching him all over, but he wasn't up to much and I thought the liquor had done its work. Mr. Smith was getting sweaty and irritable the way a gentleman does when he can't deliver and I feared the evening would come to a bad end.

All this time Mr. Stokes was sitting there as cool as could be, smoking his cigarette. He seemed to be one of those that gets their pleasure more out of watching than doing, but it's a large world, I say, and room for all of us. "Mr. Smith," he says, "I told you that if we came to a good understanding, I would offer you a sensual treat such as you could never imagine. These two beautiful young ladies are only a part of it, my good man. Let me show you the thing I told you of." He got up and went over to one of the bookcases. He touched a latch and the bookcase rolled out of sight without making a sound. There was a black curtain there and he pulled it back like he was a showman at the Exposition and there it was.

It was, like I said, the most wicked picture that was ever made. The three of us that had never seen it before stopped what we were doing and stared like mooncalves. There was a lady more beautiful than any one I ever dreamt of. She was naked except for some filmy gold cloth that you could see right through, and there were all these pillars and beautiful cushions in her room. There was the most precious little kitten sitting

in the corner. Out of the window behind her you could
see thousands of soldiers fighting out on the fields. And
it was lit up like I don't know how, so that the room
seemed to get brighter on account of the sun that was
shining down on the soldiers and their armour. I had seen
a lot of paintings, sir, and I had seen my share of French
postcards that showed all sorts of things, but I never
seen nothing like this. It made me feel all shimmery inside, like I was on fire, and it brought a smile to my face
so I almost forgot who I was and why I was there.

Mr. Smith was the first to come out of it. He suddenly seemed in a world of hurry. He had Margaret
kneel down on the sofa. I noticed he was as hard as a
man could be. He got himself up behind her and was
going at her like a dog in heat, sir.

Mr. Stokes called me over. He was sitting on an easy
chair and his trousers were open with his affair out and
ready. I saw what was wanted and I knelt down on the
floor and went about my business. I remember looking
up and seeing that Mr. Stokes wasn't looking down at
me like most gentlemen like to do. He was looking up at
the painting the whole time.

Mr. Smith made an awful noise and Margaret cried
out in such a way as to make the fat man feel gratified
at his own abilities, Mr. Stokes accomplished what he
meant to so that besides myself he was the only one that
knew. Mr. Stokes went to a closet and gave us each a silk
robe. Then we went to the sideboard and the gentlemen

each had a brandy and Mr. Stokes gave us each a glass of champagne.

We sat about making small talk, with Mr. Smith asking Margaret how she enjoyed herself and her of course saying she had been transported to seventh heaven. Mr. Stokes never said much except to lead Mr. Smith on. I began to think that Mr. Stokes was working something deep against him and I couldn't but wish him to succeed, listening to that fat little man carry on like he was the biggest bull in the yard.

Mr. Stokes had made it a point to seat Mr. Smith so that he was facing the painting. The gentlemen talked a good deal about the painting and how wonderful it was.

Mr. Smith turned his attentions to me and I kissed him back. I put my hand on his affair and I was amazed. That picture would make a dead man rise. She was the most beautiful lady that ever was, and I understood why a gentleman might feel the way he did, but I also felt tender for the lady. I can still see her quite clear in my mind. Over the years, if I'd been with someone who treated me unkind or if I was lonesome and in trouble like I am now, I think of her and I get a warm comfortable feeling. Those gentlemen only knew the half of it, while I could understand what that poor woman felt, just waiting for the next bloke to shove it in.

Mr. Smith told me to lie down on the sofa because he was going to give me what every girl truly wanted.

He told Margaret to get the butter from the sideboard.
He used me most cruelly, but I made out I liked it. And
although he pressed me hard into the sofa—he was a
very fat man and not gentle—I could sometimes see the
lady out of the corner of my eye and she was a comfort
to me. It was a queer thing but it was then that I noticed
the painter had put some mice in the painting too, and
the kitten was paying them no mind. When Mr. Smith
was done he made another awful noise and I shrieked
and wiggled so he said afterwards to Mr. Stokes,
"You see there is nothing they like so much, no matter what they say." And he said it in such a stupid and
self-satisfied way that I could have laughed at him if he
hadn't been so cruel.

Just after the clock struck eleven Mr. Stokes got up
and drew the curtain over the picture and pulled the
bookcase out so it was hidden as if it had never been
there at all.

"That is a damn fine painting," Mr. Smith said.
"You'd not have any interest in selling it, would you?"

"It has not yet come to that by any means," Mr. Stokes
said. "I'm a man of business. I sometimes fancy that if she
were still living I would sell my own mother if I could
turn a profit thereby, but I'd sooner part with my balls
than part with her. Come, ladies, good night." He shook
our hands most business-like and pointed towards the
door. Mr. Smith kissed us each and said good night. He
pressed a twenty-pound note into each of our hands.

There was no one in the dressing room and we didn't know where the old gentleman had put our clothes, so we just sat and chatted. After a few minutes he came in through the other door.

He was carrying some photographic equipment and I remembered my thought that Mr. Stokes was up to something deep. He gave us each an envelope with, said he, his master's compliments and gratitude for providing satisfaction. In it was the fifty pounds he'd promised plus twenty more for each of us so we wouldn't ever speak of what had happened. Lord, what a sum of money that was. A hundred and forty pounds for an evening's work! That was enough to keep a respectable family alive for almost half a year. Margaret and I discussed how we should set ourselves up respectable-like—as if we was two cousins living on a small inheritance. If we'd only done so, it would have made all the difference. But we didn't, and the money went where the money usually goes.

Three days later I made my way to Mr. Stokes's house, all wrapped up so as not to be recognized. There was a small park there, and I sat for a bit feeding the pigeons and saw Mr. Stokes come out. He was in an awful hurry and looking mighty grim. It was a few years later that he killed himself. I read in the papers how he had ruined ever so many people with his swindles and his dealings, but I have to say although I knew him to be a bad man he treated me fair and lived up to his word.

I've always wondered what became of that picture. I even took an interest in the sale, and I remember reading in the paper the list of paintings that were auctioned off. I had seen some of the hunting scenes that was mentioned, but there was no mention of that painting, which wasn't surprising considering the kind of picture it was. Perhaps it was never found on account of being in that secret cabinet. Perhaps it was burnt on account of being so wicked. That would have been the proper thing to do and no doubt it happened like that. But to my mind it would have been a pity. There was something dreamy-like about it, something about the way it made me feel. It made the gentlemen randy, but there was something else about it too.

It's been many years now and Lord knows I have been with enough different men and almost always on account of money, but most every time I think about that picture I get a feeling that's more like love than any other word I can find. I can't rightly explain it, except to say that I almost wish I had never seen it because it made the rest of my life seem so shabby.

"Could this be the thing itself?" Bryce asked as he put the papers down. "Stokes was a well-known collector. A number of the important Gainsboroughs, Constables, Stubbs, and Hogarths that eventually made their way into American collections passed through his hands."

"I think it is," she replied. "This could be something St. Germaine made up, but the other interviews contain nothing remotely similar. Even the most salacious ones are so dull and flat-footed that it's no surprise all the publishers turned him down. And there is something in the phrase 'lit up like I don't know how' that is suggestive of Turner."

Stokes, she went on to tell him, was born in 1869. By the mid-nineties he had established himself as a private banker in London. He invested heavily in armaments, steel, and precious metals, both in England and abroad, in the years before and after the First World War. By the time the war ended he had amassed a considerable fortune. He bought art and often sold it at a profit.

"He had good taste," she said, "which makes me think that this might be it. But by the time of our document, things were beginning to unravel. A parliamentary inquiry was looking into some suspiciously lucrative contracts he had had with the Royal Navy; there were accusations of shoddy goods and profiteering, and concerns about his dealings with the Germans during the war.

"It all came to a head in October of 1920. He had raised an extraordinary amount of money—a good deal of it from selling off his collection—and it appeared as if he might be on the brink of digging himself out of the hole he was in. The only piece missing was a freighter allegedly packed to the rafters with South African gold and diamonds. It went down somewhere in the Indian Ocean. When the news reached London, Stokes blew his brains out. There was recently a documentary about the 'Search for the Suicide's Gold' on the Discovery Channel. They didn't find anything."

They both agreed that Gina should next focus her efforts

on Stokes and his circle, particularly on those who had purchased art from him.

"But you need to move very carefully," Bryce said. "The
painting we seek could very well still be in the hands of their
descendants. We need to be careful that they don't notice
someone suspicious poking around in their ancestors' affairs."

As she was getting ready to leave she asked if they had
heard anything else about the man in Princeton.

"Ah, I'm glad you mentioned it. I am keeping half an eye on
the fellow, just in case, even though George says there is nothing
there. George asked me to send you his regards. You impressed
him quite favorably, which is unusual, I must say. He said that
if I had to 'send another rookie down on a field trip' it might as
well be you. He even forgave you for picking up that photo on the
bureau, which is also unusual. George is quite severe. "

She didn't recall that George was in the room when she had
picked up Henry's photograph. "He's awfully good," she said.

"Of course," Bryce said. "I only hire the best people." He
raised her hand to his dry lips again. "You have done well, my
dear, very well."

. 32 .

THERE IS SOMETHING UNEARTHLY, David, about this great house now that it is nearly deserted. Before, there was always a subdued hum and clatter about the place, just audible above the threshold of hearing—the footfalls of the servants as they went about their business, the sound of conversation as one was about to enter a room. But now I often hear only my own footsteps as I walk through the gallery of Greek and Roman statues. I feel like a ghost haunting the necropolis of some ancient city.

At dinner last night Mrs. Spencer forgot herself and allowed a long silence to descend on the table. "It is a damn queer business," Lord Egremont said at last, "just the four of us sitting down to our meat. It don't seem natural."

"Your nature, my lord, is to be a social creature," she said, rising to the task. "Not all men are so constituted." She looked at me and Turner for help.

"The artist is often solitary. Not like the great man," Turner said as he nodded toward Egremont, "having to deal with tenants and petitioners, other lords. He must be social to fulfill his function in this world. It's rum, but when I am in the midst of thinking about some hard problem in my studio, I find myself falling into debates within my own mind. Solitary, but not alone. Not usually agreeable company, but one must listen when the other fellow talking lives in one's brain."

"Perhaps now that we all live alone we will all become artists. Or at least," Mrs. Spencer directed one of her brightest smiles to Turner, "artists' assistants."

"No, no." Turner was more abrupt than the occasion seemed to warrant. "I am grateful for your assistance. Nor do I wish to appear more rude than is my wont. But you are not artists. You are charming and beautiful, Mrs. Spencer; you, Mr. Grant, are young and pleasant and damnably learned. You, my lord, are almost all things, but not, as you yourself have confessed to me many times, an artist."

"What I meant," Mrs. Spencer said, "was that perhaps the two of us, Mr. Grant and myself, will have some part in the creation of your next painting that might justify our thinking of ourselves as artists."

Turner put his fork down and looked at Mrs. Spencer intently. "You are a clever woman, madam. Don't spoil your reputation. Committees are only good for hanging." Turner paused and began to laugh, but his laughter was met by silence.

"I mean, you see, that there is a hanging committee—the committee that decides where to hang the paintings at the annual Royal Academy show. A committee is only good for hanging, you know." And with a quick motion he tied an imaginary noose round his neck and jerked it upward. "A joke, you see, about committees not being good for very much."

Mrs. Spencer managed to ignore Turner's rudeness and laugh at his joke, while Egremont and I each summoned up a smile. "You are right," she went on, "I cannot understand what goes on in an artist's mind. It is far beyond me. But what is it that you have been discussing with yourself these last few days?"

"Queer thing to ask a man when he is trying to do his duty by the finest venison to be had in England. My compliments, sir." He raised his glass to Lord Egremont and wiped his mouth with his napkin. "But a good question." Turner took another sip of wine. "You recall those poses I asked you to strike this afternoon, Mr. Grant?" The question was directed to me, but he looked at Mrs. Spencer as he spoke.

"I do," I said. I am not sure how much I gave away to the others, but I believe I may have blushed. I do not know what power the man has, but I had gone along meekly as Turner asked me to assume a number of poses which even now, in the privacy of my own chamber, I blush to recollect.

"I am trying," Turner said, "to see the body. How to go about it? Not usually my line, you know. Go to the North Gallery and look at His Lordship's collection of sculptures. Every feature perfect. Every figure perfect. This table is an odd one.

Half the people at it are almost perfectly beautiful. And I mean you no offense, my lord, when I mention that neither you nor I are of that party. You blush, Mrs. Spencer, but it is a fact. I do not flatter. If you walk about London you will see a thousand women before you see one half as perfect in her beauty as you. You are the classical ideal. The other nine hundred and ninety-nine are not. And the same goes for you, Mr. Grant.

"But you are monsters. His Lordship and I are the mass. No one would put us in a classical landscape. We would be in one of Wilkie's paintings, or one by Collins. Singing a song around a forge, you know, or bickering with a peddler.

"What I am trying to say is that it is damn hard to put the true body in a classical painting. I can put in a true tree or the true light as the sun sets. But when I try to put in a figure all I can see are copies of His Lordship's sculptures. In all my sketches until today you have appeared like something out of a third-rate Old Master's workshop. It is your damn beauty. Not your fault. Mine. So what I was trying to do was see you as I had been unable to see you previously."

Turner took a sip of wine and returned to his meat for a moment. When he spoke again it was more as if he was engaging with his imaginary interlocutor than with us. "All of this. This wine. This meat. This house. This countryside. And all the shades of light that illuminate them. It is all a burden. A blessing, too, of course, because, you know, we wouldn't have anything if it were not for everything. But for the artist, you see, all this is a burden, a weight. Sometimes I feel it on my shoulders, pressing me down. Or a curtain. Heavy rich stuff—some tapestry, you know. One can't see truth through it. But I do what I can. Sometimes a speck of light peeps through."

"And have you managed to catch a glimpse of the truth these last few days?" I asked.

"One never sees the truth, Mr. Grant; perhaps, at best, just a glimpse of what it might be. Sounds like nonsense, I suppose.

"Lonely craft, painting. Making the thing—the mixing, the state of the brush, the tension of the canvas—takes up most of my thoughts. But then there is the philosophy of the business. Too hard a knot for me to untie. Shakespeare, you know. A tedious answer which resolves nothing. But you deserve it for asking such a question."

Mrs. Spencer managed to direct the conversation to other topics until we had made our way through the cheese. As we rose from the table Turner excused himself and went straight to his bedroom. Lord Egremont complained that he was not feeling well and asked Mrs. Spencer to accompany him upstairs. I asked that tea be brought to me in the Carved Room.

I had Turner's conversation in my mind as I sat down with the *Iliad*, in both Pope's and Chapman's translations, before me. Only the Greek was satisfactory. I tried to see those heroes, their bodies perspiring, grimy with the toil of battle. Homer is unblinking when he tells us where the spear entered and how the viscera spilled out on the battlefield. I saw the beautifully articulated muscles of the abdomen cut apart like so much meat in a butcher shop. This truth that Turner seems to be seeking, I reflected, resides in the flesh. I thought of us together, David, and the truth that we sometimes find there. Do you know of what I am speaking?

I was so absorbed in these thoughts that I felt Mrs. Spencer's touch on my shoulder before I heard her footfall. In her velvet slippers, with a loose robe of Chinese silk over her dressing gown, she could have been one of the Percy spirits haunting the halls of their ancestral home.

"I must," she said, "have something stronger than tea." A servant appeared carrying a decanter and two glasses. As soon as he had departed, Mrs. Spencer filled the glasses and handed one to me. "You must have at least a glass of brandy. I am in danger of becoming a coarse old woman. At least it isn't gin."

Mrs. Spencer took a deep swallow, shivering as the beverage went down. "That's better," she said.

"Egremont feels poorly," she continued. "Yet I do not believe he is in any imminent danger, or that we need call a doctor. Few men have been as indefatigable and energetic as His Lordship, so he rages at his unfamiliar loss of vigor. He is well enough in public, but when we two are alone it is sometimes another matter. He has been, and is, most kind to me, but he can be demanding. I sometimes think he resents my youth and health. He cannot help it. But he is sleeping now; there is a servant in the room who has been instructed to call me if he wakes."

We sat for a while in silence. The fireplace lit up the carvings on the walls so that the wooden leaves seemed to wave in the firelight.

"So what has Turner required of you these last few days?" she asked. I hesitated as I recalled my recent afternoons in the studio. Mrs. Spencer placed her hand on my knee. "You and I, we must have no secrets from each other. Not at this time. I will be a good example and begin. Before I went up to the studio yesterday His Lordship spoke to me as he was getting dressed. He said, 'You will be paying Mr. Turner a visit in his studio this morning. He is a great man. It is my desire that you be most accommodating and help him in his enterprise.' I understood what he meant. When I arrived in the studio Turner was sitting behind his easel, preparing his paints. The couch from the Red Room had been brought up."

"I know the couch," I said. "The fabric is not so agreeable on the skin as I would have thought."

She smiled and took another sip of brandy. "Turner greeted me cordially, but, I thought, somewhat coolly. I did not wish to take the burden of what we were about to do upon myself. If Turner wanted something of me, he would have to ask for it. I sat down on the couch. We eyed each other for a moment like two dogs first meeting on the street.

"'Come,' he said at length, 'We are old friends. You are a woman of the world. I am a man of the world. I will not eat you. I have my work to do. You yours. We will begin easy.' He handed me a robe and said I should get undressed behind the screen. He had me recline on the couch and open the robe so that my breasts and shoulders were exposed. I did not know what to think. There was a battle within me. I felt humiliated and ashamed. If I were the true lady of Petworth, I would never have been lying naked in front of a man who was not my husband. But then I thought: this is so easy. I remembered my younger days, when I knew I could make men mad."

Her voice had dropped to a whisper. I looked up from the fire and, seeing the tears in her eyes, handed her a handkerchief. As she began to weep she looked more beautiful than ever.

"You are most kind. One needs friends at my time of life. How was it," she asked, "with you? You need not fear me."

Seeing me hesitate, perhaps even seeing the color come to my cheeks, she turned her face toward mine. I understood why Egremont wanted her as his mistress and why Turner wanted her as his model and muse. At our best moments I have always felt, David, that I could open up my heart to you without reserve, although I have always been conscious of the differences in perspective between us. This consciousness has, in some small way, constrained the flood of my feelings. As I looked at Mrs. Spencer I felt no such constraint. I too wept as I told her how Turner had me squat upon the couch in the most undignified and humiliating of postures. I told her how Turner had praised me for my beauty. I confessed with shame and humiliation how I had felt some perverse pleasure in debasing myself before the great man. It was the confession of pleasure that made me weep.

We sat in silence for a few minutes. Mrs. Spencer filled her glass and emptied it. "I will be spared nothing," she said. "Nothing."

. 33 .

I THINK OF MYSELF as an infrequent flyer. Whenever we go anywhere other than the Adirondacks, it's usually on Susan's miles. She knows which coffee places to avoid in Newark and that the Asian place in Philadelphia is almost worth eating in. I am not used to the anxieties and indignities of the security checkpoints or to the sight of soldiers with automatic weapons in public places.

As the plane banked and turned, I imagined that the madmen had taken over the cockpit. We would be bearing down on Big Ben and the Houses of Parliament, proof positive that the war had done nothing to make us safer. I looked out the window at the dawn-lit patchwork of the English countryside, half convinced that planes from the Royal Air Force would appear in a few minutes. I wondered if I would be able to see the faces of the pilots as they flew alongside trying to determine why Continental Flight 29 wasn't responding. I wondered how long I would remain conscious after the rockets struck. Or perhaps it wouldn't be rockets; it would be a nondescript suitcase in the hold. Either way I would dissolve into death and rain down from the sky. Blair and Bush would give a press conference. The passengers would be described as heroes and victims of terror. A fund would be set up; perhaps Susan and the children would get some money. My face would appear in *The New York Times*. Susan would be free to move in with her lover, although it occurred to me that it was only the fact of my existence that made this particular lover necessary or possible. The painting would remain in the Adirondacks; Mossbacher would find it after Susan sold the place.

I thought of Helen. She understands this violence. She knows that the men who suffer on the plain behind her tall window are dying on her account. Her cool and indifferent eyes comprehend the determination of the hijacker as he slits the captain's throat with as much remorse as I feel for the chicken that sits on my plate. She understands the look of victory in his eyes as he pushes the throttle forward. Praise be to God. It is all the same to her.

The talk on the work of the foundation went well. I am always surprised that people take me seriously as a professional person, which probably goes a long way toward explaining why I've had the same small job for twenty years. On Wednesday morning, since I was no longer on the expense account, I moved from the conference hotel to a cheap tourist-class place a few blocks from Victoria Station. The room was small and dark, painted an unpleasant shade of yellow. A television with a twelve-inch screen was mounted on the ceiling at the foot of the bed. The shower in the bathroom was so small that even though I had lost some weight it was a struggle to bend down to pick up a dropped piece of soap.

My first day on my own was cool and drizzly. I walked along the Thames toward the Tate. I put the collar of my raincoat up and allowed myself to luxuriate in the feeling of being a lonely man in a foreign city. It was six in the morning at home. I wondered if Susan was sleeping alone.

All the Turners in the Tate seemed related to *The Center of the World*, but in none of them could I see more than a hint of the truth that my painting revealed. Yet as I walked through the gallery, any doubts I had about its authenticity disappeared. There was something about the sky in many of the other Turners that I recognized at once as the same, although the effect of light seemed pale and unachieved compared with what he accomplished in my painting. There were low suns on the horizon that resembled my sun and architectural details, especially in *Rome, from the Vatican*, that seemed borrowed from *The Center of the World*. They were all wonderful paintings, but they only gave a hint of what mine revealed.

Later that day I walked to the National Gallery and looked at the Turners there. I spent a long time in front of *Ulysses Deriding Polyphemus*. The poor Cyclops is just a blur in the background, while Ulysses's gold-encrusted ship is a miracle of invention and delight in the foreground. Just above the horizon a Turner sun is setting. When I stepped close to the canvas I could see Apollo's chariot and the horses of the sun sketched in with white paint. It was a poor trick compared with what Turner had pulled off in *The Center of the World,* where the gods seemed vividly present, even if they were not represented in any visible way.

A steady rain was falling when I left the National Gallery. The crowd that had filled Trafalgar Square earlier in the day had disappeared. I pulled my baseball cap down and turned up the collar of my raincoat. The city was gray. The fact that traffic was going in the wrong direction made me feel disconcerted, almost nauseous.

I headed vaguely west toward Mayfair. A curtain seemed to be falling, but I did not understand why. I liked the city I was in; I liked the idea of being where I was. I had just seen some beautiful paintings. I possessed something more beautiful still. I was free.

At a newsstand I looked at the tabloid photos of heavy-breasted young women. They are the debased daughters, I thought, of Helen. I bought a pack of cigarettes, even though I hadn't smoked in almost fifteen years. I had wanted a cigarette ever since I arrived in England, probably to prove to myself that I was free and could do whatever I wanted. It wasn't quite as pathetic as the kiss with Ruth Carpenter, but it was the same sort of impulse. I stood under the awning in front of the store and tapped the pack against the heel of my left hand three times before I tore the cellophane off. I stuck a cigarette in my mouth and lit it. Fifteen years seemed to melt away as I performed that once familiar automatic gesture, but I coughed as I inhaled.

I let myself get lost, walking until my legs hurt. I don't know what I was thinking about, but I felt myself disappear into the rainy city. There were funny buses and beautiful buildings; cars came at me from the wrong side. At some point I found myself walking through the Wellington Arch. I read the names of the battles: Tobruk, Ypres, Khartoum. So much death, so much murder. She had seen it all, caused it all. I went into a pub to consult my map, use the bathroom, have a beer and then a few more. I smoked more cigarettes. The beer made the smoke go down easier.

It was raining harder when I got out of the pub. I put my head down and walked. I was about ten blocks from the hotel when I entered another pub to use the bathroom again, to warm up, and to have more beer.

At last the bartender said, "Hurry up, please, it's time," just like in the poem. That struck me as comic.

When I got to the hotel I leaned on the doorbell for a little too long to summon the Serbian girl who worked the night desk. She was so pretty that I wondered if she had come to London to be a model, or maybe an actress. There was something about her eyes, I thought, that almost reminded me of Helen. I tried to imagine what she thought about, staying awake all night at the desk of a cheap hotel. Did she get lonely? I can't quite remember what I said to her, but the way she looked at me as she silently handed me my key is inscribed in my mind. I went up the stairs, a trail of water dripping from my raincoat. It took two tries before I got my key into the door. I let my wet clothes fall to the floor and crawled into bed.

. 34 .

BECAUSE SO MANY of the people that Stokes sold off his art collection to were Americans Gina spent more time in New York. At first she stayed with her mother, but the way her mother careened from one crisis to another made it difficult to get anything done. One day, however, Bryce handed Gina the key to a studio apartment on Sixty-seventh Street. No one, he said, was using it, and she was welcome to stay there; no other explanation was offered. It was simply but tastefully furnished, with only two or three paintings hanging on the walls. One of them was a small early Matisse.

She spent most of her time going through records and archives associated with art dealers who were active in the years between the world wars. It was frustrating work, since she could not tell anyone what she was looking for and most of the records were long gone, the galleries having disappeared or merged with other firms.

She had been in New York for about a month when she began one of their regular meetings by reminding Bryce that he had once said that they had competitors who were looking for the same thing as themselves.

"But you had predecessors as well," she said. "Look at this."

> *Birch Lodge*
> *Saranac Lake, New York*
> *October 19, 1929*

Dear Ozzie:

I have finally gotten rid of the insufferable Mrs. R. She is a harmless soul, I suppose, but there is something criminally insipid about her. She is a good-looking woman, or she was once, but after spending an eternity with her in a parlor car, she hardly seems as attractive as everyone says. You told me she wanted a friend, but the wanting is so obvious, making love to her in the way that we genteel women do feels like taking candy from a baby.

But she is off to bed, performing, I suppose, her conjugal duties. I have been told that Rhinebeck is a lecherous old goat, and although his enthusiasm at seeing his beloved spouse and her clever friend (or so she characterizes me) was muted at best, I suspect he will make the most of the situation and get from his wife what wives are supposed to provide. He is, however, a good deal more handsome than the photographs I have seen suggested. Or perhaps it is his money; I have always found that it does wonders for a man's looks. So if it becomes necessary to serve the cause on my back, or in some more Continental posture, it will be less grim than I had feared.

From some hints dropped by Mrs. R., I have the impression that the intimate relations between my hosts are not all that they could be. I am quite sure that Mrs. R. is unaware of all the details that you have provided, but she knows that there is something rotten in the Rhinebeck Denmark. And she doesn't, poor thing, have the faintest inkling of how to make it right. I saw enough in Rhinebeck's eyes (and in the way that his gaze fixed on a negligently fastened button) to suggest that the way to his heart is not through his stomach. I doubt, from certain hints that Mrs. R. gave before the train had even left the metropolitan area, that she has much enthusiasm for the kinds of things that will keep a man like Rhinebeck interested.

As for this place—it is everything that money and good taste can achieve. It is all done up in "Adirondack" style, a charming and expensive version of American pastoral, forest division. Stuffed animals of every description hang from the walls, making the place a very paradise of slaughter. The rooms are light and airy, with wonderful views of the lake or the forest. Each room contains a fireplace, framed by artful masonry made from the local stones.

We arrived just at sunset, and Rhinebeck took us out onto a balcony. "You have come just in time," he said. We admired the view; the trees on both shores of the lake were brilliant in yellow, orange, red, and green. Suddenly the declining rays of the sun infused the trees on the island across from us with an impossible richness. The light seemed to dance on the gray-blue water. And as if that wasn't enough, there was a sliver of silver moon hanging in the perfectly blue sky. "Every evening when the sky is clear," Rhinebeck said, "I am treated to this sight. Is it not wonderful?"

Mrs. R. wept at the beauty of it all, or so she said, but I think her tears came from realizing how much her husband had been hiding from her. It is some measure of her acuity that an inkling of the truth dawned on her only then; most women would have thought it odd some time sooner that her husband had built a pleasure palace from which she was explicitly excluded!

After we had admired the view and had been given a chance to freshen up, we went to dinner. Rhinebeck so contrives things that the house staff is almost invisible, but shortly after we sat down, a plain old woman appeared, carrying a tray loaded down with venison, roast potatoes, red cabbage, and freshly baked bread. Rhinebeck managed the wine himself, apologizing as he did so for the "rough ways" of the North Country. But it was all a pretense, because I doubt that a finer plate of food could be had anywhere in the environs of Herald Square. And as for the wine—well, it was a Château Margaux from before the war, and there are few finer bottles to be had anywhere in the city.

We spoke primarily about hunting (an oddly appropriate topic, given my mission!). We started on it when I remarked that it was a bit eerie to be sitting down to eat the flesh of animals while stuffed versions of those animals, their eyes glittering in the firelight, looked down on us. Rhinebeck then told us a gruesome story about the killing of our supper

and concluded with the typical remarks of a man of his class,
viz. that it is important to see the facts for what they are,
important to look life squarely in the eye, no good taking
a sentimental view and so forth. He said he had hitherto
excluded all women from Birch Lodge because he wanted to
have at least one place where he was safe from female softness, although, if Miss Deventer is to be credited, he made
an exception for her soft female form.

At dessert (a most delicious tart of wild blueberries),
he seemed to relent. "Come," he said, "I will show you my
Snuggery and give you, even though you are ladies, a glass of
port." He then led the way to a room we hadn't seen before—
the most marvelous room in the whole marvelous place. It
was warm, cozy, delightful, and grand all at once. There
was a comfortable sofa covered with sheepskins and a few
easy chairs in front of a large fireplace in which a bright fire
was burning. A card table was off to one side, a handsome
desk on the other. There was a curious cabinet, decorated
with a hunting scene of inlaid wood, and bookshelves filled
with leather-bound volumes. There were three or four
wonderful landscapes on the walls, including a gorgeous
Corot that would fetch you a pretty penny if you could only
get your hands on it. There were decanters of wine and other
spirits on a sideboard. The whole room smelled pleasantly of
firewood and cigar smoke.

He settled us down on the sofa so that we were facing
the curious cabinet and handed us each a glass of the most
delicious port I have ever tasted. Rhinebeck stood in front of

the cabinet and looked down at us with what I thought was a smug and self-satisfied air.

"Now that you have seen this room and tasted this port," he said, "only one thing remains before you will have penetrated to the very heart of the mysteries of Birch Lodge."

He opened the cabinet with a flourish, as if he were the proprietor of a raree show. Inside was a lovely Renoir nude, one of those big pink ones. There are flowers on the wall behind her. Her right hand covers her nether regions, although a hint of dark hair is visible. One senses, indeed, that her hand is not placed where it is out of modesty, but rather that we are looking in on some very private reverie.

Rhinebeck revealed her with a kind of wink, as if he thought we ladies might be offended. He told us that we were the first ladies who had seen her in ever so many years, and that she had been painted for an exclusive club in Paris, or at any rate that is what the dealer told him when he bought her after the war. He sat down and said with amiable simplicity, "So now you know all."

Of that I am not convinced. He seemed, I thought, to be protesting a bit too much. The painting is more frankly sensual than the sort of thing you would expect to find in a museum, but many more shocking works are hung proudly on the walls of Fifth Avenue apartments. He looked hard at his wife, as if he were waiting for some expression of shock or outrage. "What do you think?" he asked.

She had been looking at the painting quite intently. With a sad smile she said that the painting reminded her

somehow of the August afternoons of her youth on Nan-
tucket. She is really a pathetic creature.

In spite of Rhinebeck's protestations, I am not convinced
that he isn't hiding something up here. I am sure, however,
that that something is not the Renoir. So I wouldn't rule out
the possibility that if this Turner of yours exists, Rhinebeck
might have it, and if he has it, it might be at Birch Lodge.
He strikes me as the kind of man who would enjoy owning
something as shocking as you claim this Turner is.

It is almost dawn. My mind has been too wound up
from the journey and too full of speculations to sleep. I also
wanted to give you some report of my thoughts and progress
as soon as I could. I have been told that the mail boat (isn't
that charming?) stops at the dock at around nine, so I intend
to put this in the bag before I go to sleep.

I will write again if I have the opportunity, but I suspect
that the next time you hear from me will be in New York.

Please know that I am dedicated to your cause and that I
will leave no stone unturned in helping you achieve your aim.

Yours devotedly,
Maria

Bryce put the letter down and smiled with satisfaction.
"Very good," he said. "You must concentrate your efforts on
Rhinebeck and his circle. But we must move cautiously. We are
getting close."

. 35 .

THOSE WERE SUCH DAYS. It was the autumn of 1830. Egremont had cleared the house, sending his son up to London on a fool's errand, which, fool though he was, Wyndham knew was merely to get him out of the way. He was convinced that I was behind the command that he depart, and he stuttered and turned crimson with rage as I bade him adieu. There was nothing he could say because his father was standing beside me. I put my hand on His Lordship's arm as I waved the bastard good-bye.

I remember the light. If Turner didn't need us in the studio, I would find Grant and make him walk with me through the park. Petworth was always beautiful, but those days live in my memory. The colors of that season seemed brighter than other autumns, the air more clear. The light of those days and the light from the painting run together in my mind. I see young Grant's face as he looked out on the view from the Rotunda. I see his back as he approaches me in the painting. I see the blue sky above the park, I see the more perfect sky above the sea.

The sun sparkled on the water of the pond the way the light sparkled on Egremont's diamonds. I wore the diamonds when Turner first sketched me. When I had been at Petworth only a month and hardly established as his mistress, Egremont called me up to his bedroom one afternoon. He had me undress and stand before him. I remember the feel of the Turkey carpet on my bare feet, the glow of the candles, the gray sky through the windows as the rain began to fall, the feel of the goosebumps on my skin in the cool air. He walked around me and considered me from all sides, as if I were a statue in his gallery or a horse in his stable. He had taken his boots off, although he was still dressed for the hunt, still smelling of horseflesh and exercise. I understood that, as old as he was, I was but the latest of many.

He approached me with a small wooden casket. He took out the jewels, the ones I wore as Jessica, the ones which Helen let fall to the floor by her dressing table. He placed them on my bosom and affixed the clasp behind my neck. I had never seen jewels like these before. They seemed to fill the room with their sparkle. They were cold and heavy against my skin, somehow heavier for the fact that I wore nothing else. He stepped back a few steps and looked at me again. I could see the heat in his old eyes as my lips parted. "Damn," he said, "you are as fine a piece of flesh as ever I beheld."

He kissed me and then pushed me back onto the bed. He turned me over and came into me. He used me hard; I could feel the diamonds cut into my flesh as he drove me down onto the coverlet.

He never stripped me down and used me like that again, but that encounter sealed my place in his affections. I became for him the woman of that afternoon, and every night when he came to me it was with that memory in his mind. Even in later years, when his powers failed, he would think of those days. He would pat my bottom or give my breasts a squeeze and say that no one had ever worn those jewels as I did and no one deserved them better. That was why he left them to me when he died. I had to struggle with Wyndham about them, but I prevailed. I was fighting for my life, while he was only fighting out of malice.

"Turner is to put you in another painting," he said. "I want the jewels in it. I want to think of that afternoon with you when I see it. So go to him and take the jewels with you. Don't fuss about. Do as he wants. I have great faith that he will out-shine even himself."

When I first went to the studio, Turner was content to sketch my face, but after two or three times he said, "Come, madam. This will not do. I know your charming face well enough from sitting across from you during many pleasant din-ners. We must come to the rest of it."

It was always said of Turner that he could not do the human figure. His *Jessica* seemed to bear that out, but as the event proved, he could paint the figure better than any artist of his generation. I never asked him why he did not do more often what he could do so well. But he knew his own nature. He had enough to do with his landscapes, I suppose; no want of subject matter in his mind. I think his sensual nature was so strong that he feared it would stand in the way of his art. I was not pleased that I had to do what was required of me, for I had grown accustomed to thinking of myself as the lady of Petworth House. But living as I had, I had bade farewell to true pride many years before.

When the day came, I undressed behind the screen while Turner prepared his materials. I was wearing nothing but a robe of China silk that Turner had been thoughtful enough to provide. I ascended the little platform and looked down. He looked up at me. "Come, madam, there is nothing to be afraid of. I will not hurt you. Besides, I'm too sensible a man even to think of it." But his lip was trembling and his voice almost broke. He was afraid, far more afraid than an old whore like me could even think of being.

I let the robe fall, taking pleasure in watching him gasp, in seeing him realize the distance between a women like me and the harborside creature who was the mother of his brats. He was such an ugly man. As I walked up the stairs to the studio I had thought about what I would do if he tested the virtue I had lost so many years ago. In spite of his nose and his dirty hands and his bad teeth, there was his genius. He was as close to a god as this fallen world possesses. I understood why those Greek girls would let themselves be taken by a bull or a swan: it was the odor of power and deity that compelled them. And I thought too that I could take a kind of vengeance on Egremont for sending me to Turner like some mere painter's model. But I was no better than he treated me. I knew that. And I was fond of Egremont and not so far gone as to forget the gratitude I owed him.

Still, when I let the robe fall I had not yet decided. Had Turner made half a gesture toward me I would have fallen. I could see that it took him some effort to master himself, but he was, in those days, a driven man. He, more than any of us, knew what it was to be touched by the gods. His nature obliged him to honor that touch and keep his mind on the work at hand.

He said nothing. He drew his hand across his brow and went to his work, leaving me to stand there just as I was. I stood very still, my hands hanging at my side, the palms turned up the way they had been as the robe fell away. His gaze was like a lover's caress, and I could feel myself yearn for him. No one had ever looked at me so intently, yet he was like a wall. Stare at him as I would, I could make no contact with the man behind the pencil.

After that first day Turner told me clearly what he wanted me to do. Raise your arm, please. Lean against the chair. Put your weight on your left leg. He was precise and polite. He knew his business. He was like old Hobb, the master of Egremont's stables. There was no horse living, Hobb said, that he could not break. It was only a matter of time and patience. Lie down on the couch, please. Move your knees apart ever so slightly. Thank you. He broke me so slowly that by the time he had me on my knees before him like a bitch in heat, I hardly felt it.

It was only later that afternoon that the memories came back to me like a nightmare remembered. I found young Grant and made him accompany me on a walk around the estate. As the recollection of my morning in the studio overcame me, I hurried ahead, as if trying to outrace my shame. Poor Grant. He hardly knew what to make of me. He must have thought I was mad. But he was kind and attentive and asked no questions. He had had his own humiliations in the studio. I cannot remember what we spoke of along the way. I am afraid I babbled like an idiot.

When I went to my room to rest, the thought of Turner sitting across from me as I passed him the meat seemed more than I could bear. Egremont and all the others counted on me to be presentable and poised. It was my duty to keep the conversation moving. I thought of Grant: how sweet-tempered he was, and how beautiful. I thought of the life that had brought me to this pass. I thought of how Turner had seen me; how I had obeyed his commands. But then I thought of Egremont's passion, of the tremor on Turner's lips when I let the robe fall and the reason I had been chosen to play my part in his great work. Shame be damned. With that thought I slept.

. 36 .

To: gbolton@madisonpartners.com
From: arthur@madisonpartners.com
Date: September 20, 2003
Subject: Change of plans

Dear Gina,

My apologies for the email, but I have just landed in
Tokyo. Call Evelyn as soon as you receive this and have
her book you on the next plane to London. On my arrival here I found a message from George. I had asked
him to keep half an eye on our friend in Princeton—call
it a hunch, but it's really more like a superstition. George
has now learned that Mr. Leiden has gone to London,
supposedly to give a talk, although why anyone would
listen to him is beyond me. Your work on Rhinebeck can
wait for a week or so. Go to London in case he makes

any moves, specifically any approaches to the auction houses, or to any of the dealers who might be interested in the kind of major work we are seeking. London would not be a bad place to sell a newly discovered Turner, so we can't be too careful. I have already arranged to have him followed from the moment he lands. Tell our people what plane you will be on and they will be in touch with you when you arrive.

I feel in my bones that we are getting close. I do not believe that a person like Leiden could stand in our way, but we must take no chances. Act carefully, and give away nothing. What we seek is ours if it is anyone's.

I know I am overreacting, but humor me.

Fond regards,
Arthur

To: arthur@madisonpartners.com
From: gbolton@madisonpartners.com
Date: September 22, 2003
Subject: RE: Change of plans

Barry was waiting for me when I arrived at the hotel and gave me a report. Leiden arrived at Gatwick two days ago and is scheduled to leave on Saturday. He took the train to Victoria and from there a cab to the Radisson. He gave a talk yesterday at a small conference about the role of foundations in advancing philanthropy; he talked about various processes for allocating resources. One of Barry's guys managed to get in; said he was sensible but dull.

After the conference was over he checked out and took a cab to a small hotel near Victoria Station (tiny rooms and German tourists). He walked to the Tate through the drizzle. According to Barry he "mooned over the pictures for ever so long, mostly the ones by Turner." From there he walked along the Embankment and then to the National Gallery. He stopped along the way to buy some cigarettes, and then had lunch in a pub. I am quite certain no one smoked in his house. Barry said he smoked a few halfway down and then put them out, like someone who was trying to quit.

At the Gallery he also focused on the Turners, spending enough time in front of *Ulysses Deriding Polyphemus* to annoy Barry. He left at five and went to a pub where he drank a lot and had beef pie.

He didn't speak to anyone that Barry noticed, nor did he make any calls. He got back to the hotel at around 10:00. Barry knows the girl at the front desk; she said he smelled something awful when he came in. She confirmed that he is leaving on Saturday. I think you are right; he is worth keeping an eye on.

Hope all is well in Tokyo.

Cheers,
Gina

To: arthur@madisonpartners.com
From: gbolton@madisonpartners.com
Date: September 25, 2003
Subject: RE: RE: Change of plans

He went to the museums again on Wednesday and got drunk again. On Thursday he got up an hour earlier than usual and walked to Victoria, where he got on the 9:20 to Pulborough and the bus to Petworth. Barry barely made it onto the train, although I had warned him that anyone who was on a "Turner tour" of London might do that. When he got there he took the guided tour and then wandered around the house and gardens for the rest of the afternoon. He had lunch at a pub in the village. Except for occasional interactions with the guide and the restaurant staff, he doesn't seem to have spoken to anyone since the conference ended.

He took the 4:35 home and went straight to the hotel. After about an hour he went to a pub a few blocks away. He ordered bangers and mash at the bar, watched football on the television, and proceeded to drink seriously and, it seemed, deliberately. He smoked about half a pack of cigarettes. He stayed until closing time, at which point he walked back to the hotel, visibly drunk.

I hope the Japanese are more interesting.

. 37 .

≈ I NEEDED TO GET closer to Turner. Seeing all the paintings in the Tate and the National Gallery was helpful, but I thought that if I could walk where he had walked and breathe the air that he had breathed, I might be able to understand my painting better. So I decided to visit Petworth House, the estate of Turner's patron, Lord Egremont.

I took the train from Victoria Station to Pulborough and a bus from there to the village of Petworth. The guidebook said that the family made the railroad go through Pulborough, rather than Petworth, because they didn't want the activity of a station town to intrude on their privacy. They also didn't want the railroad tracks spoiling their view.

The bus let me off on a nondescript town square. I walked down a narrow cobbled street, past a restaurant and a few shops that sold antiques and hunting prints. At the end of the street was a small church. There was a garden on one side, a door in a stone wall on the other. I could see that I was about to enter a large structure of some sort, although the approach to Petworth House from the village didn't reveal anything to suggest folks who had been grand enough to order the railroads around.

I had never been in a house that was anything like this; in the North Gallery the scale of the place finally overwhelmed me. The paintings were hung two or three on top of each other against a dark red background. In the center of the room was a massive sculpture of Saint Michael doing battle with Satan. The hard marble seemed like living flesh, but it was the size of the thing that provoked a visceral sense of the powers that operate in invisible worlds.

It was more a public space—a museum or courthouse—than a private dwelling. Petworth House had become a museum, but people who got up every day and had to use the toilet had lived within its walls. The guidebook said that their descendants, the Wyndhams, still lived in one of the wings. I imagined them wandering around the house after all the tourists had gone, like the ghosts of long-dead aristocrats.

There were too many paintings, too densely packed, for me to really enjoy them. The guidebook said that Turner had been a frequent guest at Petworth and that he had done some painting here. I tried to think of the man who had painted my Helen walking through these very halls and looking at these very same paintings and statues.

I kept my eye out for Turners. Just above the fireplace I spotted one called *Near the Thames Lock, Windsor*. There was a river or stream flowing away from the viewer, some trees, and a shadowy castle in the distance. There were young people skinny-dipping in the water, looking young and carefree. They were innocents cooling themselves off on a hot summer's day.

I got distracted by a large painting nearby—the kind of painting that would be just perfect for an old-fashioned Irish bar in New York. A naked woman was sleeping in a forest. She looked as though she was either thinking about sex or had just had sex. There was a chubby and corny-looking cupid flying above her. He was holding his hands over his eyes, as if he didn't want to see the naked lady, or as if he was ashamed of what she had just done. It was called *Sleeping Nymph with Cupid*, by John Hoppner, someone I had never heard of. I looked carefully at the painting to see if I could discover the nymph's lover retreating through the underbrush. Suddenly I imagined Susan lying on the bed in a hotel room somewhere, or even in our own bedroom in Princeton, in a similar posture, while her lover went into the bathroom to take a piss. It occurred to me that I was a familiar sight to the guards, the middle-aged American man looking too intently at a mediocre nude.

There was a lot of sex on the walls of Petworth House, lots of naked statues. *The Rape of Europa*, by somebody named Hilton, might pretend to be about mythology, but it was really about desire. There was a portrait of a Mrs. Robinson by Owen. No one knew who she was, according to the guidebook, but there was something knowing and worldly about the look she directed at me that seemed more like Mrs. Robinson in *The Graduate* than like someone who was alive to be painted in the early 1800s.

After about an hour, I stopped following the guidebook and just allowed myself to wander around. It was a wonderful building, suffused with grandeur and reeking of art. There were only a few other tourists, so except for the elderly docents who were stationed in most of the rooms, I often felt I had the place to myself. What would it have been like to live in Petworth House in Turner's day? I tried to imagine Turner's footfalls echoing through the empty hallways, the statues disappearing into the gloom as the light began to fade. Perhaps he would hear the soft tread of an old servant, or the rustle of a silk gown as a lady hurried off to dinner. Perhaps there would be conversation in the distance, perhaps the sound of a harpsichord and a woman singing.

Suddenly I saw her. It was Helen, but she was called *Jessica*. I somehow knew it was her, even though she didn't look like her at all. My heart started to race. She was leaning out of a complicated window casement. The background seemed ablaze behind her, as if the room was on fire, but her expression was oddly still and resigned, as if she couldn't decide whether to call for help or retreat into the flames. Perhaps she had set the fire herself and the painting captures that moment when the suicide takes her last look back on the life she is about to relinquish. The jewels and the elaborate gown she wears suggest that wealth and privilege are no guarantee of happiness. Perhaps she regrets her decision.

But when I looked closer, I saw that it was just a gold background. There was no fire. I was painfully upset to see that Turner had reduced Helen, my Helen, to this banality. It was definitely her. The jewels she wore were the same jewels Helen had flung to the floor of her chamber. But Helen's beautiful hand, a hand which was meant for touching and pleasing and for creating embroidery of unsurpassed beauty, had become, in *Jessica*, a kind of useless appendage that represented the vague idea of a hand—that thing at the end of the arm which is useful only for closing windows. What upset me even more, however, was her body. The body for which heroes met their deaths had been constricted beyond recognition by Jessica's bodice and by Turner's perverse refusal to provide an illusion of depth. I stood in front of the painting for a long time, lost in anger and confusion. Eventually I calmed down and went outside. I walked up the hill behind the house and sat on the grass beneath one of the chestnut trees, where I lit a cigarette and looked down on the view. Smoking, I realized, did not make me any younger. I kept on smoking anyway.

There was a small lake perfectly placed in the expanse of manicured ground that stretched out behind the house. There were deer in the distance, ducks swimming in the pond, an odd statue of a faithful dog on the shore. Petworth House itself, massive and grand, dominated my view. If only the sun would go down in a blaze of flame, this would all be a painting by Turner, and I would be one of those peasants or travelers placed on the edge of the composition. I imagined that Turner himself had sat on this very spot. Perhaps he had walked up here with the woman who had become Jessica and Helen. They had looked down on the great house together, feeling a sense of its power. Could she have understood what Turner intended her to become?

. 38 .

❧ "I KNEW SIR JOHN," Lord Egremont said. "He was no better than the rest of us, but he would not have done such a thing. He was always very considerate of his wife's feelings. She too was a lady of the world. Their relations were only moderately regular, but they understood each other. They continued to live happily together until his death."

We were talking about one of the pictures that hung in the North Gallery, Hoppner's *Sleeping Nymph with Cupid*, which Egremont had purchased at Sir John Leicester's sale. The painting depicts a young woman sleeping in a forest. She is naked except for bit of gauzy stuff draped most artfully between her legs. She sleeps as no young woman has ever slept, in an uncomfortable but amorous posture, which suggests either an invitation to impropriety or that an impropriety has recently occurred. A chubby and blindfolded cherub flies above her. Given what I have been told about my host's proclivities when he was a younger man, I am not surprised to find the painting in his collection.

"I too had heard those stories suggesting that Sir John's mistress had been the model for the beautiful nymph," Turner said. "You are right, sir. Sir John was a good man. He would never have insulted his wife in such a manner. But what I am about to relate is the true story of the lovely nymph. No harm now, with the present company, for I shall ask you not to spread this about. Besides, Sir John is dead three years and time has done its work. "

The four of us were sitting in the library after dinner, as had become our custom. Turner had asked for, and received, a glass of brandy. He seemed more cheerful than he had in the past few days, and more inclined to talk.

"Although not in my line, I encouraged you to purchase the nymph, my lord. Fits in well with the old Greeks. The mutable body is our link to past times. The spirit of the age may be different, but the body is the same, although it partakes of the age in which it dwells. But Hoppner understood flesh. There is a quickness to it; she almost seems to be breathing.

"There was a pretty poem, you know, written on the painting:

> As on her arm reclines the sleeping fair
> And with her breath the loitering gale perfumes,
> Love sees, or thinks he sees, his mother there,
> And near earth directs his glittering planes;
> Hovers with fond delight around her bower
> And swells the fragrance with a roseate shower.

Turner closed his eyes as he recited. I was surprised by the amount of passion he put into his recitation, but also struck by the odd places in which he put the accents.

"Lovely stuff, that. Poetry. A wonderful art, Mr. Grant. I have dabbled with numbers myself, but it's hard going for me. 'Roseate shower.' A wonderful phrase."

"You were about to tell us the true story of the lovely nymph," Mrs. Spencer reminded him.

"Ah, yes. Hoppner was kind to me when I was younger and trying to make my way. Twenty-five years ago, you know. His line was mostly portraits, so he was willing to do what he could for a poor landscape painter. One day he invited me to his studio. Sir John was there, and Hoppner was good enough to introduce me to him. We got on well. Eventually he invited me up to Tabley to paint some views of the neighborhood. Lovely locale, a fine house. Not Petworth, of course, but what is?

"Sir John was a frequent visitor to Hoppner's studio in those days. That is where he met young Molly. Pretty Molly, we called her. Sometimes Polly Molly, but why I don't know. She was no better than she needed to be, but, Lord, more beautiful than anyone had a right to be.

"She was an artist's model. Also a temporary special friend to certain gentlemen. A good-hearted girl. Sir John wished to join the ranks of Molly's friends. But Molly said no. Which seemed odd at the time, given Sir John's wealth and standing. And he was more than personable enough for a rich man. But no was her answer and she stuck to it. Sir John moped about like a heartsick mooncalf.

"But he was nothing if not persistent. A man of strong character, as you can attest, my lord. And ingenious. He hit upon the happy idea of commissioning Hoppner to paint her portrait. And the still happier idea of suggesting a classical composition. That sort of thing was not in Hoppner's line, you know, but the result was the delightful *Nymph*—his best work, in my opinion.

"Sir John felt, as most patrons do, that he had the right to stop by the studio and observe the progress on his commission. Try to discourage that sort of thing, myself. Unless, as is the case with the present company, the patron is a respectful man of taste and discretion. Not always the case, you know. Few are the benefactors of art who understand the business well enough to know when not to meddle. Fellows think that the size of their purses gives them good ideas about art. 'Wouldn't that tree look more sublime on the left—sublimity very important, don't you think?'

"But you and Sir John, my lord, are notable exceptions. Both knowledgeable and accomplished in your own line; respectful to artists and their work."

I looked over at Egremont to see how he was taking this clumsy flattery. His smile suggested that he appreciated it but was not moved. Turner continued with his story. Sir John, he said, had contrived with Hoppner that he would appear at the studio one day while Hoppner was doing some preliminary sketches of the beautiful Molly. At these early sessions Molly was clothed, and it seemed proper enough that Sir John should appear to observe the progress of the work. He took the occasion of his visits to compliment Molly on her charms and to give her small presents by way of compensating her for her labors. Turner can be very amusing when he tells stories out of school about the artist's life. As he warmed to his tale he became more and more animated, seeming to forget that terseness which is the distinguishing characteristic of his speech. He did imitations of the various parties in the little drama that had us all laughing heartily. His Hoppner spoke in a barely intelligible deep rumble, while his Sir John talked in an affected drawl which, Lord Egremont pointed out, caught the flavor of the man exactly. Best of all, however, was the way he did Molly. When he affected a high falsetto and squeaked, "Oh, no, sir, I couldn't," even the butler standing at the sideboard laughed out loud.

Molly made no objections to Sir John's attendance at the preliminary sessions, but she protested most strenuously when he arrived on the day that she was first to remove her clothes. She put on, Turner said, such a show of virtue that it appeared as if the painting might never come off. It was only a most generous gift from Sir John that saved the day. As Turner spoke, Mrs. Spencer's eyes met mine. But Turner was oblivious as to how the two of us might feel about his story in light of our visits to his studio.

Molly, Turner went on, at last agreed to Sir John's presence, but only on the condition that Sir John sit behind a curtain that was arranged in such a way that he could see her, but she couldn't see him. Molly was a good-hearted girl, Turner said, but also a sly one who knew that it was a rough-and-tumble world. No one would look out for her interests if she didn't.

Turner paused for a moment and grew thoughtful. We had by this time walked to the North Gallery to look at the painting in question.

Servants had set up lamps and candles so that we could see it clearly. "Hoppner's genius, you see, was to paint Molly in a way that flattered Sir John's idea of what he wanted." He pointed to the flesh on her raised thigh. "Lovely work here. Pink and living. Pure, but inviting. Sir John, as I said, was no better than the rest of us. A man of position, used to getting his way. Molly had not behaved as Sir John expected of a girl of her station and easy virtue. She was keeping herself dear, not flooding the market with cheap wine. But Sir John had formed his opinion of Molly not from Molly herself, but from another of Hoppner's paintings, one called *The Flower Girl*, or some such.

"It will not do to call it love. No, no. Not for a man like Sir John. But let me use the word, for I am too dull to think of another. He had fallen in love with the idea he had formed of the girl from seeing her image. And what Hoppner did here, you see, was take Sir John's idea and undress it. Hard to say which of the two was the worse, Hoppner or the girl. We painters are both whores and bawds, you know. Sometimes both at once. Sir John was delighted with his commission when it was completed. As he should have been, for it is a marvelous piece of work."

It was Mrs. Spencer who finally asked the question that had been in my own mind. "Did Molly ever surrender her charms to Sir John?"

We had begun to walk back toward the library and our tea. "Yes and no," Turner said. "I told you Molly was a clever girl. But even so, I had underestimated her cleverness, and her real wisdom, by a long shot. Most afternoons, you see, after her work in Hoppner's studio was done, Sir John would take her out for some light refreshment. A cup of tea, a glass of wine. Molly was not the first girl of her class Sir John had wooed. He knew his business. But she knew hers better. She put him off with one excuse after another. Protestations of virtue. I hardly know. But at last, when the painting was done, she said he might come to her apartment. There was a gift, of course.

"She had arranged things most cleverly. Only candles to light the way. A maid to lead Sir John in. Through one room. And then another. And then the maid steps aside and Sir John hears sweet Molly's voice entreating him to enter. He does, and there she is—a tableau vivant, if you know what I mean, lying there just as she was in the painting, with, you know, that bit of drapery arranged just so between her thighs."

Turner paused for a moment and smiled to himself. "I heard this from Sir John himself. And also from Molly," he added a bit sheepishly. "She invited him to step forward. He did so. He was a man of the world. Been to Paris, you know. Italy as well. But never so entranced as at that moment. There was the painting in the flesh. Except, of course, for that silly cherub and those murky trees. So it was even better. He steps forward until he is standing by her side. He sees her breast rise and fall. She looks at him with those wonderful eyes of hers. She had that look, you know, of always being a bit sleepy. Ripe for picking, if you follow me. And she said, 'You may.'

"Sir John told me it was the rummest thing. A world of meaning in those words, my friends. He knew exactly what she meant. A world of meaning. He stepped forward and bent down. He grasped that bit of drapery with his fingers and pulled it away. It was the same bit of cloth that Hoppner had been using in the studio. Fine and light, but with enough body to fall. Molly said there was the odd fleck of paint on it. But now she was before him in all her glory. He never touched her. She never told him not to. They both understood that it would be better so. More perfect.

"I don't know how long he stood there, but they never said another word. When he left he carried the memory with him. It was a great gift. Completed the painting, in a way. For the rest of us, that bit of drapery is always there. For Sir John, it wasn't. When Ward did the engraving that made her so famous, half the boys in London would have given a tooth to see what Sir John saw. I would rather have the tooth. But I am an old man in need of teeth and I have seen my share of artist's models."

"So, Mr. Turner. Will you paint me without the drapery?" All of us were shocked by Mrs. Spencer's question. There was an uncomfortable silence. I looked at Egremont, but I could not tell if he was angry with her, or if he felt shame at the understanding he had reached with Turner.

We all looked at Turner. He was staring into the fire as if there was no one else in the room. Mrs. Spencer repeated her question. There was something in her voice that I had never heard before.

Turner looked up and met Mrs. Spencer's eyes. "That is not the point," he said. "There is a truth beyond nudity, madam. Hoppner's is a fine painting. Molly is a pleasant nymph. But that is not what I am about. So perhaps yes. Perhaps no. It is, as I have said, a damn hard business. You have your sorrows, I mine. If you understood my struggles, you would never ask your question. But you cannot. Nor is there any reason I should expect you to. Good night! Good night!"

Turner rose abruptly and left us.

. 39 .

❧ I DECIDED TO SPEND my last afternoon in England
in my favorite room at the Tate, the one devoted to Turner's
unfinished canvases, large and almost formless fields of color
which hover on the verge of becoming. It is like being in a room
of possibilities. Before I'd found the painting, I'd felt that the
only thing left for me to become was dead. I couldn't have seen
the hope and potential that were the true subject of Turner's
unfinished work. I still didn't know what I was to become, but
I was pretty sure it was *something else*. The funk that came over
me in London and in the days following my return from England was the anxiety occasioned by being poised between one
state and another.

The unfinished paintings made me see that there was something sad about all the Turners I'd seen since I'd been in England. In none of them had Turner achieved anything like *The
Center of the World*. Only the unfinished canvases held out the
possibility of becoming what *The Center of the World* actually

was. All the others, even the greatest of them—the Dido paintings, *Rome, from the Vatican*—had, like me, done all that they
ever would. They were still great paintings, of course, but in
my painting everything was more than perfect; in the others
perfection, I now saw, was an unrealized possibility.

I had first noticed her when she was standing a few feet
from Turner's early self-portrait in the first room of the exhibit. Her name, I found out later, was Gina. She was in her
early thirties and carried herself like a movie star. Though the
outfit she wore—straight black skirt, white blouse, and high
heels—was not particularly special, no one in Princeton could
have pulled it off with the same kind of drop-dead sexiness.
She had her back to me. I followed the seam of her stocking as
it rose from her ankles until it disappeared beneath the hem of
her skirt a few inches above her knees. I assumed that she was
French or Italian. I remember feeling my wedding ring among
the unfamiliar coins in my pocket. I thought about putting it
back on, but I decided to let it stay where it was. I realized I
was staring at her and turned away before it became too obvious. Everybody in the room except her had probably noticed
the middle-aged American making an ass of himself.

After I had been in the room of unfinished paintings by
myself for about half an hour, Gina came in. I tried not to look
at her, but I found myself stealing a glance whenever I thought
she might not notice. In the line of her legs and hips there was
something of Helen. It was remarkable.

For about fifteen minutes we were the only two people
there. She was on one side, I was on the other. We each took

a step to the left at about the same moment as we moved on to the next painting. I felt as if we were dancing. The spell was broken, however, when two young Americans entered. They were in the midst of an argument about where to eat dinner. They plunked themselves down on the bench and raised their voices: he said she thought they were made of money; she said he was mean-spirited and stingy and no fun at all. The volume rose as they batted each other's faults back and forth. Between their asinine argument and the way Gina stood as she studied the paintings, with her left hand placed on her hip and right leg slightly extended, I couldn't concentrate at all. I decided I needed coffee.

The cafeteria was crowded, but I found the only free table and sat down. Taking out my guidebook, I tried to decide if I should see anything else before I left London. I looked, I thought, just like a tourist. People who go to museums are tourists. I tried to enjoy my coffee.

"Excuse me, but do you mind if I sit here?"

I looked up and noticed that the top three buttons of her blouse were unbuttoned. I felt myself starting to blush, but I guess she was used to seeing middle-aged men making fools of themselves.

"Sure," I said. I moved my coffee closer to my side of the little table and went back to my guidebook.

"You're not waiting for anyone?" she asked as she placed her cup on the table and sat down. I assured her that I was by myself. She took a sip of coffee and grimaced. "You'd think," she said, "that at these prices they could produce a better cup of coffee. Between this coffee and those people up there, it's like there is a conspiracy to ruin a wonderful place."

The coffee wasn't that great, I agreed, and those young people were hard to put up with.

"You got out while the going was good," she said. "You must be more sensitive than I am. I didn't leave until it got to his faults in the bathroom and hers in bed. That was way too much information."

I smiled and went back to my book.

"And it was such a shame," she went on. "That's my favorite room in the Tate. It was like having somebody throw this nasty coffee all over them. But look at me. I'm just as bad: you're trying to read and I'm yammering away. I'm sorry."

I looked up and allowed myself to meet her eyes for the first time. She was so attractive that I could hardly speak. "It's okay; it's nice to talk—except for waiters and hotel staff I haven't talked to anyone in three days. But I agree about that room: those unfinished canvases are my favorites."

She smiled at me. I smiled back, partly to return the gesture, but mostly at the pure pleasure of how pretty she was. I felt almost giddy as I thought that she might be trying to pick me up, and I am embarrassed, looking back, at how quickly I spun out the most improbable and lascivious fantasies.

We chatted for a while about London. This was only her second visit. She worked for an investment firm and was in London for a series of meetings. We talked about how weird it was that the cars came from the wrong direction and how the food wasn't nearly as bad as people said. She lived in New

York; I told her that I lived in Princeton. I felt myself being swept up in the pleasure of talking to an attractive woman. She had such a wonderful smile; she seemed so funny and interesting. Best of all, she seemed to find me interesting, too.

We had been talking for about twenty minutes when she said, "I think it's safe to go back; they're probably gone. Shall we go together?" I said yes and started to gather up my coffee things. She reached her hand out and placed it on top of mine. "I have to ask you a question," she said. "Are you married?" I was startled by her touch, but didn't try to move my hand away. For a moment I was tempted to lie. I wondered if she caught my hesitation and, if she had, how she interpreted it.

"Yes," I said. "For over twenty years. One kid on his own in New York, one with a year to go in college. And you?"

She made a face. "Sort of. He's seeing someone else. And he knows that I know. But we haven't figured out what to do. We don't have any kids, but it's still complicated."

"It sounds like a tough situation. I don't have a lot of information, but he seems like a fool to me."

"You're very kind," she said. "People my age don't know how to be kind. But sometimes I feel that if I was married to me, I'd want to see someone else too." She seemed to be in danger of drifting off into a funk, but she pulled herself out of it and looked at me brightly.

"Let's talk about something else," she said. "Let's go look at some beautiful paintings."

It was at this point that she told me her name was Gina. I told her mine. We walked upstairs together.

. 40 .

ABOUT TWO WEEKS AGO, Turner came down to dinner for the first time in over a week. Egremont had called for a fresh ham to be served, as he knew it was one of Turner's favorite dishes. Turner paid the meat his most gracious compliments, but the only part of the meal he did justice to was the wine. The conversation proceeded by fits and starts. Mrs. Spencer did her best, as did I, but Turner cast such a gloomy pall over the proceedings that it was all in vain.

Turner has put aside his pads and sketchbooks and has started to work on a medium-sized canvas. He often takes his meals in the studio. Sometimes, he sends his excuses at dinner, saying that he needs to take a ramble to clear the smell of turpentine from his brain. If he eats at all, he grabs something in the kitchen and eats it like a tramp as he marches along. Without Turner's company our dinners have become quick and silent affairs. I can sense Lord Egremont chafing at the lack of interesting conversation. I do my best, David, but I know that I am found wanting.

Turner's face has become thinner. This means much in someone as devoted to the table as he. On those occasions when he has sent for me in the studio, he hardly greets me when I arrive. He has given up all pretense of considering my feelings, although, to be fair, he has also ceased asking me to take those undignified poses that had been so disturbing. Usually he asks me to stand with my back toward him. Often he has me lift a heavy iron bar over my head, or do some other exercise to exaggerate the articulation of the muscles in my back. My face, I was somewhat chagrined to realize, no longer holds any interest for him.

Mrs. Spencer has been required more often. When she returns from the studio her face is cold and hard, as if she is willing herself not to weep. It does not become her. Sometimes she goes directly to her chamber, but more often she seeks me out and asks me to accompany her on a walk through the park. By an unspoken agreement we have ceased to speak of what goes on when we are alone with Turner. She leads the way and I follow. When we first start out, she is grim and purposeful in her stride, as if she were a foot soldier escaping a bloody defeat. She marches so for perhaps half an hour. Then she slackens her pace and offers up some commonplace topic for conversation. I respond. She helps me along, and soon we are in the midst of the most delightful chat. It is only when she has outrun her demons that she graces me with a smile.

At last, when the cheese was brought in, Egremont looked squarely at Turner and said, "Come, this will hardly do. How goes your work, Turner?"

Turner looked up from his port. Something like a smile appeared on his face. "I am sorry, my lord. Behaving like a beast. Never before have I struggled as I have struggled this past fortnight. It takes its toll. It goes well, damn well, although I fear it may be the death of me. There comes a time in all of my paintings—all my paintings, you know, with weight: *Dido, Ulysses, Regulus*—when I feel like one of those naked fellows in the arena. Lions all about; other fellows with spears. The crowd roaring. Thumbs up? Thumbs down? One way seems as likely as another. Harrowing. But exhilarating too. Quite out of myself. More myself than ever. It's a queer business. But that is why I have come down tonight. I am done with models, sir and madam." He looked first at me and then at Mrs. Spencer. "I thank you both. You have been patient with me. You have been skillful. And, I hope, forgiving." He raised his glass to me, and then to Mrs. Spencer. He held her eye for a moment, before turning to Egremont.

"My lord," he said. "Our two friends have been most able assistants. I have asked much of them, and they have provided it. But, as I said, I am done with them. I must now gird myself for the final battle. I will not, begging your permission, take my meals with you any longer. Not until I am done. Or undone. I will send down for what I require, but do not expect to see me. If I should happen to go out for air, do not detain me. I know myself in these times. I will not be fit company. Pray forgive me. And now I shall bid you good night."

Turner rose to go, and we all bade him good night in return. Egremont added, "Godspeed, my friend, Godspeed." Turner was visibly touched by His Lordship's condescension, but he left the room hurriedly, without saying anything further.

He was as good as his word. I saw him only once in the week following, when I was sitting in the Carved Room with my book. Hearing footsteps on the Portico, I looked up and saw Turner, dressed against the rain in an oilskin coat such as a sailor might wear. He marched off into the wind, gesticulating to some internal interlocutor.

Mrs. Spencer and I were much together during this time. If the weather was fine we walked, but most often we sat together and read or engaged in desultory conversation. I began work on that article which was eventually published in *The Westminster Review* and which you were so kind as to say you admired. Sometimes Egremont joined us, although mostly he busied himself about matters of the estate. Time seemed suspended between the days that had been and the days that were to be.

It was about ten days after Turner had last joined us for dinner, the evening of October 23, 1830, when a servant entered and handed a note to Lord Egremont as the three of us were at our evening meal. He read it and handed it to Mrs. Spencer, who read it in turn and then handed it to me.

My lord,

I have completed my labours. I beg Your Lordship's atten-dance tomorrow morning, when the light is best. I shall send word when I am ready. I have done all that I can do.

Believe me,

My dear Lord Egremont,

J.M.W.T.

We all looked at each other. "We shall see," said Egremont, "what all this huffing and puffing is about. He goes too far, I think. But the morning shall tell the story."

I hardly slept that night. I felt like a child on the eve of some great holiday, or a soldier on the eve of some great battle. When I arrived in the breakfast room, Mrs. Spencer was already there. She confessed that she too had passed a sleepless night. A few minutes later Egremont arrived. He called in Mr. Gregs and made a great show of going over accounts as he drank his coffee, but he too seemed distracted and on edge. Mrs. Spencer whispered to me that His Lordship had also tossed and turned all night.

The coffee was cold, and poor Mr. Gregs had hardly ever seen his master so contrary by the time John, one of Egremont's most trusted old servants, arrived. We had been waiting for about an hour by then. He stood before Egremont with his hands folded deferentially in front of him. He spoke awkwardly and formally, as if Turner had asked him to memorize his little speech.

"My lord," he said, "Mr. Turner most humbly requests the honor of your presence upstairs in the studio."

Egremont forgot his dignity to the extent that he was up and out of his chair before old John had quite finished. When he left the room Mrs. Spencer reached over and grabbed my hand, looking decidedly ashen. "I feel that I will be undone. But there is nothing for it but patience. The die was cast long ago."

We had only been alone together for about ten minutes when old John returned, moving as fast as I had ever seen him. "Madam," he said, "His Lordship bids you come upstairs at once. At once," he repeated. "I have been in his service these sixty years and never heard him so agitated. Please, madam, hurry."

Mrs. Spencer turned pale. She rose quickly and rushed off, only turning at the door to give me a pitiful look. I felt sorry for her.

Alone except for a servant who had come to clear away the breakfast things, I felt superfluous. I began to feel, David, that my time at Petworth must soon come to an end and that my dream of Paradise was over. I had taken part in the production of something momentous, but I was not a central character in the play; I was not even one of those peasants who tells the hero which way the army went. If I was anything I was a prop or a bit of decoration, perhaps an empty chalice sitting on a sideboard.

As I was engaged in these gloomy reflections, standing by the window overlooking the park, I saw Turner walking down toward the pond. He had his hands thrust deep into his pockets and his hat pushed back on his head. There was a spring to his step that I had never seen before. He appeared to be whistling.

I asked for more tea and took up my book. I think I sat for about an hour; I read perhaps four pages, although, when the hour was up and old John came in again, I had no idea what I had read.

He stood before me in the same formal pose he had taken when he spoke to Egremont earlier. "Mr. Grant," he repeated, "Mr. Turner most humbly requests the honor of your presence upstairs in the studio." He bowed and indicated that I should follow him. I did as he requested, feeling more than a little foolish, as if I was a child enacting some pantomime. When we reached the door of the studio, John bowed again and with the same gesture pointed to the door. "Mr. Turner, sir, bids you enter." As soon as he spoke these words he turned on his heel and left. It was an absurd performance. I would have laughed except that I was almost overcome with anticipation and dread.

I opened the door to the studio. Turner had set up a black curtain on the small platform where I had posed for him. All his painting materials had been put away and the room seemed curiously bare and imposing. The late morning air came in through the open windows, but the breeze could make little headway against the smell of paint and spirits that was Turner's stock-in-trade. An ornate cord, such as you might find on a bell pull or a tapestry hanging, was attached to the front of the curtain.

Turner, who had been standing behind the screen where I had changed out of my clothes when I was posing for him, stepped forward. He must have used the back entrance when he returned from his walk. He bowed to me gravely, but there was a sparkle in his eye. He pointed toward the cord. "With my compliments, sir," he said. "But first allow me to take my leave."

The curtain fell to the floor. The painting was sitting on Turner's easel, adorned with a simple gilt frame. There was a second black curtain behind it. The light flowed in from the windows behind my back, but my face was suddenly warm from the light that poured forth from the painting and illuminated my soul. I felt an understanding in my body like that I felt when you first took me to your chamber and introduced me to the mysteries of love. It was the purest moment I had ever known. I saw not only Helen in all her glory, but into the heart of the life the gods have given us. The vast chasm between Homer's world and Homer's truth and our world and our truth evaporated in an instant. Everything seemed clear and beautiful and holy.

When you took me to your chamber you gave me the greatest gift I had ever received, but I remember well my doubts, my sense of sin, my sense that no matter what we did, you were you, dear David, and I was mere sinful Charles Grant. What we had that night was as deep a pleasure as our fallen world allows, but when I looked at Turner's painting my sense of sin, my sense of self, disappeared. I was left with nothing but light and beauty.

I could not so much see the beautiful gods as feel their presence. They lived in the light. I knew their invisible hands directed the golden ships that I could see on the far horizon. It was their hands that directed the flight of the spears which the heroes hurled at each other on the plain beneath the many-towered city. I cannot do justice to the clarity of the vision. It was less that I could see what I have just attempted to describe than that I knew it was true.

In the foreground I saw Helen in her chamber, in a high tower overlooking the battlefield. She is the source of all light, but I cannot describe the trick of paint that made it so. The world of gods and heroes rages outside on the plain, but for that Helen has no regard. She is light. She is sublimely indifferent to the pain and suffering of the entangled armies. Her eyes are only for her lover Paris, who approaches. Her eyes, which I could only see reflected in the mirror, met mine as I viewed the painting. I saw myself in the figure of Paris who approaches her as she lies ready on her couch. It was my flesh as Turner had painted it that approached the divine beauty and they were my eyes that met her gaze. I saw that I had been perfected, but I knew that I was lost.

. 41 .

:⊷: THE YOUNG COUPLE had disappeared, to continue their quarrel elsewhere. We had the room of unfinished Turners to ourselves. At first we just wandered from painting to painting. We paused a moment before each one, and then, as if by some sympathetic magic, moved on together to the next one. For the longest time we didn't say anything. The beauty of the colors was made more pure by the beauty of the woman who was standing next to me, moving when I moved. The sound of her breathing and the smell of her perfume got all mixed up in what I saw on the canvas. It was like a diluted version of looking at *The Center of the World.*

After we had made a relatively quick circuit of the room we started talking about the paintings. We had to lean close together to make out each other's words. Her hair, I thought, smelled like light.

"I don't think these are unfinished," I said. "They just are what they are. Turner was interested in the play of light and color. He used these canvases to work out his ideas about those interplays. When he had taken the idea to its logical conclusion or to some place where it just couldn't go any further, he was done. He must have resented the fact that his audience wanted him to put in all those castles and mountains. He had to represent stuff that his audience would recognize as an appropriate subject for art because he had to make a living."

I went on and on, half amazed that I was making as much sense as I was. I don't remember half the things I said, but I remember the way she looked at me, as if what I said mattered. She told me she didn't know much about art, but everything she said seemed really smart.

At last the spell was broken when a museum guard announced that it was closing time. I looked at my watch.

"I had no idea it was so late," I said.

"Neither did I. I have to get back to my hotel and put together my slides for tomorrow's meeting."

We stood together for a few moments on the steps in front of the Tate, watching the low sun break through the clouds. One of the river ferries was pulling off into the Thames.

"It is almost a Turner sunset," she said.

"Which way is your hotel?" She was staying at the InterContinental near Hyde Park Corner, she said, but she was going to walk even though it was a bit of a hike. "It's my last day in London and I thought I might as well see some of the street life."

I told her that my hotel was in that general direction, although it wasn't true. When I asked if she would mind if I kept her company, she smiled at me and said she would be delighted.

As we walked up Vauxhall Bridge Road we continued talking about Turner. We wondered what he would make of this modern city: the cars, the smog, the jets inscribing white contrails against the sky. At some point the conversation changed gears.

"At first I felt like some character in a bad TV show," she said. "I'd be sitting in the apartment waiting for him to come home. Then he'd call to say he had to stay late at work. Don't wait up for me. When he finally got in I thought I could smell some other woman's perfume on him. It was driving me crazy. In the morning I'd ask him if he'd been with someone else and he'd get angry. He kept saying that if I didn't trust him I should leave. And so I didn't leave, and I felt guilty for suspecting him. But then he goofed up on his email, and I got a note that he meant to send to her. All sorts of porn star details; it was gross. He couldn't deny it; he moved out. We still talk, but it never goes anywhere."

"He's a jerk and a fool. You need to make a clean break of it. I don't know much, but I know he doesn't deserve you."

"I'm such an idiot about this stuff."

"It's difficult," I replied. "I think my wife is sleeping with someone else, too. I'm not sure, but I think so. But I don't want to leave either."

"You wouldn't happen to have a cigarette, would you?" she asked.

I was so glad I had bought some. I took out my pack and shook one out for her. I held the match for her and then lit my own. It was like in the movies.

We walked along in silence for half a block. Perhaps I had lost enough weight to make a difference. I almost forgot that I was nearly old enough to be her father. We were both, I thought, bathed in light, and that made all the difference.

She stopped suddenly and grasped my hand. Her touch was soft and cool, but strong and determined.

"I like talking to you, but if we are going to talk, we have to talk about something else. Please."

I nodded. Of course she was right. I was about to make an ass of myself and she knew it.

"So," she said, "wouldn't it be wonderful to own one of those Turners? Just have one in your living room so that you could look at it all day?"

I think I paused for a moment, as a flash of alarm and suspicion crossed my brain, but then I looked at her and was overwhelmed by her smile. "It would be too much for me," I said. "I think I would disappear."

"I don't understand," she said. She stopped walking and looked up at me.

"I'm too small," I said. "My life and my heart are not large enough. If one of those canvases could fit into my living room it would take over everything."

"But they are just pictures," she protested.

"No," I said. "I've been in London for almost a week. Most days I've gone to the Tate or the National Gallery. I've spent I don't know how many hours standing in front of those Turners. I can't explain it. I feel overwhelmed by the beauty and the light, by the divinity on the canvas. I would disappear." I was, of course, talking about *The Center of the World,* not the Turners I had just seen. Looking back, I see that this was the first hint of the true nature of the risk that the painting posed for me.

"You are an odd person," she said.

"If you knew me in New Jersey, you'd think there was nothing odd about me at all. A typical middle-aged guy, who works at a decent white-collar job. Two Volvos—one wagon, one sedan—with a combined two hundred and fifty thousand miles on them. But there's something about being here in London, cast off from my moorings, that makes me think about stuff I usually don't." I paused and looked at her. Her face was a gift. "I'm sorry. You wanted to talk about Turner and look what I've done."

Her laugh made me smile. "I guess," I said, "it would be nice to have one of those watercolors. I think I could handle that."

We managed to chat contentedly as we walked along, avoiding any deep waters. She told me about her work and her colleagues; I did the same.

"Here we are," she said. "That was a nice walk. I needed to get some air and stretch my legs. But I'm sorry to have bored you with my pathetic troubles. You're a good listener. Can I buy you a drink in the swanky hotel bar by way of thanks?"

I looked into her eyes and saw a promise of some happiness that was more profound than any I had thought to know in this world. Her eyes were Helen's, and the skin under her shirt would be as soft and fragrant as a goddess's. I stood there like an idiot for I don't know how long.

"I don't think so," I said at length. "I have to pack and get organized before my flight tomorrow."

She took my hand. "You're probably right. You may be an even better guy than I thought." She stood up on her toes and planted a kiss on my cheek before I knew what was happening. "Good-bye." I watched her disappear into the hotel.

I put my hand on the place where her lips had touched me. I could still feel the warm pressure and the hint of moisture, and wondered if there was a trace of her lipstick on my face. Who would ever have known? How could I have been so faithless as to turn away from Helen's gift? Had she taught me nothing?

. 42 .

I CANNOT SAY HOW much time passed with only the four of us in the deserted house. But I do recall the day that Turner told us at dinner that he had no further use for me. It was time, he said, for him to shoulder the work alone. I felt, I confess, some pang of disappointment. I could not tell if it was because I had come to love my shame or if I felt regret that my small part in the great work was now come to an end.

Turner was never a man who paid much regard to appearances, but now he seemed no longer part of our world at all. His conversation, always rough and eccentric, descended to the level of grunts and nods. When we saw him it was at dusk, just as the light was failing. He would leave the house quietly and walk through the park for a while, seeming more like a ghost than a man.

Grant, Egremont, and I ate by ourselves. Do what I could, none of us had much to say. Grant, bless him, would speak of what he had been reading. I would try some observation about the state of the park and ask Egremont about the progress of his improvements. In the past this was a topic that had always excited his interest, but now he was impatient and short-tempered. Our meals were over quickly. Some evenings he asked me to read to him, some to play the harpsichord, but neither words nor music had the power to keep his attention for long. He had me come up to the bedroom, and we would both toss and turn into the early hours. Sometimes I would wrap myself in my gown and walk the halls of the great house like the spirit of one of Egremont's ancestors. Sometimes I would find Grant in the library and interrupt his studies. One night when it was warm I stepped out onto the Portico and looked up. I could see the light in Turner's studio and his shadow on the window as he paced back and forth.

I remember the date—it was October 23, 1830—and that Egremont, Grant, and I had just sat down to our dinner when old John came in and handed His Lordship a note from Turner. He would be most appreciative if we would gather in the breakfast room in the morning at about eight o'clock, when the light was best, so that he could call us up one by one to see what had been accomplished.

The three of us looked at each other. My chest grew tight for a moment as I thought of how my two companions would see me in the morning. Grant and I exchanged a glance, and I knew that similar thoughts were going through his mind.

"We shall see at last," Egremont said, "what all this fuss is about. Turner has genius, to be sure, but these last days he has carried it with too high a hand. But perhaps the end will justify all. We shall see."

Our meal was brought out and we all picked at our food. After a few minutes Egremont put down his fork. "I have no relish for my meat. If this is all that comes from Turner's tricks he shall have hell to pay. You two may continue, but I will take a walk with the dogs."

In the morning we all gathered in the breakfast room at an early hour. Egremont and I had hardly slept. Grant did not look well rested either. We attempted to make conversation, but the effort failed.

At last old John came in. He bowed and walked a few steps into the room, where he stood stock still, like a character in a play. "My lord," he said, "Mr. Turner begs your company in the studio."

Egremont rose quickly and rushed out. An expression of surprise appeared on John's normally impassive face as he saw his master move so quickly at another man's behest. He followed Egremont out the door. I looked at Grant. He returned my look. "Our fates," I said, "are hanging in the balance."

Hardly ten minutes had gone by before John returned. He seemed frightened and asked me to come upstairs as quickly as I could. Without pausing to ask any questions, I rushed toward the door. I looked back at poor young Grant. His beautiful face looked like death. My mind was full of terrible thoughts. Egremont was of an age where he might have a stroke at any time. I thought that he might be lying on the floor demanding my attendance. As I ran down the corridor toward the studio, I saw Turner walking toward me. He looked thinner and pale, but there was a queer smile on his face. But I did not stop because I could hear Egremont calling my name with a kind of desperate urgency.

Egremont, a mad gleam in his eyes, was pointing at a canvas propped up on the easel. I feared he was in the midst of some species of fit. "Look at this, damn it, look at this!" he cried.

What I first saw was light. The world and my own mind suddenly grew quiet. All my fears vanished. Petworth House itself, the room I was standing in, the life that had brought me to this place and the moment I was living in all disappeared. There was nothing but the light. I cannot describe it except to say that it seemed I was seeing light itself.

Gradually the images out of which the painting was composed emerged, resolving themselves into something I can remember. I was in the center, but I was not myself. There was a sea beyond, a field below, a room filled with unbearable beauty, and I knew that all of them existed only for me and because of me. Beautiful boats returning from glorious lands dotted the sea, beautiful men struggled on the plain. I could see the sweat on their glistening bodies and the blood that flowed from their wounds. I wanted to weep for the horror and the shame of it, so many beautiful young men, so much suffering and dying. But I could not be sad because I could hear music, simple and sweet, yet like no other music I had ever heard, ringing in the air. I knew that it had been produced by the lyre, the lyre I had flung down and that was leaning against the side of the dressing table. It was such beautiful music! In all the years since I first saw the painting I have only sometimes been able to make out small snatches of it, but in that first moment I could hear it clearly. And I wondered if it was not the lyre, but the sound of the gods themselves, speaking to each other as they hovered invisibly over the battlefield, that I heard.

I became aware of Egremont saying something and pressing up behind me in a kind of dream. I found myself on the couch on which Turner had had me pose. I could not speak nor take my eyes off the painting. I could feel Egremont fussing with my dress and then with my under things. I lifted myself up for him and he came into me. I saw Grant more beautiful than I had ever hoped to see him, I saw my own smile in the mirror urging me on. I met Egremont's thrusts and felt the heat of all the love I had ever hoped for and all the love I could remember. I dissolved into the blue of the sea.

· 43 ·

To: arthur@madisonpartners.com
From: gbolton@madisonpartners.com
Date: October 11, 2003
Subject: RE: RE: RE: Change of plans

Yesterday I met Barry at the Tate and had him point our
guy out to me. He's less prepossessing in life than even
the photos in his house would suggest. He was wearing ill-fitting slacks and a sweater. Not a lot of hair, and
what there was needed to be cut. He has a funny shuf-
fling sort of walk, and there is something odd and hesi-
tant in his movements. He seems an unlikely candidate
for a blessing, but, as you have pointed out, the only ones
who could truly deserve this are those who seek it.

He stood out from the other tourists in that he seemed
to be struggling with the paintings. He stood in front of

each one for a long time, often circling back to the same
paintings over and over again. I felt that he was looking
for something, much as you and I are, but that he isn't
sure what it is. There was a puzzled and desperate look
on his face.

I first let him see me in the room with the unfinished
paintings. I wasn't quite dressed as if I was going to meet
Mr. Ashford, but I confess to having taken some pains
to make myself appear interesting. The cafeteria was
crowded, so I had a reasonable excuse for sitting down at
his table. He wasn't wearing his wedding ring, although
I could see the mark it had left on his finger. It was easy
to get him to talk; it always is with men who have their
wedding rings in their pockets.

I have to admit, I half warmed to him as we made small
talk. I said that I worked for an investment firm and was
here from New York on a short business trip. He told me
about himself; nothing that wasn't true, but nothing we
didn't know. I had expected, frankly, for the floodgates
to open and for him to pour out his life story. Middle-
aged men are somehow drawn to me. I can't tell you all
the things I have learned in airport departure lounges
or, God help us, on the plane itself. I thought my charms
had deserted me. I said I was happy I'd had a chance
to get to the Tate. I told him that Turner had been my
favorite painter since I studied art in college. It was so

refreshing to get to see the Turners after two days of sitting in hotel meeting rooms and staring at PowerPoint presentations.

He finally lit up a bit and said that Turner was very important to him too. It was only his second trip to London. He had been once before while he was in graduate school and had been longing to get back. He was on a business trip too, he said, and I could see the lightbulbs begin to go off as he thought about two lonely Americans in London.

We chatted about Turner. He is no expert, and very naive in terms of his art historical understanding, but he's not stupid either. He is one of those people who sincerely believe, I think, that art can reveal "the Truth." He doesn't know what truth he is looking for, but seems to believe that if he stares at Turner long enough it will reveal itself. It is sort of sweet, actually.

I was getting tired of him, so I told him I had to get back to my hotel. He asked me where I was staying; he said his hotel was on the way; would I mind if we walked together. This was the first thing he lied about. We continued our conversation about Turner on the way. It occurred to me that if I appeared to share his enthusiasm he might reveal any secrets he had in an attempt to make himself interesting to an attractive young woman. When

we got to the InterContinental, I asked him if he wanted
to come in for a drink. For a moment I thought he was on
the verge of revealing something, or perhaps just taking
the plunge that middle-aged men always want to take.
But he said no to the drink and went on his way. I went
into the hotel bar to wash my hands and have a glass of
wine before heading back to the apartment.

Barry had been following us and he picked him up at
the hotel. He continued walking away from his hotel
toward Hyde Park, then toward the Brompton Oratory,
and then back up toward Bloomsbury before heading
back to Westminster. He gave Barry quite a tour, and
he told me he may put in for a new pair of shoes. He
stopped at a number of pubs and eventually at a cheap
Indian place for dinner. At closing time he was at a pub
not too far away from his hotel. In the morning he was
on the early flight out of Gatwick.

He's a sad guy; one of those middle-aged guys who
missed the party and knows it. If he had been touched
by the thing we seek surely something would have
rubbed off. He's got no patina whatsoever.

How do you like Singapore?
Cheers,
Gina

. 44 .

THE JEWELS, I REMEMBERED, had been dropped carelessly on the floor. They were the same jewels I had seen on Jessica's neck at Petworth. No other woman had ever earned such a treasure, and no queen had ever been so careless of her fortune.

It was early October and I was back in Princeton, feeling as though I was disappearing from my own life. My dreams of Helen and my regrets about England were on the verge of overwhelming me. I thought of Helen sitting at the little golden table, dressed in nothing but nearly invisible silks; I thought of Gina turning her back on me and walking into the hotel. Helen picks up the jewels and examines them: gold and diamonds from India, rubies from Persia, emeralds from Egypt. Gina takes the lift up to her room, undresses, and takes a shower. She sits in her nightgown and works at her laptop. Helen sees the fire that glows from within a perfect gem and lets it fall to the floor, where a kitten paws the bauble. Gina hits save, takes her nightgown off, and slips into bed.

Helen was the saddest woman who ever lived. My own sorrows and complaints seemed petty and hardly worth considering compared to hers. The golden cup from which she and Menelaus had drunk on their wedding night was on her table, but it was filled with shells she had picked up when she wandered on the beach after she first arrived in Troy. There was a jewel-encrusted knife on the table that had once been given to Menelaus in tribute. She had whispered into his ear and the knife was hers. Men are such fools. Sometimes she thought of taking the beautiful blade and cutting into the flesh of her perfect cheek. If only, she thought, men did not always find me so beautiful, if only their foolishness did not make my beauty a burden.

And Gina's beauty must be a burden to her as well, I thought. While she was trying to make things work out with her stupid husband, men were probably falling all over her. I felt like an ass for not getting any contact information. All I knew is that her name was Gina. How many Ginas were there in New York? How many were that beautiful? Even if I found her, what chance would I have?

My memory of what had happened in London changed as time passed. Gina became more willing to spend the night with me, while my refusal to cross the threshold of the hotel seemed simply idiotic. I spent hours staring at my computer at work, lost in these and similar thoughts. I made a couple of serious errors in the process—a note from a major donor went unanswered, there was an extra digit in an award letter that I sent out. And at the same time, I was worried about how to find the money to fix the house at the lake. Should I just sell it to Moss-bacher? And should I sell the painting? I could be rich beyond any dreams of money that I had ever had, but the thought of parting with the painting was more than I could bear. I needed to see it again, but I was trapped in my house in Princeton with Susan. And underneath it all, the bass notes that anchored my mania, was the thought that Susan was seeing somebody else.

As time passed I became more and more certain of it. She often had to work late in those days, and she occasionally spent the night in the city. It's clear to me now that her "infidelity" was an excuse to justify the essential lie that my life with her had become. Because the face that I showed her was false, I became certain that hers was false as well.

We quarreled frequently in those days, mostly over things that had nothing to do with what mattered. Usually the subject was her perception that I had become sullen and uncommunicative.

"I cannot live with you if you won't talk to me," she said.

"What is there to talk about? I'm fine. You work a lot; I work. We've been married for over twenty years: we've said all the things that need saying," I would answer, and so back and forth, with the truth about the painting gnawing at me like an ulcer.

I had not, I confess, expected her to take the initiative, nor had I allowed myself to see how bad things had become. It was the coward's way out: I didn't have the courage to take any action so I did nothing until the situation became unbearable to her.

One Saturday morning she was in the kitchen drinking coffee when I came downstairs.

"I am not happy being here with you," she said. "Something is going on. I don't think you're messing around with Ruth Carpenter, but something happened in London and you're not telling me about it."

"Nothing happened in London. I gave a talk. I walked around. I saw some pictures."

"I don't think you're lying, but I don't think you're telling the truth either."

Her friend Julie had taken a three-month assignment at the Chicago office, she told me. Susan was going to stay in her apartment in exchange for watering the plants and feeding the cat. It would give us both, she said, time to think.

"I've packed my bags. I'd like you to drive me to the station."

It occurred to me that I ought to play the injured husband and let her know that I knew why she wanted to stay in New York, but the world of possibility I saw opening up before me rendered me dumb.

"Don't you have anything to say?" I saw that tears were starting to form in the corners of her eyes. "I was hoping you would ask me to stay."

"It's not a bad idea," I said at last. "You're not happy; I'm not happy. Some time apart might be good."

I carried her bags up the stairs to the platform. They seemed heavy with the weight of our marriage, but also with possibility. The platform was crowded with people going to a matinee. I wondered who would be there to witness her leaving. Word gets around pretty quickly in Princeton.

When the light of the train appeared in the distance, she planted a kiss on my cheek. "I want to love you," she said, "but I need you to talk to me. Call me when you want to talk. And take care of yourself."

She struggled onto the train with her big legal briefcase and the two suitcases.

I watched the train recede into the distance. I touched the place on my cheek that was still wet with her tears and wiped it with the back of my hand. I got in my car and headed straight for the mountains. The world was before me.

. 45 .

❧ WHEN I CAME DOWNSTAIRS I found them all gathered in the Carved Room. Lord Egremont himself handed me a glass of champagne. "Come," he said, "this will do you good. We have been toasting Mr. Turner's great success." I took the proffered glass and raised it in Turner's direction before swallowing it off in a gulp.

"I thought that you might never come down," Turner said. There was a sparkle in his eyes that had only something to do with champagne.

I looked at Turner as I held out my glass for more. "I am overwhelmed, sir. How long was I in the studio?"

Turner smiled and took out his timepiece. "Well over an hour. I thought we might have lost you."

"I had no idea. Time has been altered," I said. "If you had said ten minutes, if you had said a year, I would have believed you."

"He has outdone himself, has he not?" Lord Egremont said. I turned to face my host. He was seated in an armchair, with his arm around Mrs. Spencer's waist. I had never seen her look more beautiful.

"I hardly know what to say," I said. "It is not a painting that you have made. It is something else altogether."

"But you like it?" Turner asked with a laugh.

"Like it? I suppose I do, but it is not the sort of thing one likes. It is like breathing or sunshine or fire or water. It exists. It is true. It is most beautiful. I can think of nothing else to say."

Turner beamed like a schoolboy who had just stolen a sweet without being noticed.

"I had always known," I said, "that the world was beautiful and we were blessed to be alive in it. But I had never quite felt what that meant until now." I drank some more champagne. My hand, I saw, was shaking. "But," I went on, turning to Mrs. Spencer, "has not Mr. Turner played us a cruel trick? Will this world suffice now that we have seen what we have? Can we live knowing what we now know?"

I must have seemed half mad to her, for she detached herself from her lord's grip and came over to me. "You are overexcited," she said, putting her hand on my shoulder. "I felt that way myself when I first saw it. You will soon become yourself again. It is only a painting, although a very great one." Her touch calmed me.

I asked for tea, the champagne having gone to my head in a way I found disagreeable. I sat down and looked across at Turner. It was impossible to reconcile the ugly little man in the greasy suit with the vision of Helen that he had created. He was in the midst of telling one of his vulgar stories about his travels—this one involved a French countess and a chamber pot. As he reached the conclusion Mrs. Spencer and Lord Egremont joined him in his laughter.

Turner reared his head back and brayed like a donkey. He has only a few teeth left and of those that remain most are broken and all are dingy.

But gradually, as the conversation of my friends enveloped me, I came out of the dream into which I had been plunged and felt more and more like myself. I was even able to say a few sensible things about Turner's masterwork, which pleased the artist and earned me grateful looks from both Egremont and Mrs. Spencer.

We had been thus together for about an hour when Lord Egremont said he wanted to go up to the studio and discuss some matters of business with Turner. When I recollect this moment, I seem to remember that Egremont nodded at Mrs. Spencer in what seemed a purposeful way, but whether or not that was the case, Mrs. Spencer proposed that I should accompany her on a walk about the grounds. "The weather," she said, "has turned fine. We two have much to discuss. And the exercise will do us good. Come, let us go to the Rotunda."

My heart sank at these words, for I knew somehow that they meant my days at Petworth would soon come to an end. But I said that nothing would please me more than to revisit that wonderful spot in her company, and gave her my arm.

We walked along in silence for a time, but gradually she managed to draw me out on the beauty of the scenery and other neutral topics. I was in a kind of daze, with the images from the painting commingling in my mind with the beauty of my surroundings. I could not tell if what I had seen in the painting had made the world more beautiful or if this beautiful world had become nothing more than a pale reflection of what Turner had shown me. When Mrs. Spencer spoke, and I turned to look at her face, I saw Helen, the idea for which so many heroes had died, so many cities had been destroyed, so many empires sacked. It was a miracle that I could keep my feet steady.

On reaching the Rotunda we stood for a moment and admired the view. I felt tears forming in my eyes. When I turned to look at Mrs. Spencer, she was looking straight ahead and tears were running down her cheeks as well.

She turned to me. "His Lordship bade me tell you that it is time for you to leave us." Her eyes met mine for a long moment, but then she burst into sobs and threw her arms around me. I too began to weep, and we held each other for I do not know how long, until the paroxysm passed and we sat down on one of the little carved benches and busied ourselves with our handkerchiefs.

When we were both somewhat collected, she turned to me and took my hands in hers. "Those," she said, "were the hardest words I have ever spoken. You will understand I had no choice. But you must believe me when I say that I will be eternally grateful for your kindness and sympathy. I could not have survived this time without your company. It breaks my heart. But this is the way of the world, especially for the likes of us."

I told her that I had known this moment would come, but that I had tried to delude myself into thinking it could be avoided or postponed. I told her that her company had meant a great deal to me and that I would be forever in her debt. I told her that she was the most beautiful person I had ever known, and that her beauty had reached a painful pitch of perfection since I had seen her reflection in Turner's painting.

"Egremont," she said after a few moments, "is also exceedingly grateful to you. He recognizes that Turner's great work could not have succeeded without you, and he too feels in your debt. This painting has delighted him beyond all measure, beyond all the other works in his collection."

"As well it should," I said, "for we have witnessed the creation of something extraordinary."

"His Lordship," she went on, "has come, like me, to delight in your company. You have brought both youth and sense to Petworth House, he says, and he thinks you are a young man of great promise. He wishes to support you as you make your way in the world. You will find, when we return to the house, a check for five hundred pounds, as well as a promise that every year at this time you will receive three hundred pounds as long as Lord Egremont lives. There is, of course, a condition. There always is for the likes of us. You must never, as you are a gentleman, speak to any living soul of Turner's painting and the time that we have passed together."

This offer made me feel like a common whore, making cheap what was most dear. Mrs. Spencer saw my thoughts in my face and redoubled the pressure on my hands.

"I know what you are thinking," she said. "You must not, for my sake. Knowledge of this painting must never come out in my lifetime, or I would be a ruined woman. I am no Helen, I know, but I can be recognized in that painting down to the very mole on my upper thigh."

"But I need not be bribed," I snapped back, "to protect the honor and reputation of a lady I admire. I am a gentleman, after all."

"Don't be a fool," she said. "'Lady' and 'gentleman' are very precarious words. This is your great chance. If there are any sins, the greatest is to turn your back on good fortune. The world is too cruel." She fixed her eyes on mine for a moment and her tone softened. "And besides," she said, "you must do this for me and the sake of the pleasant hours we have passed in each other's company. Although the money is Lord Egremont's, you must think of it as a gift from me also. We must part, but in the years to come it will give me no small joy to think of you making your way in the world and knowing I had some small part in assisting you."

I saw a depth of love in her eyes that I had not seen before, and felt I was in communion with a creature half divine. I raised her two hands to my lips and kissed them.

We walked back in silence; the time for speech had passed. When we arrived at the house I found that all my things had been packed except for my books and papers. Egremont's carriage was waiting to take me to the coach.

I went up to the room which had been mine and gathered my few remaining possessions, taking one last look at the portrait of Lady Mary that had kept watch over me. I wanted to take a final look around the galleries, but I saw that my departure, like a well-conducted execution, was to be swift.

Mrs. Spencer came out, flushed but still radiant. "His Lordship," she said, "is feeling indisposed, the events of this morning having been quite taxing. He sends you his compliments and his most profound thanks." She handed me an envelope that was closed with Egremont's seal. "I do not know when and if we shall see each other again. I hope, at the very least, to hear of you. I will not now repeat those words I spoke at the Rotunda, but know that I meant them from the bottom of my heart."

"I fear," I said, "that these days at Petworth, and my time with you and Turner, have made me into some creature 'rich and strange.' I doubt that I shall know myself when I return to the larger world."

"Do not fear it. There is a goodness and a beauty in you that will prevail against all odds."

I thanked her again for her kindness and asked after Turner. She said she was surprised that he hadn't appeared, as he had been informed of my departure. She needed to go back to His Lordship, but she would send a servant to fetch him. Then, taking me by the hands again, she kissed me on the cheek and, quicker than thought, was gone.

The driver told me that we must be off in five minutes or we would certainly miss the coach to London. I waited as long as I could before climbing into the carriage. Just as the driver was about to set his whip to the horses, I heard a cry, and saw Turner running as fast as his short legs would carry him.

He was flushed and out of breath when he arrived at the carriage door. He thrust a small portfolio through the window.

"Sorry. Time and its fleet wings, you know. You are a good fellow and I am much obliged to you. I thought these might be of interest. With my compliments."

I grasped his hand and told him that I admired him above all other artists and that I had been privileged to play a small part in the creation of his masterpiece. Turner brushed my compliments aside, but I could see that he was pleased. The driver, meanwhile, reminded us most urgently that I was about to miss my coach.

"Off with you, then! Time and tide, you know, and the London coach waits for no man. Godspeed!"

The carriage rattled off. As we drove down the drive I turned and saw Turner waving his handkerchief. He was but a small figure dwarfed by the imposing bulk of Petworth House.

We reached the inn with only a few minutes to spare. I took my seat on the coach and soon I was on my way. I had hardly thought what was to become of me, David. My departure had been so sudden that I had time neither to despair nor to plan. I knew I wished to return to your arms, but I felt, and the sequel proved me right, that it would be hard for our friendship to be what it had been. I was hardly civil to the two other passengers, as I thought of the small set of rooms that awaited me. An uncertain world, I reflected, was before me, and Paradise behind, never to be regained.

At length I opened the envelope that Mrs. Spencer had handed me. True to her promise there was a check for five hundred pounds. Also a note:

Dear Charles,

*I had not the courage to say this when we parted, but
we must never see each other again. As you are a gentleman,
please do not seek me out. If I seem cruel, you must believe that
I am acting according to what is best for both of us. I hold you
more dear than my poor words can express.*

Godspeed.

I sat back in my seat and watched the countryside go by through my tears. I do not know if my fellow passengers noticed, but I was beyond caring. When my eyes were dry I opened the portfolio Turner had handed me. There were three sketches inside, carefully separated by soft white paper, as well as a note hastily scribbled on the back of the artist's card:

With my compliments, and in memory of our time together.

J.M.W.T.

The first sketch was the portrait of me that he had done that rainy morning in the Carved Room. There was a kind of agony in my expression that seemed more appropriate to the way I felt now than to how I had felt when the likeness was taken. It was as if Turner had seen what I was to become after the events at Petworth. The second was a pencil sketch that showed me as a handsome young man. I had an air of easy confidence that I had never seen when I looked into the mirror. There was a small inscription in the upper left corner of the drawing: "To

Mrs. Grant. Compliments of the artist, J.M.W.T." I felt a pang of guilt when I saw that Turner had been considerate where I had not. I had only written to my poor mother once or twice during the whole time I was at Petworth and had received half a dozen letters in return. I resolved at once to go visit her after I had got myself settled in London.

The last sheet was a portrait of Mrs. Spencer. She was seated on the red velvet settee I knew so well from the studio, wearing a loose dressing gown, negligently fastened to reveal the Egremont family jewels adorning her bosom. It was a good likeness of her, unlike *Jessica*; anyone who saw it would have immediately recognized Lord Egremont's mistress. Yet there was something, mostly in her eyes and perhaps her lips, that hinted at Helen's glory. I was quite confident that Turner had given me one of those preliminary sketches that had occupied so much of his time and effort in the early days of his work. The image before me was poised between the memory of the woman I admired and the Helen that I had seen so briefly earlier that day. For me, and for me alone, this sketch would be both a remembrance of the happy days at Petworth and a hint of that secret and forbidden glory that is *The Center of the World*.

. 46 .

IT WAS MUCH MORE beautiful, much more wondrous than I had remembered. It was as if I had never seen it before. No one alive had ever seen anything like it, I reminded myself. There was no me, no marriage, no wife in New York fucking some guy who looked no better than I did. Sometimes my eyes would leave the plane of the painting to focus on something in the barn or something that I could see through the barn window. I would become aware of an old chair that needed a bottom or the crosshatch of branches against the sky. As I focused on these things, I came back into being. I had a plan to bring the painting with me to New Jersey; I thought of Susan taking a shower in Julie's apartment as she waited for her lover. As I turned back to the world inside the frame, a sentence containing the word "I" would half form in my mind: "Those sandals by the foot of her couch are encrusted in jewels beyond price. I wonder how she walked in them?" But then the sentence disappeared and I disappeared and there were only the sandals and the jewels and the light which created them.

Toward late afternoon I wrenched myself out of the painting. I wrapped it in its canvas and placed it carefully in the car. I put the bedstead back in front of the recess in the wall. It was just before midnight when I arrived home. I went in to make sure that Susan hadn't changed her mind and that I had the house to myself.

I set *The Center of the World* up on the bureau in the bedroom, adjusting the light as best I could. I piled the pillows up on the bed so I could see the painting, like a pasha looking over his harem.

I could sense the rise and fall of her breasts and almost hear the passage of god-touched blood as it coursed through her veins and infused her skin with life and color. If I had thought about it I would have realized that I had never been so happy, but I was too happy to think. Soon I no longer saw her image. She was simply present to me and I was complete.

I called in sick on Monday. I suspected that everyone in the office knew my wife had left me. They would understand if I took a few days off, and they wouldn't say anything when I came back. It was the sort of thing that happened all the time.

But I *was* sick; incapacitated by wonder and ill with happiness. I had fallen into perfection. My marriage, my children, my job, and all the stuff that I worried about faded away. Everything that mattered was in front of my eyes.

By Wednesday afternoon, however, I found myself gradually awakening to the sense that there was a world beyond

THE CENTER OF THE WORLD

the picture frame that I needed to attend to, just as there was a world outside Helen's chamber. Out there on the plain was where the work of living went on, where the battle was fought, and, farther off, where the grain was grown. In the distance I could see the small towns that housed the farms and the workshops where the silk that adorned Helen was spun. The gods were there too, although more difficult to see than on the battlefield. They were in the light that fell upon men and women and allowed them to do their work.

On the Thursday after Susan left, I went back to work. I told my colleagues that I'd had the flu. They all nodded sympathetically; no one mentioned Susan. Work seemed better than it had in many months. I felt that what I was doing was useful and interesting, and that if it weren't for the good work of the foundation, a number of useful projects would remain undone. I did manage to leave every day promptly at five. When I got home I went upstairs to be with the painting. Some nights I forgot to eat dinner. I lost a few more pounds and had one of my suits taken in.

I talked to Susan a few times a week. At first I couldn't imagine a greater happiness than being alone with the painting, but gradually the absence of her familiar voice over morning coffee and her warm body in the bed beside me began to bother me. Although I still didn't mention the painting to her and was very much aware of what I wasn't speaking of, I was more comfortable now. She was doing well too, discovering a life for herself in the city. At first there were only references to colleagues, but then so-and-so, a friend of a friend, would enter the picture. She was getting connected with a network of fifty-something women, mostly well-off, working, and divorced, who had drinks after work and sometimes went to a movie.

"You sound good," I said during one of our calls.

"I think it's not having the commute," she said. "I read this article the other day, where these economists did an analysis of what makes people unhappy, and having a long commute was way up there on the list. But I miss you. I miss our house. I miss the life we made for ourselves. Are you taking decent care of yourself? You sound better."

I told her I missed her too. We agreed that we would both take the day off and she would come out to New Jersey on Friday.

. 47 .

HOW LONG IT WAS before I came back into the world I could not tell, although later we determined that I had been in the room for about half an hour before I spoke. Egremont was beside me on the couch; we were both still looking at the painting. He kissed me on my brow. It was an uncharacteristically tender kiss, but I was not surprised.

"I am beyond words," I said.

"Yes, he has outdone himself. He has outdone the lot of them. Nothing like it."

"And you," I said.

"Yes," he said. "I cannot tell you how I felt. The years slipped away. I remembered when I first set eyes on you, when I first set eyes on Wyndham's mother, when I first set eyes on Priscilla, down by the outbuildings before you were born. Lord, it all came flooding over me at once, and the feelings too. I feared it would not last, and that is why I called you so impatiently. I hope you are not angry."

"No." I returned his kiss. "For a moment I feared you had suffered a fit or a fall. And then when I saw it, I stopped thinking altogether. That is the most remarkable thing. It was as if I had ceased to be."

"Yes. Everything became quite beyond words."

"I feel the whole world is somehow here before us. Do you see those birds there, on that tree? What extraordinary creatures. I fancy I can almost hear them singing."

He looked at the place where I had pointed. "No," he said, "I had not seen them. You are right. They are remarkable. All the colors of the east and yet harmonious. And yes, I can almost hear their song, deaf as I am. But did you see there, down on the battlefield, the fear in the faces of the common soldiers as they flee from that hero in bronze? I feel quite cut up for the poor chaps. They shall be carrion ere long."

We spent the better part of an hour wrapped in each other's arms and admiring the painting. The years slipped away—he took me once again—and I opened myself to him as if I was first in love. We laughed and made jokes like two children. It was the sweetest hour of my life.

I felt a pang in my heart as I thought of young Grant waiting in the breakfast room, but then a great rush of envy as I realized that he was going to see the painting for the very first time. We dressed and made ourselves as presentable as we could, but I blushed like a girl as I thought that all the servants would know what we had been about when they saw the state of my hair.

When we returned to the sitting room we sent the servants out of the room. Egremont looked at Turner as sternly as he could.

"You have played me a nasty trick, sir. I had proposed to pay you good money for your labors, but I find that you have cheated me." A look of alarm began to cross Turner's complacent face, but Egremont went on regardless. "I had asked you, sir, to put my jewels in your work and you have not done so. Do you expect to be paid the full measure when you have defied me on my only specific request?"

Turner saw the humor in Egremont's eyes, and his alarm was replaced by delight. Recognizing that Turner had seen through his joke, Egremont clasped him around the shoulders. I offered him a kiss. Egremont called in for tea and a bottle of champagne.

"You have outdone yourself, sir. You have outdone all of them, past and present. There is nothing like it." We went on in this vein for some time. Turner drank in the praise as a thirsty man drinks water.

"I thought, yes, it would more than do. But had my doubts. Not my usual line, you know. Not like any of the others. I thought perhaps I might be mad. See the thing for one thing when in fact it is another. Enthusiasm can lead one astray—it's hard to trust it. Sometimes right, but sometimes madness. There is a fine line."

We both assured him that there was no question that he had succeeded. "Glad it pleases. Would have broken my heart had it not. Or else I'd have thought you were mad. Either one. But as for those jewels: they are there, you know. On the floor beside the dressing table. I tried to think the thing through. Helen. The greatest beauty in the world. Men give her trinkets all the time. But she is Helen, nothing can increase her beauty. Nothing larger than infinity, you know. So I put them in—to please you, my lord—but not in the usual place."

Turner drank off his glass of champagne with satisfaction and smiled as Egremont refilled his glass. "Good stuff, this. Thank you, my lord. Those jewels—another joke between us. In Rome I spent many hours in the Gallery Doria where there are a couple of paintings by Caravaggio. One of them the Virgin, the other the Magdalene. Old Caravaggio used the same pretty girl for both. A sly trick, I thought. His Magdalene is sitting on a low stool, wearing a gown of rich brocade with gold stitching. Garb of her trade in Caravaggio's day, I suppose. But next to her on the floor are all her jewels. Just strewn about, a whole casket full, as a sign of her repentance, you see.

"So I put Helen's jewels on the floor too. Not as a sign of repentance, however. Helen never repents. The whole world is in flames, and she the cause. Those jewels are very fine, my lord. No family in England has any finer. But dull compared to Helen herself. It would be like her, don't you think, to just toss aside a kingdom's worth of jewels. Great cruelty in great beauty. Not in your case, Mrs. S., but in the idea of it, you know."

We chatted on like this for about an hour, until poor Grant came down. He was speechless in his admiration, although he managed to say more that was sensible than either Egremont or I had been able to. He knew that the end was coming. It would be my task to tell him so, not a task I relished, but I managed it when the time came. Helen had already given me the strength I needed.

. 48 .

ON THE LEFT-HAND SIDE, near the bottom, I could sometimes make out a sheet of paper. It had blown off Helen's table, or perhaps she had dropped it there. When I went up close to the canvas it vanished, but when I stepped back it appeared. When I saw it I could not make out the Greek letters, but sometimes I was almost able to understand what she had written. Often this understanding came to me when I was away from the painting, or concentrating on some other part of it. As I was waiting for Susan at the station, I understood that Helen had been writing an appeal to Priam. She told him that she wanted this war to be over. She had seen so much and suffered so much. She could no longer bear the sight of the men out on the plain below, dying and suffering on her account. But then she had heard Paris's footfall in the corridor, and the sheet of paper lay forgotten on the floor as she prepared for the arrival of her lover.

A wave of fondness washed over me when I saw Susan step off the train. "You look great," I said.

We planted kisses on each other's cheeks, but then we kissed each other as if we meant it. I think we were both surprised and pleased by that.

"I like what you've done with your hair. I was half afraid you were going to turn into some blond TV-show lawyer. I think I'd let myself forget how pretty you are, gray and all."

"And you look good, too," she said. "You look like you've lost a few more pounds, but it might be time to have a piece of cake."

"I've been too sad to eat," I said. She smiled and gave me another kiss. I felt that we were falling into the comfortable old rhythms. It was easy to forget how good all that was.

She only had her briefcase with her, so I saw that she was planning to go back to the city. I was already a little bit sad about that.

I suggested we go to town for coffee. Susan held down a table while I got two large cappuccinos and a piece of cake to share. She had picked a table in the back of the room, as far as possible from the students pecking earnestly at their laptops.

We chatted for a few minutes about Susan's new life in New York. I liked looking at her, my wife of twenty-four years, but I suddenly felt a spike of nausea as the image of Susan in the hotel room in Cleveland rose up in my mind like bile.

"Tell me," I said. "Are you having an affair?" I don't know where I got the courage to ask the question, but I saw the piece of paper that had fallen to the floor of Helen's chamber as I spoke.

She paused with her fork halfway to her mouth. As she spoke I focused on the bit of carrot cake that hung there.

"Don't you think you have a lot of nerve asking me that question? In case you've forgotten: you were the one kissing Ruth Carpenter. It occurred to me that maybe you wanted me to come out here so you could tell me you'd been seeing somebody."

"Fair enough," I said. "But you didn't answer my question: Are you having, or have you had, an affair?"

She hesitated for a moment before speaking. "No," she said. "I am not having an affair. Someone kissed me once and I kissed him back. And it felt good. But I didn't take the plunge. So now it's my turn: Are you having an affair?"

I thought of Helen waiting for me in the bedroom. I thought of Gina and the kiss she gave me at the door of her hotel.

"No," I said. "I've been tempted, but I haven't. What you saw was both the beginning and the end of my romantic adventures with Ruth Carpenter."

"I wondered if you'd gone to London to meet somebody. And when you came back I thought you had. You seemed sort of shifty and guilty, if you don't mind my saying so. That's why I left; I couldn't stand it. You seem better today."

"I know I was acting oddly," I said. "I was feeling guilty. I met a woman in the cafeteria at the Tate. She was trying to pick me up. She was really pretty. Maybe in her late thirties. We had a nice conversation. It was a beautiful evening, and I walked her to her hotel after the museum closed. When we got there she asked me to come in for a drink. I said no and went back to my hotel by myself."

"So why didn't you go in with her, if she was so nice and pretty?"

I shrugged. "To be frank, I don't really know, although, as I've thought about it, it's not clear that she was actually willing. How come we don't sleep with other people? We're married; it's a habit; it's what we said we wouldn't do. But it would have been false—a fantasy out of a bad movie. We're the real deal."

I saw the light in her eyes and all the happiness we had shared. I knew what I had to do.

. 49 .

THOSE WERE AMONG the sweetest days of my life, even with all the suffering, even though Wyndham and the brats came back. Grant was gone. Turner was gone. We had fewer guests than previously. The house was often quiet. People said that the cause was Egremont's great age, but he was in love for the first time in his life and had no patience for trivialities. So was I. It was a time bathed in light.

Egremont had a special cabinet designed to hold what we simply called "the painting." It was installed in his bedroom. Every morning as the sun rose, I would open the cabinet and we two would lie in the bed, sometimes reading, sometimes chatting, sometimes falling back into delightful slumber. We would take our coffee thus. At length we arose—Egremont went to the fields and I to my occupations around the house.

Our guests often said to me that Egremont seemed to have aged. In the past, they recalled, he had been out in the fields as soon as the sun rose. It was still remarkable, they said, for a man of his age to get out at all, but they noted that he seemed less active than before.

But the fact was that the painting had made him younger and, as he often said, more sensible. I remember one afternoon about a month after Turner had departed. We had gone up to his bedroom and I had opened the cabinet. We spent about an hour looking at the painting, pointing out beauties we had not noticed before. Then Egremont took me. I took my pleasure in him as well, for he had become most kind in this way. His skin was dry and almost transparent. His body hair had all but disappeared. The muscles that had been toned by so many years in the saddle hung upon his bones in loose folds. But bathed in the light from the painting, he was sweetly beautiful to me. And I had never felt so beautiful either. We were like two gods.

"If this is witchcraft," he said as we lay exhausted amongst the pillows, "I am happily damned." He kissed me gently on the forehead. "With one possible exception," and here he nodded at the painting, "you are the fairest woman that ever lived. But you are her as well, so we need not trouble ourselves with the distinction. The good fortune is mine. To think that at my time of life I have spent the last hour as I have spent it is hardly short of miraculous. When I was young, there was nothing I feared more than the decline of my powers. I remember thinking that men ten years younger than I am now were only toothless idiots, gelded old fools.

"I cannot describe to you the bitterness that was in my heart, when my old fool failed me. It had done me such good service over the years, always ready to do a man's work. When

I first met you it was still serviceable, but when it failed I was full of wrath and sorrow. I had ceased to be the man I was. I am sorry," and here he kissed me sweetly again, "that I was cruel in those days, but my rage must find an outlet."

We both looked at the painting again. We knew that it could not last. The painting can do much—it has great power, but no art, no matter how exalted, can stop the flow of time. We lived two years in that happy dream; and none of it, not the restoration of Egremont's vigor or my own sweet pleasure, was sweeter than the kindness he showed me in his final years.

It was about two years after the painting was completed when Egremont first grew ill. It began innocently enough, with some discomfort in his throat and fits of sneezes, but it soon grew to a fever. His breathing became labored. His mind seemed to wander. We sent up to London for a doctor. After he examined the patient he took me aside and said that I must prepare for the worst. His words almost broke my heart, but I would not believe them. I felt in my heart something I had never felt before. I had come to love this man.

That was a terrible time. I never left his room for almost three months. With his last bit of strength and lucidity Egremont had forbidden Wyndham to enter on pain of forfeiting his inheritance. The doctors saw how his son disturbed him with his presence and enforced the edict. Wyndham thought I would steal the very bed linens, and he set up his desk outside the room. He wished to be there to provide assistance, he said, but I knew the truth. His idea of assistance was to repeat my commands to the servants so as to make it appear that they came from him, or to question any decision that might result in expense and the diminishment of his inheritance.

But he was a weak man, and I was stronger than I had ever been. I still cannot understand how such a puny thing could have been fathered by a man like Egremont, but I did not pause then to work out the puzzle. I simply told him what I was going to do and he retreated before my wrath and contempt. I hardly know where I got such force of will. Sometimes, when I looked at the painting, I thought the very gods were giving it to me; sometimes I knew it was simply love that made me strong.

There is nothing worse than a proud old man in the grip of illness. Egremont was not an easy patient. He used his last bits of strength to rage against his weakness, to fight against the need he had for care. He would allow no one but me to attend him. I bathed him as if he were the child I had never had.

In the darkest hours of his illness, the great lord of Petworth almost stopped breathing. His chest moved slowly up and down, occasionally he tried to speak, but I could not make out the words, nor even tell if he was waking or dreaming. His eyes were sometimes open, but he gave no sign that he could see. When Dr. Haddon saw him in this state he told me, speaking as if Egremont was no longer in the room, that the end was nigh. Wyndham remained just outside the door; I could almost hear the clink as he counted the money that was to be his.

When the doctor left I opened the cabinet and sat down beside the bed. I looked at Egremont. He seemed such a poor and mortal shadow of himself. I looked at the painting. I had never felt before that life was so wonderful and that I had been so fortunate. Egremont had been most kind to me. He had taken in a tainted woman and made her into a semblance of a lady. And, in those last years, he had given me his love. I took his thin hand in mine and began to weep. But then I felt a fleeting pressure. His eyes met mine for a moment, and he moved his head ever so slightly and looked at the painting. I cannot tell if he saw it too, but when I turned I saw the fleeting figure of a god beckoning to me and urging me to have faith. For these many years now, I have been trying to see that figure again, but though it has never reappeared to me in all its full vividness, the god still lives in my mind. He was in the upper right corner of the canvas, just above the place where the sky touches the battlefield.

Upon his recovery Egremont did not remember seeing the vision, but I am convinced that his health began to return when the god called to him from the canvas. It was by no means an easy recovery. For about two weeks I was wrestling with powers much larger than myself for Egremont's life. It was a lonely struggle, and I hardly know how I, who had been so weak and so selfish for so long, found the strength and the will to persevere.

The doctors thought I was mad, but the victory was mine. When the London doctor next returned, Egremont beckoned to him and he leaned over the bed. Egremont's words were clear enough: "How much, sir, did you charge to say that I was dead? Be off with you. If I am to die I shall do so without your assistance; if I live, I shall do so without it as well."

From then on his recovery was slow but steady. Spring had come and I was able to throw open the windows and let the air into the sickroom. One day, as we were at our breakfast, Egremont asked me how long it had been since I had gone outside.

I told him that I had not left his side since he fell ill about three months before. He took my hand and patted it gently. The tears that began to form at the corners of his eyes were the greatest gift I had ever been given.

"I have been too selfish," he said. "You must get out and take some air. It will do you good. Besides, I wish to speak to my son. Call him in and leave us."

I thanked my lord and did as he had bidden me. At the beginning of his illness I had all the looking glasses taken from the sickroom. When I passed the great glass in the hallway, I saw how I had aged. I had lived so much in the painting that I had come to think that time had stopped. With a shudder I saw that it had not.

The air was sweet and warm. The smell of earth rose from the grass about me as I walked toward the bench overlooking the pond. Happy as I was to be in the air, it was a struggle to make my way up the hill. I had to stop along the way to rest.

I pressed my hand to my breast and looked down upon Petworth House, my heart beating as though it would burst. When I thought of the pleasant hours I had passed in this very spot, my tears started to flow. I wondered what had become of young Grant. He had written once from London, but I had never replied. Also, truth be told, I felt that the painting had somehow carried me beyond whatever he might have been to me.

I sat there for about an hour. Perhaps I dozed a bit. I remember looking at the sky and seeing it as if for the first time. How beautiful is the world, I thought—more beautiful even than the painting, but the painting's sky gave form and meaning to the air around me, while the water of the sea beyond Helen's window taught me what water was. I wept again for the wonder and amazement of it all.

When I returned to the house I saw that Egremont had not been improved by his son's visit. But Wyndham was looking down at the floor like a puppy who had been beaten. He wished me good day with a painfully forced courtesy, assuring me that his only desire was to further his father's wishes and that he knew that Lord Egremont's wishes and mine were the same. He would endeavor, he went on, to do me any service that he could. I had merely to ask.

I bowed and thanked him. I had no more trouble from him while his father lived.

. 50 .

WE SAT DOWN TOGETHER in our familiar living room. I took her hands in mine. "But I have been unfaithful, in a sense," I said. "I haven't slept with anyone else, but I haven't told you the truth. I *feel* as if I've been unfaithful. I am ready to talk to you about it."

I watched the expression that formed on her face. At first she seemed relieved, but then she seemed sad, more for me than for herself.

"For the last year or so I've had this feeling that my father was right, that I'm a loser and a failure. My life has seemed to me like a string of accidents. Even the good parts—our love, the kids, the life we made for ourselves—seemed random and pointless. I was going to die and the fact that I had lived wasn't going to matter one way or another. My whole life could have happened to someone else.

"I told you about the girl I met in London. I didn't sleep with her, but for a long time since I've been back, I thought I should have. In my mind I've done all sorts of things with her. And it would have been okay because I was convinced that you were sleeping with someone else too. When you went to Cleveland I thought you were with someone, and I was obsessed with ugly visions of you and whoever it was in the airport Marriott."

"But I told you," she said, "that I haven't."

"And I believe you. And I need you to believe me about the girl, too." I stopped to catch my breath. "Last summer, you know, we were up in the mountains. We were having a pretty good time. You had to go back to the city for some meetings, and I stayed up at the camp to clean out the barn."

"And things have been different since then," she said. I was surprised that she associated any change with that time, but moved on.

"Something happened to me up there which didn't feel like an accident," I said, "and my life has been transformed." I told her about finding *The Center of the World* in the barn and how I guessed that it had been hidden there since before my father bought the place, back when the house was part of the Rhinebeck property.

"It has shown me the heart of things; I have seen why the blood flows in our veins and why we have children. And I have wanted," I said, "to keep it all to myself, but now I understand that this greed, this lust, is killing me and driving us apart."

Susan looked at me very earnestly.

"And even if we don't keep it, we could sell it for twenty million dollars, thirty million dollars, more money than we could ever count or spend. It could change everything for us. I would never need to even think about Mossbacher. But what I am trying to say," I went on, "is that I saw hope. I found hope. I don't always see it, but I've caught a glimpse of it, and I believe there is at least a reason for it to exist. I will die. You will die. Our children will die. But perhaps there is a reason not to give up. That is what my Turner tells me. There is beauty in the world and there is beauty in the space between men and women. We have seen it, you and I. We have seen it when we were younger and there is no reason that we cannot see it again."

I had grown more and more excited as I spoke, becoming animated at the thought of the two of us dwelling together in that light. She, meanwhile, seemed to grow more and more alarmed.

"Look," I said. "I know I sound crazy. Words are not enough. I want to give you this gift. I love you. We can talk about it later. We can talk about if we want to keep it or sell it. I want you to go upstairs to our bedroom. I am going to wait down here. You will see the painting on the bureau. Call me when you want me to come upstairs."

She looked at me and raised her eyebrows.

"No, really," I said. "Trust me. I want you to go upstairs. You can tell me I'm nuts later."

. 51 .

⟨⚬⟩ **WHEN SHE RETURNED** to New York after seeing Henry at the Tate, Gina put him out of her mind and concentrated on Rhinebeck and his affairs. Bryce forgave her indiscretion with Henry; he called her into the upstairs library almost every evening to think about what they ought to do next. It became a matter of faith for both of them that Rhinebeck had owned *the* Turner, as they had come to think of it, and that it had been among those paintings dispersed after his death. Did it stay within the Rhinebeck family or had it been acquired, somehow, by Maria Overstreet's employer in the days immediately following the car crash that claimed the lives of Rhinebeck, his wife, and Overstreet herself?

Maria Overstreet had worked for Oswald Lambert, a gallery owner who operated on the edges of legality. It seemed reasonable to associate a painting as scandalous as the Turner with a character like Lambert, who was eventually forced to close up shop and move to Paris when stories about his financial and moral laxity became too widely known in New York.

But it was also possible that Rhinebeck's brother Rupert had kept it for himself, or that he had sold it quietly while he was selling off his brother's assets to establish a trust for the benefit of the two Rhinebeck boys, who both died young and without issue.

The trail forked, thus, at Rhinebeck's summer place in Saranac Lake. In early November Bryce suggested that Gina drive to upstate New York to consult the real estate records associated with the property in order to identify families into whose hands the painting might have fallen.

Before she made her trip she consulted histories of the Adirondack Great Camps and found out that in 1908 Rhinebeck had purchased a twenty-acre lakeside lot and begun the construction of Birch Lodge, famous in its day as one of the most expensive construction projects ever undertaken in the Adirondacks and as a haven for Rhinebeck and a select group of his most intimate male associates. The property consisted of the main building and a series of more or less elaborate outbuildings: guest cottages, boathouses, dormitories for staff, stables, and a house for the caretaker. After Rhinebeck's death the place was all but abandoned. In the end Birch Lodge was sold to a family from Cleveland, who held on to it for a decade before they broke it up into a number of smaller parcels.

Gina told the town clerk in Saranac Lake that she was doing research on Cornelius Rhinebeck for a book on New York financiers. He offered her a cup of bad coffee and a seat at a metal desk. Systematically she worked her way through the old ledgers.

She followed the trail as the property made its tortuous way through the legal limbo that followed the death of Rhinebeck's children. She noted the name of the family from Cleveland, then the names of the families that had purchased pieces of the parcel. She was about to close the ledger when she saw, at the bottom of the page, a familiar name. The property that had been the housekeeper's cottage was sold in 1952 to David and Irene Leiden. She turned the page. In 1970 it passed into the hands of their son, Henry.

She recalled what he had said when she had asked if he would like to own a Turner. "It would be too much for me," he had said, "I think I would disappear." At the time she had taken his comment as an eccentric expression of admiration, but now it struck her that he was speaking from experience. He had seen it.

His clumsy approach to the professor in Princeton, his interest in Turner, the photos of him and his wife sitting on a dock beside some blue water: it all made sense. The detective had mentioned a summer place in upstate New York, but if George had provided the name of the town, she couldn't remember. She felt like an idiot, but she kept calm and continued writing dates down carefully for fifteen minutes, so that the clerk would never suspect that the attractive young woman in front of him had just made an extraordinary discovery.

She drove down the Northway and then the Thruway in a kind of delirium. It wasn't until later, until after it was all over, that she was able to see how illogically she had behaved. The obvious thing, of course, would have been to drive the few miles to the lake house and take a look around there.

She turned her phone off and drove straight to New Jersey. She knew that she should inform Bryce of what she had discovered, but she needed to do this for herself and to present this thing to Bryce as the product of her own pluck and initiative. She checked into a hotel on Route 1 just outside of Princeton. The next morning she waited until she thought they would both be at work before she went to Leiden's house.

When Gina broke the glass of the back door to let herself in, the sound was as loud as anything she had ever heard. She stood for a moment waiting for sirens and policemen. She went in.

It was propped up on the bureau in the upstairs bedroom. The felt and visible world disappeared. Everything became gray and irrelevant, except for the painting in front of her.

She collapsed onto the foot of the bed. She had never before seen light like that; she had never before seen light itself for what it is. There was the ocean out beyond the battlefield; she now knew the life that teemed within it, as well as the death that threatened every day. In one glance she seemed to comprehend everything that Homer knew about the sea.

The face reflected in the mirror was Helen's. She saw all the great queens and goddesses in whom men had ever believed. She saw Nefertiti and Venus. She saw the force against which all men were powerless. She saw herself as she wanted to be. These realizations broke over her like waves upon the shore during a storm. Beauty is power as well as truth. Helen was the force that set the heroes at each other's throats. She was the force that propelled the sap through the trees. She was the idea behind all action, but prior to all thought.

She sat in the Leidens' bedroom for twenty minutes, but it could have been an hour, a day, a lifetime. The room slowly began to impinge on her consciousness. She became aware that Helen would not sit there goggle-eyed while the prize of a lifetime lay before her. She took the painting down from the bureau and placed it on the bed. She wrapped it carefully in the bedspread and carried the clumsy bundle down the stairs.

The detective grasped her by the arm so firmly that the pain forced the air from her lungs. "You are very pretty," George said, "but you've been bad, dear, very bad. But Mr. Bryce said it was to be expected. Things will work out if you come along and behave. I'll take the dingus, if you don't mind. Just come along to the car here."

She burst into tears.

. *52* .

THERE WAS ONLY a small party seated at the dinner table: Wyndham and his family; Mr. Gedding, the member from Pulborough; and Mr. Bainbridge, who had ridden over to talk about a scheme to build a canal. We had just finished our soup when Egremont suddenly looked about him with a puzzled air. He half stood up and then sat down abruptly. We all looked at him.

"I am not well," he said. "I wish to go to my room." He turned to me. "Come up with me. And you," he turned to his son, "be ready to follow. I will send for you." I could see that Egremont was making a great effort to speak clearly, but even so there was something altered about his voice. He motioned for me and I helped him from his chair. "And my friends," he said. "Thank you for your company and your conversation. All of it. It has been most edifying. Good night."

I called to some of the servants to help us, but even so it was only with great difficulty that we made our way up the stairs.

After we had settled him in his bed, I said that I would call for the doctor.

"No. I have no need of a doctor. I am past all that. As we walked up the stair my right foot was like a stone. Summon my son—I wish to speak to him. Call in the oldest servants—I wish to say farewell."

I did as he bade me. When Wyndham entered, Egremont asked me to step outside. I stood in the corridor for about ten minutes, feeling as if my fate were being decided. When the door opened Wyndham motioned me to enter. He looked pale and very angry.

Egremont spoke with even greater difficulty. His voice was becoming slurred. "I have asked my son to treat you with respect. I hope he will do so. I have asked him, too, not to trouble himself about the sickroom. I wish to spend my final hours with you."

My eyes welled with tears as I felt the feeble pressure of his hand. Wyndham stood stock still. "May Jesus Christ have mercy on your soul, Father," he said. He bowed and left the room.

Four or five of the servants came in. Egremont thanked them for their many years of service and bade them adieu. He told them that they had all been remembered in his will.

After they had gone he motioned for me to open the cabinet. I sat down beside him and asked if there was anything further I could do. His words were now very difficult to make out, although he did not seem to be suffering in any way. "No," he said, "I am past all help. It has been good. I wish to die here with you and with these wonders before me. Everything is here." I held a glass of water to his lips; he took a small swallow.

"They call me," he said. I looked at the painting. I could see the invisible gods hovering above the battlefield. I looked at Egremont. There was an expression of great peace on his still face. He tried to speak again, but I could not make out his words. I felt a gentle pressure from his hand. He shook his head and smiled. He looked at the painting, his eyes bright.

We sat thus for about two hours. He could no longer swallow. I occasionally moistened his thin lips with a cloth. He struggled to keep his eyes open, but that was the only sign of discomfort I saw. At length he seemed to sleep. I held his hand and watched the slow rise and fall of his chest.

As the night progressed his breathing grew more and more shallow. I remained by his side, holding his hand, although I suppose I may have dozed for a brief while. When the morning light filled the room I blew out the candles and turned off the lanterns. I watched as new beauties came into focus in the dawn's light. Suddenly Egremont gave a start. He raised his head slightly, his eyes opening. His lips moved, but no sound emerged. An expression of wonder came across his face as the light from the painting illuminated the room. His head fell back into the pillow. The great lord of Petworth was no more.

. 53 .

◄❧► SUSAN CAME DOWN the stairs. "What on earth have you been talking about?"

It was as I had feared. She couldn't see what I had seen; either I had been deluding myself or there was something in her nature that made her incapable of perceiving the truth.

"*The Center of the World*," I said, "the painting on the bureau. Couldn't you see at least a hint of what I am talking about?"

"What painting? There is no painting. Are you okay?"

In her utter disbelief, I saw a horror that it had not occurred to me to consider. I rushed up the stairs and saw the void. I checked under the bed, in the closet, behind the door.

How could the gods do this to me? How could they toy with me in this terrible way? That is what they always do— give us a glimpse of meaning where none exists. It would have been better, I thought, if I had remained ignorant. I felt frantic with rage and bafflement. My breath came with difficulty and tears streamed from my eyes.

Susan stood in the doorway. I was standing at the foot of the bed. I stared at the place where the painting had been, gasping for breath. My hands hung at my sides, but every few seconds I lifted them up as if I wanted to grasp something that was no longer there.

. 54 .

IT HAS BEEN seven years since I was last at Petworth, seven years since that fevered autumn of 1830. As you know, David, my life has been one of modest success and ordinary heartbreak. My duties at *The Westminster Review* have not brought me fame, but they have earned me the respect of a small circle of influential men and women. Most men would, I suppose, consider me fortunate, but since that evening in Cambridge when you said you would see me no more, I have felt like a stranger in this world. My mother is gone, Mrs. Spencer is forbidden me, and you have rejected me. My past life seems a kind of remembered glory, even though to the eyes of most men, it is only in these last few years that I have begun to realize my promise. But everything seems empty, a pale shadow of that truth I remember glimpsing in Helen's eyes. Where are those golden ships that would carry me off to distant lands? Where are the beautiful gods that order the flights of arrows over the plain?

When news of Lord Egremont's death reached London, I decided that I would attend his funeral. I owed him much; it was his generous support that had allowed me to make my way in the world as far as I had. I wished to pay my respects to his memory. And besides, I thought the funeral would give me a chance to see Mrs. Spencer without violating the terms of the promise that I had made. I had had Turner's portrait of her framed and hung in my bedroom, but I longed to see her in the flesh once more. Time, I thought, might have softened her resolve and perhaps we might be friends again.

The morning of Egremont's funeral broke cold and gray. By midmorning a steady soaking rain was pouring down on Petworth. I had resolved to write a short piece for the *Review* on the event. It seemed to me that the hundreds of mourners gathered at the small cemetery in Petworth village had come to mourn not only one of the great men of his age, but also the end of the age itself. England would never again see an English life lived on such a scale, nor an individual who patronized the arts and useful sciences on such a scale. The English Maecenas was dead; he would return no more.

I found Turner at the center of a group of painters and sculptors. Over the years I had seen him only occasionally in London, and I felt he was happy enough for our meetings to be infrequent. He seemed, however, very glad to see me on this sad day. He grasped my arm and looked at me most earnestly.

"Ah, young Grant. Although not as young as you once were, either. Those were great days that we lived through, great! Come stay by me." The years had not been kind to Turner.

He was much thinner than when I had last seen him, and he seemed worn down. When I inquired after his health he claimed that it had been tolerable until a few days ago, when he had come down with a bad cold. "Damn rain," he said. "When I was younger I never minded it, but now it soaks through to my old bones." I held my umbrella over the aged artist and did what I could to protect him from the storm.

Wyndham and his wife stood under the shelter of the church porch as the crowd of mourners made its slow way toward them. I looked up at one point and saw that the long line of black umbrellas stretched perhaps a hundred yards between us and the old stone church and perhaps half a mile behind. I was in the midst of a number of painters and sculptors who had benefited from Lord Egremont's patronage. Jones, whom I had met in the early days of my stay at Petworth, stood next to us. He remembered me and said a few kind words. The artists present sincerely lamented the loss of their great patron; the conversation I heard around me was full of stories of his generosity and good taste. Turner stayed aloof from the general talk. "These fellows," he said, "are mourning a patron. Only I knew him as a friend. The great have few friends by nature of their position. But I was one." He said that he was composing a poem in Lord Egremont's honor. "But in my mind, you know, while all these fellows are talking."

The rain poured down, the line moved slowly forward. Just before we reached the church, Turner asked me if I had any paper about me. All I had, I told him, were some proofs for my latest review, which I had been going over in the coach. That would do, he said, so I handed them to him and he began scribbling in the margins, though it wasn't easy, owing to the dampness of the paper and the way the wind was blowing the rain about. He mumbled to himself as we shuffled along.

"Don't worry, Mr. Turner. You will soon be free from this obligation and able to resume your studies." Turner looked up with a start. He was standing on the church porch, facing Wyndham, who had an oily smile smeared across his face. Jones had interposed himself between me and Turner, so I too was surprised to find myself so near the head of the line.

Turner stuffed the offending piece of paper into his coat pocket. "Most sorry, sir. Attempting an ode. A poem, you know, on your father. 'Talent, genius, exceeding rare, / mold in the earth in the funeral bier.' Those were the lines. Trying to jot them down before I forgot." Turner tapped his forehead with this finger. "I'm getting old, you know. Tend to forget things now. But your father was a great man. I loved him dearly. My heart is quite broken at our loss. There will never come amongst us one like him again. I offer you my most heartfelt condolences."

Wyndham looked at Turner coolly and regarded the artist's outstretched hand as if it was something distasteful. After an unconscionable delay he touched it briefly, returning none of Turner's sincere pressure. "Most obliged," he said.

"And there is one matter I would like to discuss with you. A painting of mine. A portrait of Helen. Done especially for your father. Would very much like to see it again. Perhaps even buy it back."

Wyndham's face quickly took on a look of undisguised contempt. "I had expected the vultures to descend, but not so quickly, sir. Not so quickly. As for that painting, I know the work to which you refer. It is a memorial of my father at his worst, hardly a fit topic of conversation for a solemn occasion like the present. Or for any occasion. But I can assure you of one thing, sir: it shall be destroyed. Good day. There are many worthy people who wish to pay their respects. It will not do to keep them waiting in the rain."

Wyndham turned from the greatest artist of the age and directed his attention to Jones. Turner stumbled away, too staggered to speak. Wyndham was exceedingly gracious to Jones. I believe he prolonged the conversation more than was strictly necessary, so as to underscore how abrupt he had been with Turner.

When my turn came I did my best not to allow the way in which he had treated Turner to affect my demeanor. I offered my sincerest condolences and told him how much I admired and was grateful to his father. Then I asked after Mrs. Spencer.

Wyndham started and looked at me more closely. "Mrs. Spencer," he said, "is not here. Her whereabouts are a matter of indifference to me. I recognize you now. You were of that party that took advantage of my father in his dotage. I further recall that my father, sir, once felt compelled to apologize for referring to you as a sodomite. If I had been in his position I should not have felt myself under any such obligation."

I also felt staggered, but something arose in me that quite surprised me. I thought of Egremont and those days I had passed at Petworth with Mrs. Spencer. I thought of those evenings the four of us had talked in the Carved Room, those walks with Mrs. Spencer to the Rotunda, the kindness Egremont had showered upon a young man with few prospects.

"You, sir," I said, "are not worthy of your great father."

I moved quickly off the porch to Turner's side, but not before I had the satisfaction of seeing the sanctimonious little man turn crimson with rage. Turner was so shaken he could hardly speak. He took my arm when I reached him and asked me very earnestly to accompany him back to London. He had hired a private coach for the occasion and offered me a seat. We found his carriage among the sea of them standing near the inn in the village.

I settled Turner on the seat opposite me. He was silent and shivering. I relieved him of his sodden rain cape and wrapped a blanket about his shoulders. Then I went into the inn and procured a sip of brandy. These efforts soon had their effect and after a few miles Turner was more comfortable.

"I am much obliged to you. You always were a good chap and I see that you still are. An evil day, Grant, an evil day for J.M.W.T. Egremont was like a second father to me. My own father was a good man. He stretched my canvases when I was younger. I'd send him off to buy pigments when I needed them. Like a studio boy, but without the expense. And he drove a better bargain with the merchants than I ever could. A double savings. Started out as a barber, you know. A mere barber. But Lord Egremont was a different order of father. The Greek or Roman sort, the head of the tribe, the dispenser of order and all that is good. A philosopher king in his way. It is a great loss.

"And to think that puppy will destroy my Helen. The murder of a favorite child, that's what it is. A brutal, heartless man. I heard what you said to him. Truer words were never spoken. Good for you, and my compliments. I hardly know how I did it. I've looked at the sketches, but they don't add up. Such a moment. Such a gift. It occurs but once. I feel my old heart cracking in my ribs."

. 55 .

AFTER A FEW MOMENTS I was able to breathe normally. I stared at the spot where the painting had been when I left for the station. There was a faint mark on the wall behind the dresser where the back of the frame had touched the paint. There was a slight depression on the bed. The bedspread was missing.

I was aware that Susan had walked up behind me. I could see the carvings on Helen's lyre and sense the touch of the craftsman who had shaped the wood. I could see the clouds that gave shape to the sky, the light fall on Helen's thighs, the gods. I saw that the world was beautiful.

I sat down on the bed. The rage and bafflement that had consumed me began to dissipate. The color of the sea remained. The light remained. The fury of the soldiers on the battlefield and the invitation in Helen's eyes were all still there.

I felt Susan's hand on my shoulder. "It's been stolen," I said. I turned to look at her, watching me with pity and fear in her beautiful eyes. I saw that she was more beautiful than she had been in the early days of our marriage; I hoped she could find something in me too. "We can make this work," I said.

I pointed to the place where the painting had been. I was suddenly calm. "I had something," I said. "But someone took it. It doesn't matter. Maybe I can explain. Maybe not." I leaned forward and kissed her. At first she pulled away, as if she was concerned that there was something wrong with me. But I think she recognized something in my eyes and in the sudden repose of my face that allowed her to see a kind of beauty in me that she hadn't seen in years. As we kissed I felt a heat that we had not felt since before the children were born. I saw the gods in the light that poured in through the bedroom windows. She responded to my urgency and before long we were pulling off each other's clothes as if we had never been married.

. 56 .

IT WAS TWO DAYS before the funeral. Egremont had been dead for five days. Wyndham and I had exchanged only a few words, but they were sufficient for me to understand that I was to be out of the great house before any of the guests arrived. This arrangement suited me well, as I had no desire to be the object of either his condescension or his scorn.

All my belongings, such as they were, were packed and in the carriage. Thanks to Egremont's love and the work of his solicitors my modest provision was secure. I had the world before me and Paradise behind.

I went down to the Carved Room where Wyndham had set up his desk in order to meet with the legal men and to work out the settling of the estate. It was here that he held forth as the new lord of Petworth. I think he felt that the majesty of Henry VIII, as depicted in Holbein's portrait, would rub off on him, but the old king's air made it all too clear that Wyndham was nothing more than a misshapen jester trying on regal robes.

He protracted his conversation with the steward as long as possible before turning to me. "So," he said. "You are still here. I'd thought I heard a carriage on the drive."

I waited until the steward had left the room before sitting down. I regarded him for a few minutes before speaking.

"You and I," I said at length, "do not love each other. Neither of us, I fancy, sees any value in pretending otherwise. I grant you that you loved your father in your way. I too loved him. And of his affection for me the lawyers have provided you ample evidence."

"All of that," he said, "is neither here nor there. You have been, against my better judgment, provided for. We have agreed that you should leave before the funeral. The funeral is the day after tomorrow. Yet you are still here."

"There is one matter that must still be resolved between us. The painting in the cabinet in your father's bedroom. My things are packed, my carriage is ready. You must help me with it. We have always kept it from the sight of the servants, and it should remain so."

"It is a vile thing. You have no right to it. I should destroy it."

"No right? You forget your father's words. Your father commanded you, as you are a gentleman, that I should have it."

"He was old and in his dotage, debauched by you and your bewitchments. You spoke to the worst parts of his corrupted nature. I would be well within my rights to destroy the thing or even to keep it for myself."

I stood up so that I would be able to look down on him. I had found over the years that in spite of all his bluster he was a timorous soul. It usually did not take much to make him give way.

"You are the heir of Petworth, but a bastard. It is well known. Between your birth and your character, you will not have an easy time taking up your rightful place amongst the gentry. A scandal will not make your way smoother. And I must let you know this: if I do not get that painting, there is no shame so great as to deter me from exacting revenge on you."

I stared down at him until I could see in his eyes that he was about to surrender. "Come," I said. "We need not be about this all day. You would just as soon be rid of me, and I would just as soon depart. There is no reason we cannot make things easy. Do as you ought to and we are done. You must come up-stairs and help me."

He stood, and I followed him up the stairs to the great bed-room. I had prepared cloth and cord and laid them out on the bed. Taking the key from the chain about my neck, I unlocked the cabinet and handed it to him.

"I have no more need of this," I said. "I will open the door. You must help me lift the painting out. Together we shall place it face down on the cloth. We shall tie it up with the cord and you shall be rid of me."

He nodded his assent. I positioned him in front of the cabinet and opened the door. Something passed across his face when he saw the painting—I could not tell what—but he grasped the frame and did as he was told. I made quick work of tying up the bundle, and it was soon in the carriage.

The servants had come out to say good-bye to me. I held my hand out to Wyndham, but he kept his own resolutely behind his back. He enjoyed having them notice how he cut me. His wife was nowhere to be seen.

"Very well," I said. I spoke softly so that we could not be overheard. "But there is no need for us to part on such terms. I wish you no harm and am prepared to remain indifferent to your insult. You need not fear me nor doubt my discretion. Consider this painting locked in a tomb, for it would doom such honor as I have were it ever to be seen in public. Among the living only you, Turner, young Grant, and I have seen it."

"To call that a painting, madam, is an insult to those noble works of art which adorn this great house. But it does nothing to change my opinion of you." He took a few steps back to the house and then turned to face me for the last time. He raised his voice so that all might hear. "I have known you to be a debauched and covetous whore for these many years. My opinion is unaltered."

He turned and walked into the house.

"I loved your father with an honest love," I called to his retreating back, "and for that you must not blame me." I thought of the light that illuminated the field of battle and the way the gods seemed to embrace the struggling heroes. I thought of Helen and the look of power in her eye. His insult meant nothing.

The servants seemed genuinely sad to see me go, for I had always been kind to them. They knew, I think, that with my departure the great age of Petworth had come to an end. Tears were shed on their part and on mine. I shook hands with them all, having already made them such small gifts as it was in my power to offer. Sally, who had been my special attendant, wept most piteously as she clutched the small box that contained the earrings and the lace collar I had given her.

I turned to look for one last time at Petworth. I had been fortunate to have passed so much time in Paradise. I put my hand on the bundle that lay on the seat beside me, reflecting that there was an even greater Paradise before me.

. 57 .

Dear David,

I scarcely know why I am writing to you after all these
years, but I feel some need to justify myself and explain.
You can hardly understand the extent to which you were the
great planet about which the puny moon of myself revolved
for so long. Or perhaps you did understand, and you chose
not to let me see that you knew. It no longer matters.

In a week I shall be going to America. I do not think I
shall ever return to England. There is nothing for me here.
My mother is gone, you are gone, the days I spent at Petworth are gone. Lord Egremont is dead. I get no relish from
my work at the Review, even though I have been honoured
for my accomplishments and men of note esteem me. It all
seems like stale beer, or soup without salt. I have been offered a position at a journal called The Atlantic Monthly,
which is published in Boston, Massachusetts. I shall see if a
change of scene will do me good.

Do you remember the day I first visited you in Cambridge on my return from Petworth? I had gone up to London from Petworth to settle myself in my rooms. London seemed monstrous and overwhelming. I felt, for reasons which you will perhaps understand when you read the enclosed narrative, out of sorts with the world and defeated by its ugliness. But then I thought of you and recalled the joy that we had felt in each other's arms. I resolved to visit you at once. It would have been wise, I know, to have written to tell you of my coming, but like the fool I was, I listened to the promptings of my heart.

When I arrived at your rooms you were busy about your work. Though you received me cordially and called down for tea, you explained that you were preparing an examination and needed to complete it by the following day. I remember seeing your well-thumbed edition of Herodotus on your writing table.

As soon as your man left the room I put my arms around you. But as my lips found yours, I felt a reluctance in your body that shattered my heart. You escaped from my embrace as quickly as you could, muttering something about the servant returning with the tea things. Yet even had Puck or Mercury been in your employment there was no danger that we should be interrupted so soon.

You directed me to one of your chairs and sat across from me. We spoke, as I recall, about the state of the weather and university gossip. I explained that I had left Petworth, probably for good, but you did not enquire about my stay there.

When your man came in with the tea, you asked him
to secure a room for me at the University Arms Hotel. For
months I had been dreaming of spending the night with
you, but I saw it was not to be. I would have cried then if
your servant had not been present, and perhaps because you
sensed this, you detained him for longer than was necessary.
You asked him about the arrangements he had been making
for dinner, about the state of your wardrobe, about I forget
what else. But I saw that you were keeping him in the room
so that I would not be able to reveal my pent-up feelings.
Despite your stratagem, and despite my best efforts at self-
control, I thought your man might hear my heart crack.

When at length he left, you started in on a tedious tale
of an insignificant scandal in the bursar's office. I don't
think, David, I had ever heard you talk so quickly and to
such little purpose. You wanted, I knew, to prevent any
conversation on the one topic that was nearest to what was
left of my heart.

I chafed under your chatter for about half an hour, when
there came a knock on the door. Edward entered, and I saw
the look you gave him and the look he gave you. I saw what I
had been to you not too many years before.

Edward was, as you said later, a very promising young
man. He was beautiful—perhaps not as beautiful as I was,
but handsome enough in a different, darker style. But his
conversation, as I recall, was insipid. He was so young. He
knew so little. I could see by the way he looked at you that he
adored you. You had given him what you had given me. I had

never thought that a broken heart could break again, but I was wrong.

When he left we had our moment of truth. You said that you feared that my stay with the "great people at Petworth" had spoiled me for life with a humble scholar. You said that I had fallen in love with luxury and you with a simple heart.

I could not speak, as you recall. We said good night and I went to the University Arms, where you had been so kind as to procure a room for me. I passed the most miserable night of my life.

I thought of Helen, and of our love. I thought of the world that was and the world that could be. I had glimpsed such glorious things, but I knew that night that I would never see them again.

You don't understand what I am talking about, nor did you have any desire that night to understand what had happened to me at Petworth. The enclosed manuscript will explain some part of my story. I have soldiered on since then, but it has been a heartless trudge through the desert. Perhaps it will be otherwise in America.

Charles Grant

P.S. As you are a man of honour I ask that you destroy the manuscript after you have read it.

. 58 .

HANNAH KNOCKED on the bedroom door. "There is a gentleman here to see you, ma'am." I closed the cabinet and saw, once again, how the light in the room was diminished. "He says his name is Turner."

"Tell him," I said, "that I am indisposed."

"I have already done so, ma'am. He is most insistent." She handed me a note hastily written on a page torn out of a sketch-book. It must have pained him to rip it out. On the back there was a drawing of a London street scene.

Dear Madam,

It is most cruel of you to have hidden yourself away as you have. But now that I have discovered you, we must speak. I will not take up much of your time if such is your desire. Please believe me

your most humble and obedient servant,

J.M.W.T.

"Very well," I said. "Bring him into the sitting room and make us some tea. Tell him I will be down in a few minutes."

I dressed with care, although I knew that no pains of mine could disguise how much I had aged since Turner had last seen me. As I saw my face reflected in the mirror, I thought of how different it was from the face in the mirror of the painting. I did not relish the thought of this meeting, but if I had hoped to avoid it I should have moved to New York or Johannesburg.

Steeling myself as best I could, I descended the stairs, but nothing could have prepared me for what awaited me. Although it had been only three years since we last saw each other, Turner appeared twenty years older. He had made some effort to make himself presentable for the interview, but his coat, although recently brushed, was greasy and worn at the elbows. His hair was dirty, and the soles of his boots were caked with mud. There was a wildness about his eyes that I did not recognize from our days at Petworth.

I held out my hand. "How good of you to come," I said. "You are looking well."

"Nonsense," he said. "Pardon my rudeness, but not at all the case. Don't feel as bad as I look, but don't feel well either." He smiled at his own pleasantry, showing even fewer teeth than before.

We both sat down as Hannah entered with the tea. We waited in silence until she left.

"You, on the other hand, are looking well. Time has passed, to be sure. If not a thousand ships, then still nine hundred." I felt he had been rehearsing this small witticism for weeks and that he would have made it no matter how I looked.

"You are too kind," I said. "But it is only through your art that I could launch even a single ship."

"But you inspired me. Without you not a single ship would have been launched." Turner looked about him for the first time. He paid me a few pretty compliments on my taste. "Have you lived here long?"

"About three years. I went up to London a few days before Egremont's funeral. Wyndham had no use for me at Petworth, and there is that about him which spoils perfection."

"Abominable fellow. Cut me cold at his father's funeral. That was the last time I saw Petworth. It was raining, I remember, a horrible day. I caught a dreadful chill and shook so that my very bones felt as if they would crack during the ride back to London. I have so many fond memories of the place, and you not the least of them. But why did you not let me know you were in London? It is most cruel."

I looked at him for a long while. "You men cannot understand what it is like for a woman like myself, a woman of a certain age with a certain reputation, with her beauty gone. I had no prospects and no one to depend on. One feels entirely cast out.

"Egremont," I went on, "was kind to me until the very end. We understood each other better than most married couples do. He left me with a modest sufficiency that just enables me to live quietly in this out-of-the-way district. You will forgive me, I hope, for not seeking you out. I have sought out no one. I have wished for nothing but to be alone."

Turner looked at me for long moment. "You sound like that fellow—what's his name? Horace? Retired to the country, but in the city, you know. But fair enough. Lord knows I have spent a good deal of my life trying to stay out of the general view. Operating in public is a damn nuisance. That's why my time at Petworth was the best of my life; each of us kept to himself, but there were times, too, of fellowship. The best time of my life.

"But you do yourself an injustice—you would still make a good model. Perhaps not Helen now. Dido instead."

"The ruined and scorned queen? How apt. But I have no relish for such employment. I cannot think of our time together at Petworth without shame."

Turner colored. "I only meant, you see, that you are still an attractive woman."

"You are very kind. But tell me, how did you find me?"

"A bit of a long story. Not a day has passed since good Egremont's death that I have not thought of you. I even inquired of your whereabouts to Wyndham, who returned my letter unopened. A few days later his solicitor wrote to say that any further attempts to annoy his client would be dealt with severely. That's all poppycock, of course. Then, it must have been about five weeks ago, I ran into Garret at the Royal Academy. I doubt you would recall him, but he was once a guest at Petworth. We were chatting about those days when he mentioned that he had seen you. Just from a distance, you know. He paid a few compliments to your looks, both past and present. He didn't want to make a fool of himself by running after you, so you never knew you had been spotted. I was more interested than I let on, Mrs. Spencer, so I asked him, casual-like, where he had seen you, and he mentioned this district. After that I made it a point to be about here as much as I could. Two days ago I saw you when you were out marketing and followed you here. Not the behavior of a gentleman, I admit, but I was not prepared to speak just then. I felt like a damn schoolboy, in fact. Didn't wish to intrude, in case you were with someone else."

I reminded him that he could have written.

"I thought of that," he said. "But in the end I allowed my desire to run ahead of my manners. Not for the first time and probably not the last. But it was policy also: much easier to turn away a letter than a broken-down old painter."

"I confess that you are right. I value my privacy and the life I have made. But now that you are here, I am glad to see you. Heartily glad," I said. "We had such times at Petworth."

We sat in silence for a few moments, sipping our tea. Turner's shoulders slumped as if he was carrying a heavy weight.

"So how have you been? I see your name in the papers. You are still considered the lion of British art."

He snorted. "More like the mouse. I don't read the papers; I just do what I can. My digestion is horrible. Sores and whatnot about my gums; pain in those teeth that remain; stiffness in my joints. I have coughs, cramps, and palpitations. All the evils flesh is heir to. I grow old.

"But those were fine days at Petworth. You, young Grant, Helen, and the gods. I felt most fully in my power. I have sought those moments since then and only found success in the world, which is a damn poor thing compared to what I was seeking."

"It was a Paradise for me, too," I said. "Looking back, I feel ashamed that I ever experienced a moment of unhappiness there. But I do not complain much—I have no one to complain to. A life of quiet independence suits me."

"But we were great friends. We had many fine moments together."

"You need not remind me," I said. "When a lady is stripped of her clothes and set up on all fours like a dog in the street, she tends, no matter how great a lady she pretends to be, not to forget."

"Oh, dear," Turner said. He wiped his brow with a dirty handkerchief. "I have made a mess of it. For all the world I did not mean to offend you. Far from it. Of all the women I have ever met, you are the one I admire most. Do let us be friends."

I felt pity for the old painter and was sorry that I had spoken as I had. "You must see the thing from my point of view," I said. "When Egremont's bastard put on his cloak of virtue and threw me out of the house, I was left alone in the world with nothing but my small sufficiency and my shame. I did not have, as you do, genius and a name in the world to carry me through. Indeed, I find it hard to hear you complain of your diminished powers, when most men would trade everything they have for a tenth of what remains to you.

"Knowing each other as we do, or, rather, knowing how well you know me, it is foolish for us to be anything but honest with each other. I bear you no ill will, but I must ask you to understand my situation as it appears to me."

"I do," he said. "At least I'm trying. But did you not feel, as I did, as Egremont told me he did, that we were touched, all of us—you, young Grant, myself—by some awesome fire? Not me alone. I never worked like that—not before, not since. All these years—just me and my materials. It's why I prefer landscape, don't you see, as a rule."

Turner shook his head sadly. "You know, at the funeral, I asked him about our Helen. That is when he cut me. He said he would destroy it. Do you think him capable of such a thing?"

"He is a monster," I said. "I think him capable of anything."

"But even that?"

"He would cut off his own finger if he knew it would grieve others. You must understand. He could no more appreciate your Helen than you could speak Japanese. He could not see her because he could only see that the life his father lived was so much greater than his. His soul is not large enough to encompass your genius."

"The rack is too good for him," he said with sudden vehemence. "But it breaks my heart. It breaks my heart." After a few moments he grew calm and I saw that tears had formed at the corners of the old painter's eyes. "Of all my paintings, it is the one I loved best, though it was least like the others. I have tried many things in my day and accomplished much. But never anything like that. It is murder.

"I have the sketchbooks, you know, from that time. I look at them often, trying to capture the spark, to see that light. But only a shadow's shadow remains."

Turner looked up from the floor and stared at me intently. "It's queer. You are not now what you were. You are still a stunner, no matter what you say, but, I grant you, not the same. It was those days: the light at Petworth, Egremont's bounty, young Grant's beauty and your own. I was able to catch a glimpse of something.

"It was your face. I tried to capture stages of passion and delight. Some of my best work in pencil, you know. Not the sort of thing to exhibit, but very good."

"I wonder," I asked, "if I might have one of those sketches? It would be a sop to my vanity, but no great harm in an old lady looking back at better days."

Turner seemed taken aback by my request. He looked at his hands and avoided my gaze. "Those sketches are part of a sketchbook, you know. I make it a rule not to take things out. They are the tools of my trade. And they are not finished—not worthy of your esteem."

"I understand," I said. I poured him more tea.

"You actually believe he burnt it?"

"That is what he said. You know what I think of him."

"My eyes have grown dim," Turner said. When he looked at me then my heart nearly broke. "Even now, looking at you, I can no longer see her. It is gone."

I summoned up some of my former skill and managed to direct the conversation to happier matters. We chatted about the weather and some of the other guests we had both known at Petworth.

"It was good of you," I said at length, "to come and seek out an old forgotten lady."

"Not forgotten. You have been much in my mind. I hoped we might become friends again, even create between us some small version of those happy days. It would be good for us both."

I shook my head. "You are very kind to think of me in such terms. But I am convinced that this retirement is best for me. You do not know how hard I have struggled to make this life. Please forget I live here. Tell no one that you have seen me."

He looked at me strangely. "Rum. But you are not like other women, and I respect you for it." He rose to go.

"I wonder," I said, as we stood by the door, "if you have heard of young Grant?"

Now Turner seemed anxious to get our parting over with. "No. A year ago I heard he had taken himself off to America. Why I don't know."

I held out my hand to him. He touched it briefly.

"Well, good-bye," he said.

"Good-bye," I replied. I watched him through the door as he walked down the steps. The vigorous dogtrot that I had seen when he was rushing across the fields of Petworth was no more.

Afterward I went up to my bedroom, locked the door, took the key from about my neck, and opened the cabinet. As I lay on the bed, bathed in the light from the canvas, I knew that what I had done was wrong, but as Helen looked back at me from her mirror, I knew also that it had been needful.

. 59 .

TWO WEEKS LATER we found a large box at our door. It was filled with money, bundles and bundles of wrinkled twenties and fifties, just over three million dollars when we finally counted it. The letter was in a plain envelope, the paper on which it was written was unremarkable. The ink was blue and the elegant cursive script was precise and unquestionably legible.

Dear Mr. Leiden,

I owe you neither explanation, justification, nor compensation, but I understand, I believe, the vacuum you currently feel in your life. If you have any sense of injury—as I suspect you do—it is, although natural, unjustified. You had no more right to that painting than I do and, from a moral point of view, mine was the greater claim. If possession is ninety percent of the law, the law was on your side. Now it is on mine. You had your chance; now I have mine. The ease with which I was able to acquire your possession suggests that you were not an appropriate steward of that which even you recognized as a work beyond compare, a work which, in some profound sense that even I cannot yet grasp, changes everything. You may rest assured that The Center of the World is no longer propped up on a bedroom dresser as if it were a second television!

I do not know how it came to be in your house (although I have a strong suspicion), but it seems safe to say that the main element of the "how" was chance. You were lucky, more lucky than you or perhaps anyone deserves to be. You are still lucky, because you have seen what no more than a handful of people have ever seen.

So while your claim to ownership was based on luck, mine is based on will. I have been actively seeking this painting for many years. Through intense study and scholarly intuition I came to suspect its existence; through painstaking work and patience I transformed my imaginings into physical fact.

You will probably think this comically arrogant coming from one who, from your perspective, is nothing more than a thief, but I think I have some right to claim that I have willed this painting into being, or at least into visibility. My act of creation is, in its own way, on a par with Turner's. Turner willed the painting onto the fabric of the canvas; I willed it onto the fabric of time and history.

And you? You did nothing but have the advantage of mindless propinquity. Your father—not you—purchased a

house in the Adirondacks. Do you even know that this house
was once the property of Cornelius Rhinebeck? Do you know
that Rhinebeck was one of the great New York collectors of
European art of the nineteenth century? I suspect that for
some reason the painting was being stored in your father's
house when Rhinebeck met his untimely death in 1929.
There it sat until you stumbled on it. The painting, for
reasons that are easy to imagine, was not part of any official
inventory and did not pass into the hands of Rhinebeck's two
sons, both of whom died many years ago and without issue.
So I feel quite comfortable dismissing any claims that you
might care to assert—if you could.

There is no justice in the fact that you possessed the
painting as long as you did. What did you do to deserve such
a gift? I have some information about you. You are one of
those people who go about their business and make no great
difference in the world. I suspect you have no great feelings
either. How else could you live the life you do? I wonder,
therefore, what you felt as you looked at The Center of the
World.

This painting is a lightning bolt hurled from the past
and anyone (including you) standing near its point of impact
must feel the heat and hear the thunder. So surely you felt
something. You were probably blinded by Helen's sexuality.
What did you make of the anatomical precision of Turner's
brushwork? Did you see the play of light and shadow in
the sea or the exquisite fall of the transparent drapery on
Helen's thigh or the masterly deployment of pictorial space?

Even if you were unaware of the hundreds of small elements that contribute to the painting's greatness, you must have appreciated some part of its glory and wonder.

None of this really matters, although you have become in my mind something of a curiosity, an odd footnote in the history of art. You are one of a handful of individuals who have ever seen this wonder. You are one of an even smaller number who have seen it since the creation of the modern world. You and I are joined in a small and exclusive fellowship. We are products of the twentieth century—the great wars, the genocides, the atomic bomb, AIDS. All these things have a place in our consciousness, but so does The Center of the World. It has shown me truth more profoundly than I had ever imagined possible.

Did you feel what I felt? Have you been transformed? As I write I can look up from my desk and see The Center of the World. Whenever I look at it, I see some new wonder or find myself lost in a totality whose boundaries I cannot map. For you, this painting has become a memory. You will never see it again. Could you perceive the thing for what it was when it was before you? Can you recall it now that it is gone? Will you only regret your loss or has some gift remained? I hope the latter.

I think you understand that The Center of the World must always and forever remain a secret. Although you made a clumsy attempt to establish its worth, the indirectness of your approach suggests an awareness on your part that the very nature of this painting requires that it remain hidden. The worst thing that could happen would be for it to enter into the world and be degraded by reproduction. The thought of its image on a coffee mug or a beach towel turns my stomach. I suspect you share this feeling.

In fact, in spite of who and what you are, you are a kind of hero. If you had rushed The Center of the World to market, all would have been lost. You understood, I believe, that it is not meant for general consumption, but I doubt that your understanding will take you so far as to allow you to comprehend that it was not meant for you either. There is a fitness in the way things have worked out that almost inclines one to a belief in Providence. You do not have the depth of interest or understanding that I do. I am far better equipped to allow Turner's masterpiece to fulfill its destiny than you are. That is a fact.

All of this will be small consolation to you, but I have attempted to mitigate your sense of loss with the cash enclosed with this letter. I am of course under no obligation to you, but I feel an uncharacteristic wish to reward you for what you did.

I also wish to demonstrate that I am a man of considerable resources. My ability to find this painting in the haystack of the world should give some sense of my reach and grasp. Although I am predisposed to think of you with kindness and pity, please know that if you make any movements toward me—any movements whatsoever—I will know of them, and you will immediately feel unpleasant consequences. I am a ruthless man. I know more about your children than you do; your wife is an open book to me. In the bourse where such matters are traded, a stranger's life can be had for $20,000, plus travel expenses. You and your family are such strangers.

Imagine your feelings for the painting. Now imagine them multiplied a hundredfold—no, a thousandfold. You may now only begin to understand my feelings and the lengths to which I will go.

You have been blessed. Very few have come as close to the truth of things as you have.

I bid you farewell.

. 60 .

OF COURSE IT WAS wrong. I never saw Turner again. He wrote me a few times over the years, but received only a short note in return, begging him to write no more. And then he died, and shortly afterward Wyndham died, too. One of the brats now rules at Petworth. I only learn of these things through the newspapers that Hannah brings in every morning.

I have outlived so many. My breath fails when I climb the stairs. Many days I lie in bed all day. I listen to the sound of the air passing in and out of my lungs. I have no desire or need to see a physician.

Hannah too is growing old. She is becoming a middle-aged woman, and she is more plain than ever, but I treat her well. She remembers the life she had before she came to me. She has no family. I have told her to go, to find another life. But she is content. All this will be hers when I die. To whom else should it go?

The light still remains. It grows richer with each passing day, each passing hour. New things appear. The old somehow remains, at least in memory. I grow more beautiful. The skin on my hand is mottled, the flesh sags around my neck.

I no longer look at myself much, or even at Paris's smooth skin. I look toward the sea. The ships seem more and more wondrous, their cargo more and more precious. Where are these riches bound? At times I seem to see beyond the picture's frame: there is the merchant pacing on the dock, waiting for the arrival of the cargo; there is the sailor's sweetheart, burning to see him again. Where are those towered cities? The sweet smoke of sacrifice rises to the sky. The people pray. Sometimes the gods smile; sometimes they do not.

I see the gods over the battlefield. I see them in the light of the sky, in the spaces between the edges of the clouds and the sky, about the borders of the sun. I feel all the yearning I have ever felt, and all the joy as well.

Hannah will bring me tea. I have never shown her what is in the cabinet, but surely she suspects something. The servants always know. It has been so many years. She must know, but she has never spoken of it, never asked me. She has been silent and respectful through all these years, a faithful servant indeed.

She will find the key about my neck when I am gone. She knows where the letter to my solicitor is.

There is more in the light than there ever was. The colors grow richer. The wind pushes the marvelous boats along. I can smell the sea. There is nothing but light.

ACKNOWLEDGMENTS

· · ·

The following friends and early readers provided comments on various drafts and, most importantly, encouraged me to go on. Thanks to Doug Baldwin, Connie Cook, Bob Cumming, Logan Fox, Jessica Hecht, Carl Klompus, Jane Mallison, Ray Potter, Saundra Young, and Ingeborg Van Essen. Additional thanks to Ray for making an important introduction.

I would also like to thank Ida Lawrence, Steve Lazer, and Fran Morecz. You didn't know about this book until it was done, but I could not have written it without your support.

Chris Calhoun, my agent, did everything that an agent is supposed to do and is a nice guy as well. Thank you.

I am especially indebted to Evelyn Toynton. Her care, good sense, and attention were great gifts. Thanks to Marjorie DeWitt, Yvonne E. Cárdenas, and Sulay Hernandez of Other Press. I also want to thank Judith Gurewich for believing in me and my book.

But mostly I want to thank my wife, Barbara Fishman, for being my friend and lover for all these years. Nothing would have been possible or worth doing without that.